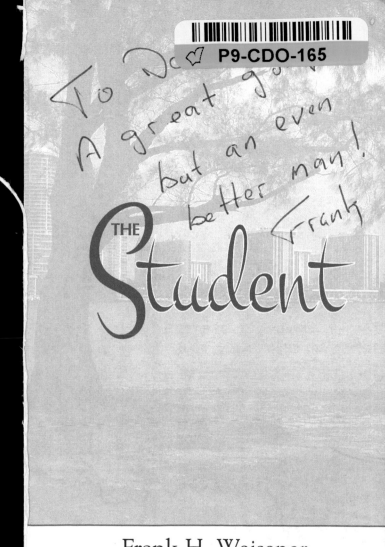

THE Student

Frank H. Weisener

Copyright 2015 by Frank H. Weisener

Published by Frank H. Weisener

weisenerf@gmail.com

ISBN:

Printed by Eagle Litho, Miami, Florida in the United States of America.

This book is dedicated to my loving wife, who has put up with me through thick and thin. My wonderful children who never fail to amaze me with their inner and outer beauty. My parents who have allowed me to live and made me what I am (it's all entirely your fault). And last but certainly not least - Christa and "Doc" who have extended their trust in me and helped me achieve things I thought unattainable.

Chapter One

Sabine Sander, Miami (Monday, March 2nd, 2015)

Once inside the room her captor pushed her down onto what felt like a mattress. He easily pinned her down with a knee to her chest and started to work her shorts and underwear down her legs. She immediately started kicking and bucking frantically, but without saying a word, her captor struck her with his hand upside her head hard enough to make her feel like she was going to pass out. Stunned she laid prone long enough for him to finish the job and quickly shackle her right ankle to a heavy iron chain, tying her up like a rabid dog in a junk yard. He got off her and in one swift motion pulled her to her feet, cutting her wrist restrains and yanking her polo shirt and bra off. She was still fighting dizziness, and just stood there on wobbly knees. With a hard shove he sent her back down onto the mattress and took off her sneakers and socks. After what seemed like an eternity, she heard a heavy door close. She carefully untied the cotton bag her captor had pulled over her head and saw - nothing. She was engulfed in utter darkness. Heavy metal on metal clanged outside of what she assumed was some bolt or bar securing the closing door. Gingerly she got up, but without any light illuminating her surroundings she lowered herself back onto the mattress, and sat there dazed, tears streaking down her face. At least she could breathe easier. She peeled the duct tape off her mouth and took a deep breath. What was happening to her? Why was she here and who was holding her imprisoned?

She started crying uncontrollably. Imprisoned without a shred of clothing on her she felt, and was, naked and utterly vulnerable. Dark thoughts started entering her mind. Maybe her captor was one of those serial killers. She was at his mercy, shackled in a dark room, sitting on a mattress, ready to be raped and then what - butchered? She felt lonely and desperate and started to scream in fear and frustration – as loud as she could – but there was no response from the outside. Since her screams sounded muffled even to her own ears, she figured that there was heavy insulation in the walls. Exhausted from screaming she lay down and continued sobbing quietly.

She must have – inexplicable in her current situation - fallen asleep. When she woke up she had no idea how much time had elapsed since the masked man had put her into the room. The room was still pitch-dark and she was unable to make out anything; she couldn't even make out her hands in front of her face, let alone any walls or the door she'd heard earlier. On her hands and knees she started to feel around the floor next to her. It was concrete as far as she could tell. She moved in one direction until the chain stopped her from advancing any further. Straining at the chain, she started to move around towards her right, always keeping the chain tight, trying to reach as far as it allowed her, which felt like a mere three feet at best. Yes, finally there was something she was able to touch. The wall seemed to be covered by some sort of plastic sheeting that she immediately tried to - but couldn't - rip off. She continued her circle, touching and feeling. Her fingers touched something plastic, further exploring the object she found a lid and figured it was a small camping toilet. She tried to move it, but it was somehow secured to the concrete floor.

How could she have been so stupid? She was normally very careful walking back to her car after classes. Maybe it had been the excitement of her brother being in Miami. She'd seen a guy hanging around, following her for weeks. She had been on high alert, but he had nevertheless been able to take her by surprise. He'd popped up behind her car, wearing a Bill Clinton mask, and forced her into her own car at gun point.

Her heart had been beating so fast, she'd thought she was going to have a heart attack. He'd ordered her to start the car and drive off the campus. They had exited onto SW 107th Avenue and following his directions she drove across the street into a shopping center. It had been after 11:00 p.m. – her last class – and the parking lot in front of the Drivers License Office had been deserted except for a lone dark car. He'd ordered her to stop next to the car, then pulled a roll of duct tape from a small gym bag, ripped off a generous piece and affixed it over her mouth. He'd continued by slipping a dark cotton bag over her head, securing it with a drawstring. He'd exited the car, opened her door and ordered her out, made her walk a couple of steps, lifted her up, almost gently, and placed her into the trunk of the other car. Once she was inside of the trunk he'd tied her wrists and ankles with zip-ties. She'd heard the metallic click of the lock engaging as the trunk lid closed. She had tried to scream but the duct tape had prohibited it. She'd immediately started to work her tongue against the tape, trying to get it wet, trying to create some space between the tape and her mouth.

The car had reversed out of the parking space and her ride had begun. After some turns that made her bang her shoulders against either side of the trunk, the car had started to travel in a straight line and at a higher speed, indicating to her that they had merged onto a highway. The closest highways from the campus were the Florida Turnpike and the Palmetto, and she assumed they had gotten onto one of them. However, she had no idea as to which direction they had taken. The odor of gasoline had given her a headache and after what had seemed to her like hours they had reached their destination. He'd lifted her out of the trunk, cut the ties around her ankles and made her walk a few steps.

Now she was in a dark room, naked and terrified. Sabine tried to calm herself, tried to evaluate her situation, rationalize. Who was her captor, and more importantly, why had he abducted her? Her parents weren't rich. As far as she knew she hadn't really upset anyone in all of her life! Why? Why had she been captured? It took her a few minutes to realize the obvious answer – he was going to kill her. She started crying again. Just then she heard the metallic sound of the door being unlocked.

Chapter Two

Benjamin Walker, Miami (Monday, March 2nd, 2015)

While he'd thought about it many times, somehow, surprisingly; in his more than four years in Miami he'd never found the time to drive down to the Keys. Well, things had changed and he'd now had to make the time and was actually, despite the circumstances, looking forward to finally getting the chance to do so. He much needed a change of scenery that would allow him to sort things out in peace and quiet. A friend had told him that the first eighty minutes of the three hour drive would be rather boring, but that it would get progressively better. He loved living in Florida; it was a great place to live. Sure, it was humid and outright muggy for a few months, but luckily the current month – March - held the best of both worlds; warm and dry. Either way, it sure did beat the weather in Hamburg, Germany. Hamburg was a truly beautiful place – but should have never been opened up for civilization. The weather was just not meant for people to live in. Well, really, it wasn't that bad. Unfortunately the summers tended to be pretty short – but what the summers lacked in duration, the winters made up for. On the flip side, just like many other places that weren't blessed with tropical weather, it made up for this with culture. The Staatsoper, the Schauspielhaus, and the Thalia-Theater were staples of the cultural cloth that Germany was made of. The Alster lake, really a dammed river, gave an especially nice touch to the center of the City. Actually divided into the inner- and outer Alster, it provided spectacular scenery for visitors to downtown Hamburg; and a splendid, beautiful view for all those who could afford to live around the outer Alster. The Neuer Wall – one of the more expensive shopping districts in Europe added to the allure of the city, making it very attractive to millions of tourists from all over the world. Heck, just the fact that it had been civilized for more than a thousand years was kind of neat.

Thinking about Hamburg was causing all of his not so distant memories to flood his mind.

Through bits and pieces that he had picked up throughout his childhood, Benjamin had been able to put together quite a bit of his parent's past. His mother, Christina Krop, had met his dad, Henry A. Walker, when she was twenty-two years old. Well, from what he gathered, technically his dad had met his mom. He had been on leave from the Ramstein Air base near Kaiserslautern, Germany.

Henry and his buddies had started to investigate the Red Light District in Hamburg on a Friday evening. She had 'performed' at a club on the Reeperbahn. More specifically, she had been working at a club that only had two performers on stage. Yup, his mom and her then boyfriend had been the performers. Benjamin had once overheard his dad tell a friend that it had almost made him sick to his stomach to watch her give the guy an hour-long blowjob that never came to a happy ending. His dad however had somehow managed to instantly fall in love with her.

According to what his dad told his friend: He'd watched her perform for as long as he could, but had eventually gotten tired. After all, how long can you watch a guy not come? She had looked so disgusted, he'd almost felt like getting on stage and handing her a barf-bag! When he had refocused his attention to his friends – to his surprise, they had left without telling him, he guessed, due to his being transfixed watching the non-performance. Henry had been upset about them having left him behind, but eventually had been able to navigate his way back to the 'Hamburg Hauptbahnhof' from where their train was going to leave. Not a small feat considering his blood alcohol level.

On his next leave love smitten Henry had been dumb enough to look for her – successfully. He'd found her in the same establishment 'performing' with an old dude! Why, Benjamin could never fathom, but his dad had pursued his mom and eventually married her.

Snapping back to reality he forced himself to pay attention to the scenery he was afforded on his drive to Key West. When he hit the 18-Mile stretch he suddenly realized that there was actually a reason for him to be afraid for his future. He was only twenty three years old, and he would certainly not enjoy a prolonged stint in a State detention facility. He should have called the cops right away, but had been too rattled after the encounter. While he had always considered himself a cool and collected guy, last night he had lost his cool – well, in his defense, he'd been afraid and pushed. A few months ago he'd figured out that pretending to be gay tended to double his tips as a waiter. So he had developed a rather convincing gay persona. The three guys at the corner table had been his last customers of the night. As a matter of fact, they'd come in only minutes before the restaurant had been going to close down. They'd ordered potato skins, fried mozzarella sticks and margaritas. The kitchen staff had cussed him out for having taken such a later order, but had it ready within a few minutes anyway. It was anybody's guess what they had done to the food – other than preparing it – but he'd served it with a smile. He'd immediately recognized that they were gay. Two of them had been an obvious couple. The odd man out had looked not only drunk but also mean. It had been too late for him to drop his 'gay' act, so he'd continued with his charade. By the time he'd served them their food he'd known that the drunken guy was going to be trouble. He had been making crude and openly sexual comments every time he had checked on them.

When they'd asked for the check he had sighed in relief. Thank God, let this be over, get out of here and let me go home.

Alas, he hadn't been that lucky. When he'd finished cleaning up some fifteen minutes later and exited through the rear door, the drunken odd man out had been waiting for him.

"Hey good looking!" the guy had opened.

Benjamin had been somewhat perplexed by the guy. Not only had the dude startled him by being behind the restaurant, but he'd had the fly on his pants open, with an erection greeting Benjamin hello.

Really?

"Man, please leave me alone." Benjamin had asked him politely, since after all, he'd been a guest.

"Don't be coy! I know you want me! I've seen you checking me out!" the guy answered while moving his piece around.

"No man, I am actually straight. Have a girlfriend waiting for me at home." Benjamin had lied.

"What the fuck – you've been leading me on!" the guy exclaimed with a forceful voice that led Benjamin to believe that there may be trouble ahead. Benjamin realized that the guy may have not been as drunk as he'd originally thought. Trying to set the record straight he told him: "No, no!"

Surprisingly, the formerly uncoordinated guy had quickly tucked his penis away and started to advance on Benjamin with a speed not common to the drunks he'd encountered before.

Wham – the guy had decked him with a hard right hook to his chin. Benjamin had seen stars lighting up in front of his eyes. He'd almost lost control of his bladder. Primal instincts had taken over and sent his adrenalin level sky high. Without realizing what he was doing Benjamin had kicked into high gear! He'd kicked as hard as possible at the guy's left knee. There hadn't been any immediate reaction so he'd followed with a desperate punch to the center of the man's face. He'd made contact with his nose and knew instantly that he'd broken it in a bad way. The guy had howled out in pain but was still standing and Benjamin had been so afraid of the repercussions that he just continued to go after him. A left jab to the face; a hard right in the stomach; a knee to the face and the guy had finally started to crumble to the pavement. A couple of kicks to the head and Mister Asshole lay still, collecting his thoughts on the street. Benjamin had been breathing hard from the rush of adrenaline when the fear hit him suddenly and he'd started to realize what he was doing. Shit, the guy had stopped moving. Benjamin had felt panic rising in his gut, his stomach felt like it was boiling, and he'd unloaded the cheeseburger he'd eaten earlier into the 30-gallon, luckily lid-less, garbage can next to the rear door of the restaurant.

The last image of his mom had shot through his head. This guy was lying just as still. He'd contemplated – but had been too afraid - to call an ambulance when Mr. Asshole had started to stir. Thank God, the guy had still been alive. Benjamin had made up his mind he wasn't going to call an ambulance, let alone the cops. He'd locked the back door to the restaurant and high-tailed it out of there.

Shit, what if the guy was seriously injured he'd thought? Maybe he'd cracked his head. On the spot he had decided to get out of town for a few days.

The memory of the guy lying prone on the dirty pavement behind the restaurant had triggered the image of his mother, and his mind started drifting back to his past and his parents.

Chapter Three

Benjamin Walker's parents,
Hamburg, Germany (September 1988)

Benjamin's parents: Henry and Christina had gotten married a week after his dad had gotten out of the service. It hadn't been much of a wedding, but they had a good time. His mother's parents had been there. They had actually approved of his dad even though they could hardly communicate with him. Big deal, while they hadn't really known exactly what his mom had been doing before she had met his dad – they'd had their suspicions.

They'd spent their honeymoon on Sylt. The decadent island that was known as the playground for the rich and famous.

Sylt had the famously nude beaches where the elderly citizens liked to display their junk. They had stayed in Westerland, the less glamorous part of the island. However, they had ventured to the nicer parts. They'd had coffee and cake at the Go-Garten on the 'Whiskey Mile' in Kampen, paying as much for two slices of apple pie cake as they would have for two sirloin steaks elsewhere. Sitting outside by the street they admired the Porsches, Maseratis, Bentleys and Rolls Royce rolling by slowly, allowing the less fortunate to dream. Afterwards they had gone to the "Cliffhanger". They'd had a good time. Henry hadn't really enjoyed all the old guys drooling all over Christina, alas – she'd been beautiful and he'd decided to let it slide and take their attention as a compliment.

Unfortunately reality had started to settle in soon after. They'd moved into a small apartment in the Grindel Hochhaueser in Hamburg. Centrally located, it was still somewhat in the no-where-land of Eimsbuettel. Henry had figured that he would easily be able to score a job as a mechanic at the Airport in Hamburg-Fuehlsbuettel. However, they hadn't been hiring. In 1988 he had only been able to get a job in the harbor as a 'Festmacher', the guys who caught the vessels heavy anchoring ropes. Not glamorous, not very well paying – but a job!

It hadn't mattered – his dad had been in love with her. She'd been his queen! Getting to work had been a mission though. He had to catch the "102" bus up to Rothenbaum Chaussee, transfer to the U-Bahn Hallerstrasse – transfer again at Jungfernstieg to get to Hafenstrasse where he transferred to a shuttle boat to get to the harbor.

Benjamin shook his head and tried, unsuccessfully, to snap out of memory-lane. He could still almost visualize his dad sitting on the sofa, complaining to one of his drinking buddies: He hadn't been able to get the job he had wanted. While he had been able to learn German, his accent was still very thick and communicating with the locals had been difficult. Christina had gotten pregnant, but he had discovered that his wife had still been turning tricks. Not only that, she'd been snorting cocaine and occasionally used heroin. Should he just accept her faults?

When they had gotten married he had hoped that she would follow through with her dream. Become a travel agent, leave all the dirt and smut behind. Well, that hadn't worked out that well. But he'd still believed in her. Maybe it had been his fault? Maybe he had needed to be more supportive, foster her dreams, and remind her of them.

In order to pay their bills however, he'd had to go to work. That was the scary part for his dad. What was she doing at home – more precisely whom was she doing at home. More importantly, what about his baby boy? He hadn't anticipated this. All he'd wanted was a real life with the love of his life. One of his dad's friends had gone as far as giving him the business card of a divorce attorney. There hadn't been a chance in hell his dad would have ever done that. Not only had he still loved her, he'd adored his son.

He remembered how much fun his dad had been. He had loved his dad – that was for sure. They had gone to the local FC St. Pauli home games on the Heiligengeist Field to watch their favorite soccer team. While they would have liked to support the team on away games, it hadn't been in the budget. They had loved the fact that St. Pauli had been the perennial underdog. The FC St.Pauli had the best and most lubricated fans in the league. The Millerntor Stadium at that time had been one of the few that were still offering alcoholic beer. Most of the others only offered alcohol-free beer. The fans had been known to make generous use of this fact, but had been surprisingly non-violent.

Occasionally they'd gone to the Hamburg Stadtpark to kick a soccer ball around. His dad had introduced him to baseball and football, but he'd much preferred soccer. Thinking back to those days always gave him joy. He happily remembered the sun filled afternoons on the meadow below the Planetarium. From there you had a magnificent view of the lower part of the park. Hundreds of people throwing Frisbees, playing paddle ball, kicking soccer balls or just bathing in the sun. At the bottom of the meadow was the Stadtpark See. It was a small natural lake which, during the summer months had been open for swimmers. The Stadtpark was an oasis in the middle of a bustling metropolitan city of more than 1.8 million people. There were bicycle path snaking through the forest of old pines, maple and oak trees. Bar-B-Q pits were available on some of the many meadows throughout the park.

Unfortunately too often those beautiful days ended with them getting home and his dad falling into depression because his mom had been gone – destination unknown. Well, they'd had a pretty good idea of her whereabouts. Chances were that she was out scoring cocaine or turning tricks in one of the many other apartments in the Grindel Hochhaeuser. Benjamin hadn't really cared anymore, but his dad had always taken it hard. He'd started walking around the apartment, eventually he'd always started to roam the corridors of the building, listening for her voice. Luckily he never found her on those excursions. His dad had been strong. Years of heaving those heavy ropes had made him as strong as an ox. Had he ever encountered his mom in the presence of another guy in one of the other apartments – Benjamin's money would have been on his dad.

His dad had never talked bad about his mom to him though. He'd just put up with her no matter what, but it had taken its toll on him. He had started drinking. He wasn't a violent drunk. After he'd had his fill he would generally just pass out on the sofa or in the bedroom. Oftentimes he would be out of beer and go across the street to a small bar, the Eckstube, on the corner of Grindelallee and Hallerstrasse. He would bend the bartender's ear for hours about his unfaithful wife. The guy must have been a saint, deaf or the most patient man in the world. When his dad had had enough he would come stumbling home, look at his wife – if she was home – shake his head and go to bed. How he had managed to always somehow get up at 5 a.m. and make it to work was anyone's guess.

Christina, his mom, must have hated his dad. How else could she have trampled his feelings like that? How else could she have humiliated this strong proud man so many times?

Benjamin had understood that she had a drug problem and that she had given up on all her dreams and hopes, but why did she have to drag down his dad with her? Benjamin's loyalties had been squarely with his dad. He just felt sorry for his mom. But all that had come to an abrupt end one cold winter night.

On December 15th, 2005 Benjamin's world had changed. It had been a typical December day in Hamburg when during the day the sun had been invisible. It had been uncomfortably cold and foggy and after 4 p.m. only bats had been able to see any object more than ten feet in front of them.

Henry had had another meltdown over Christina's absence when he had returned from work, frozen stiff from working outdoors since 7 a.m. He had gone to the Eckstube and gotten his usual fill of seven beers, seven shots of Korn and a handful of pretzels. What had been unusual about that day was the fact that Henry had opted not to cross at the traffic light located at the intersection, but to make a beeline for the apartment building, thus effectively taking a shortcut of approximately seventy yards. Benjamin had later been told that his dad never saw the taxi coming. The Mercedes Benz had not been traveling at an excessive rate of speed, as a matter of fact; it had been going at only about twenty five miles per hour. And while most people believe that small children and drunks don't break any bones when they fall – due to them being relaxed – Benjamin's dad hadn't been that fortunate. He had flipped over the roof of the taxi and landed on his head, snapping his neck and killing him instantly.

It had taken the Hamburg Polizei until 1 a.m. to locate the family that was living only two hundred fifty yards away from the scene of the accident. Benjamin had woken up to the doorbell and while half asleep had been told that his dad had died in an accident. He had been devastated; his mom had been out. The officers had inquired about his mom's whereabouts but he hadn't known, hadn't cared. They had left a female officer with him to comfort him and to notify Mrs. Walker about her husband's demise. When his mom had finally returned home at around 3:00 a.m., he'd lost it. Before the police officer had been able to get out the first word he had jumped up from the sofa and punched his – obviously intoxicated and high – mother right in the face. She had crumpled to the floor while the officer had scrambled to her feet. There had been blood, lots of it, pouring from his mother's face. He hadn't cared, he'd attempted to kick her, but the officer had pulled him back before he'd been able to strike again.

Fifteen minutes later the ambulance and a couple of police officers had arrived and the paramedics had determined that his mom's nose was not broken, and that she didn't have to go to the hospital. They had been so very concerned with his mother's well being. He hadn't given a shit about his mother. What had been wrong with them? His dad had been killed, his mother had been the ultimate cause of his death and they had been concerned about her! The police officers had asked her if she was okay with Benjamin staying with her, or if she wanted a social worker to come over. One officer went so far as to ask her if she had wanted him arrested. His mother had declined. She had said that she was okay and that she felt safe with Benjamin in the house.

Chapter Four

Sandra Restrepo, Miami (Friday, January 30th, 2015)

It had been hard to miss her. She definitely stood out in his class. She was a Columbian beauty standing at approximately five feet and five inches tall. Her long black, almost straight hair fell to her midsection. She had the ability to unite across ethnical lines – there wasn't a guy in the room whose attention she didn't capture upon entering the class room. There may have been a couple of Chinese students that seemed to have a different taste. However, the rest of the class, including him, paid rapt attention whenever she was in sight. No surprise there – her face and figure could have graced the cover of any number of magazines.

She was definitely a candidate for his purposes. The fact that she had a boyfriend, who naturally was sitting next to her during class, didn't concern him. The guy wasn't even that good looking. He was barely a hand width taller than her with a pasty face and sagging shoulders. What was wrong with her? Well, he was going to mix things up a bit. Over the next couple of weeks he learned their schedules, modes of transportation, and where they lived. Maybe he should have become a detective?

It was a Friday night when all the stars aligned and he followed them onto Key Biscayne. They had made a U-turn under the William Powell Bridge and pulled onto the side of the road that allowed an unobstructed view of the waterside of Brickell Avenue. Parked under the tall Australian Pines they were sitting in the car necking. He parked a hundred yards away and contemplated the timing of his next move. There was really no reason to prolong the inevitable. He would have to go out there and get her. Take her home to his place and convince her that they were the perfect match.

He didn't consider himself a violent person, but he did possess a large hunting knife and a .38 caliber revolver. He had brought both items along to convince the boyfriend to peacefully abandon his place. Gathering the additional gear he had stored in his trunk a few days ago, he put on a Bill Clinton Halloween mask and exited his car. It was after 10:00 p.m. and pretty much pitch black between the trees.

Nevertheless he made sure to walk up to the rear left door of the Chevy Impala at an angle so that he was not visible in the rear view or side mirror.

His plan, as he realized walking closer to the car, was flawed. He was going to open the rear left door, slide in and control the situation. But what if the doors were locked? This had the potential of turning into a bad thing. Cautioning himself not to panic – he could always use the gun to smash in the driver's side window and force his way in - he calmed down. No problem - he was in total control.

Approaching the car he became aware of Pasty-face moving in on his Columbian beauty. He already had his face glued to hers and his hands where nowhere to be seen. He realized that he was just in time to prevent the guy from advancing any further. Placing his gym bag softly on the ground, he lifted the door handle and was relieved to feel the mechanism engage and the door open right away. In one swift motion he yanked the door open and slid into the rear seat, pointing the gun at Pasty-face.

"Hi there." he whispered to them "I am gonna take over from here."

"What the fuck?" Pasty-face replied while Columbia started screaming.

"Ssshhhh" he said pointing the gun at Columbia, but failed to achieve the desired result. She continued screaming even louder. Afraid of attracting any attention from other lovebirds that may pull in close or from motorist driving by; he decided swift action was in order. He quickly placed the gun on the seat next to him, reached around and pulled Pasty's head against the headrest, exposing his throat which he proceeded to slit with his hunting knife. The ensuing pulsating fountain of blood gushing forward onto the windshield and dashboard was amazing.

Columbia gasped and passed out, which allowed him to turn the switch on the overhead light to the off position, exit the car, grab the gym bag and come around to her side. He opened the door, retrieved some cable ties which he placed around her wrists and ankles and stuffed a gag into her mouth, securing it with duct tape. Glancing over to the driver's seat, he was certain that Pasty wouldn't give him any trouble. Closing all the doors, he walked back to his car and drove it over next to the Chevy. He quickly picked Columbia out of the seat and placed her gently in the trunk of his car.

Back to his place, forward to their mutual future....

Chapter Five

Benjamin Walker, Hamburg, Germany (Spring 2006)

It had taken Benjamin quite a while to adjust to his new life. A life without the one person he had really appreciated – his dad! His mom had never even mentioned the incident following his dad's death. His grades in school had never been great to begin with – but then they really began to slip. The Helene-Lange-Gymnasium, the closest High School only minutes away from where they'd lived, had been an elite school. While they had a policy of weeding out those that couldn't keep up, in his case they must have felt sorry, because they had really gone out of their way to help him out. A school counselor had been assigned to talk to him; his teachers had offered to give him free tutoring. But in the end it was the neighbor's cat that had gotten him back on track.

The Grindel Hochhaeuser had a strict 'no pet' policy. Strict to the point, that when an animal was seen outside of the apartments, it was subject to removal. When Benjamin saw his neighbor's cat in the hallway, he'd known somewhere deep down inside of him that this was an opportunity to do something to release some of his pent up anger. He'd felt something strong, an urge developing inside of him. He'd known he had to do something that meant something. Why, how – he hadn't had an idea, but it was an opportunity nevertheless. What was he going to do? Since the cat had been familiar with him, it hadn't been difficult to pick her up. In the end he had gone back to his apartment and gotten some solid string that had been left over from securing a package they had sent to someone or other. Manipulating the noose he'd tied over the cat's head had been a bit of a challenge, but he managed it after coaxing the cat for a little while. The elevator had been empty and he had quickly hung the cat from the overhead light cover that had a metal grid covering the fluorescent lights. Once he'd let go of the cat, which he had hung at about six feet off the floor, she had put up a remarkable fight. Twisting, turning, jerking and flipping. What a show! He'd started laughing out loud. He had been truly surprised by how long the cat had held on, but after a few minutes it had been over. He'd hit the button for every floor, all fifteen of them.

The next day at school he had felt like never before, relaxed and in-tune with the world. Soon thereafter his grades had started to improve. His counselor had been delighted; his teachers had given him compliments. Life had gotten back to a degree of normalcy. Though he had still despised his mother for what she'd done to his dad.

Benjamin had felt liberated after the cat's sad demise! But his mother had continued to get out of hand. She hadn't cared anymore. Not that she'd ever been the most caring or attentive parent, but after his Dad's death she'd deteriorated at an accelerated pace. She had started bringing her Johns back to the apartment. Benjamin learned to go straight to his room after school. Most of the time, his mom had been shacked up in her bedroom with a "friend". He had known what was going on! After suffering through two years of constantly changing "boyfriends" he'd decided that he had to correct the problem. His mother had picked up a constant boyfriend. Benjamin had suspected him to be more than just a boyfriend – something closer to a pimp. What a prize that guy had been. One afternoon

Benjamin had come home to hear his mother whimpering in her bedroom. Upon entering her room he had found her naked, handcuffed to the bed. She was in tears. While he'd thought that she must have lost all shame over the years, he had been surprised that she'd seemed ashamed to have her son find her like that. She was lying spread-eagle on the bed. The bed she had shared with his dad! It had been too much for Benjamin. He had turned around and left the room locking himself in his own room.

Two hours later, he had gone back and un-cuffed her. She had started to cry, called after him when he left the room. No way was he going to turn around and look at her, listen to some of her drug induced idiotic stories.

However, a plan had started to form in his mind... He could liberate himself, and her, and the pimp! Sure, he was only barely seventeen, but he could probably survive on his own. His dad had left – god bless his heart – a life insurance, thanks to the Harbor Union, that had been worth seventy-five-thousand Euros, which he'd wisely left to Benjamin and not his wife. He'd also had an aunt in Hamburg. His mother's sister had lived only a couple of blocks away on Hochallee. He had known that the authorities wouldn't have let him stay by himself at his age. But he did have an aunt! While all their interaction had taken place during the few holidays they'd spent together, he thought she would most likely take him in. A few more final touches and his plan would be ready for implementation.

Chapter Six

Jerome Water, Miami (Wednesday, April 25th, 2015)

He'd gotten lucky – his dad had this inexplicable affinity for everything Native American, so he had wanted to name him Geronimo – but his mom had put her foot down. Thank God, he would have never been able to live down that name. Not that he was unsympathetic to the Native American cause, just that he wasn't a Native.

His mom was the most caring person he'd ever met. His dad was alright but had constantly been pushing him. Everything was a competition with him. His dad had discussed his future with him multiple times before he even knew what he wanted to do. 'They' had settled on him becoming a Certified Public Accountant with a minor in Finance. However, just like everyone else in America he was profoundly changed by the events of 9/11/2001. Watching the Twin Towers collapse rocked him to his core. His teacher had turned on the TV in their classroom and he had witnessed firsthand the devastation of the despicable terrorist attack. He and his classmates had seen people jump from the Towers to escape the flaming inferno that used to be offices. They had seen the collapsing towers fill the streets of Manhattan with dust that choked people that couldn't get away fast enough. They'd watched first responders collapse in the streets overcome by respiratory problems and grief.

Later he and his parents had watched the American Flag being raised by fire fighters on the rubbles of the collapsed Towers. He had been ready to sign up with the Marines, ready to just get suited up and go over to whatever country that had perpetrated this heinous crime and kick some ass. While the Army accepted applicants at the age of sixteen, he was only thirteen at the time and had to delay his thirst for revenge. By the time he'd finished High school, he had settled on becoming a law enforcement officer. Naturally his dad hadn't been too happy, but eventually had come around and supported his decision, after they'd compromised on him getting an AA in Business Administration first. He'd continued and received his Bachelors Degree in Criminal Justice eighteen months later.

Being called up to the Homicide Division to be trained as a Detective, was a big deal to Jerome. After having put in three years as a patrol officer at the MDPD, he was ready to solve all kinds of crimes. At least he thought he was. Deep down inside, however, he knew he was a rookie who didn't really have a clue. Luckily he was assigned to Detective Eric Poole, a veteran of the department.

The first case they caught together had ended with Jerome not making it in time to the kitchen sink but instead distributing his breakfast all over the crime scene. Det. Poole had been surprisingly understanding, ripping a few paper towels from the roll in the kitchen and sending him off to wait in front of the house that featured the crime scene. This hadn't been the way he'd wanted to start his career in the department. Poole had been cool about it though.

"Don't sweat it man, we've all done it on the first case." he'd reassured him.

"Thank you, Sir!" he'd replied in between heaves.

"When you're done vomiting you can start calling me Eric."

As seemed to be true for a lot of cases, the spouse, in this case the husband, turned out to be the murderer. Poole had taken the husband to an interview room and had started sweating him. Eventually the guy had tripped up and confessed. Case closed.

Chapter Seven

Benjamin Walker, Hamburg, Germany (May 2008)

How ironic, after all it was his mom's boyfriend who'd given him the idea for his plan. It was only appropriate for him to recreate the handcuff incident where he had found his mom tied to her bed. What sick and deranged person would handcuff a woman to her bed and leave her there to be discovered by her son? It had been a Monday morning when he had put all the pieces of his devious plan into place. For the past two months he had monitored the comings and goings of his mom's boyfriend. Yes, her boyfriend, because after all he had put her through, was still putting her through; she hadn't been able to break away from him.

Benjamin had found the four sets of handcuffs Jakob had used on his mom the night he'd found her, right in her dresser covered by her underwear. He had bought some latex gloves to make sure he wasn't going to leave any fingerprints on the cuffs, or any of the other equipment he had needed. He had taken the U-Bahn from the train station Schlump to St. Pauli, the Red-light District. After walking down the Reeperbahn for a few minutes he'd found a store that had sold all kinds of sex toys and accessory. He had been looking for, and had found, one of those leather headgears that the masochist's liked to use. First he had been wondering how to purchase the gear without touching it. Then he'd realized that he could always wipe it down once he got home. In the end he had just grabbed it, paid for it and taken the ride back home.

After he'd cleaned the headgear with bleach, just to make sure none of his prints were left on it, he had stored it in his dresser together with the handcuffs he had removed from his mom's room.

It had only been a matter of timing. He had known that sooner or later his mom would come home plastered beyond repair. Sure enough, he only had to wait a couple of days before she came home, dropped into bed and was out like a light.

He had taken no pleasure in it, but what he had done had been necessary. He had handcuffed his mother to the bedposts; stuffed two potatoes into her mouth, put the mask over her head and secured his handiwork with a scarf that he had wrapped tightly over her mouth and nose, the only parts of her face left exposed by the headgear. He'd thought that the potatoes had been a nice touch, like the balls his mother had handled.

The amazing part had been that his mom had not even moved while he'd prepared her to die. Not once, not a moan, not a twitch, she had been just lying there – until she'd run out of air – and suffocated.

Benjamin had gone to his room after he'd completed his task. He'd felt at peace with himself and the world. It hadn't really been his fault after all. His mother had killed his dad – not directly, not literally, but by pushing him over the edge. Maybe he could have forgiven her eventually, but she hadn't repented, hadn't changed her lifestyle. She had been dragging him down with her.

He'd perfected his master plan over the last few weeks. Had gone over every step, every emotion he was going to display. He mentally went through the whole process again. He'd been very careful not to touch the handcuffs without gloves, since he'd figured that the pimp's fingerprints were still on them. When making the phone call to the police he would have to be credible, act like the victim of a crime. While he knew the pimp's name, it was Jakob, he'd never been able to say it out loud or even say it to himself in his mind.

Well, Jakob was going to have a bad day. Benjamin had called the Polizei at 7:00 a.m. crying hysterically. He'd been barely able to give the address to the dispatcher before he had faked a very believable nervous breakdown. He'd shown the police officers to his mother's room before he'd suffered another breakdown. A very nice and beautiful female police officer had finally been able to calm him down. Through his tears he'd been able to glance at her very well developed breast that luckily hadn't been camouflaged by a bullet proof vest.

Interrupted by some more crying and sobbing he'd finally been able to recall how he'd woken up to go to the bathroom and on the way back to his room had wondered about the open door to his mom's bedroom. He'd explained to them the horror he'd experienced when he'd walked across the hallway to close the door, only to discover his mom with that hideous mask and the scarf wrapped around her head. He'd called 110 – the emergency number – immediately.

It hadn't taken the police officers too long to befriend Benjamin enough for him to share his suspicion with them. The only person he'd been able to identify that had access to the apartment had been Jakob. No, he hadn't known Jakob's last name or address, but he'd known his favorite bar. It was only a few of blocks away. "Die Tuba" in the Isestrasse had been his hangout. Benjamin had actually been to the place in the past. Wooden floors, wooden tables and benches, narrow, steep stairs down to the restrooms that had taken its toll on a few patrons after midnights!

The officers had gotten lucky; Jakob had been at the bar for his liquid breakfast. Naturally he'd denied any involvement in Christina's demise, he'd even cried when he'd heard about her death. The police hadn't believed him. It had taken the German prosecutors only eight months to charge and then convict him of murder in the second degree. Germany's laws are based on rules; there are no cases of precedent, previous rulings or other distracting factors. You break the rules – there's a set of consequences you will suffer or so he had believed. To Benjamin's dismay these rules had been applied very leniently. Jakob received only seven years for manslaughter, five with good behavior. So much for the German justice system, and it's -

what he had believed - legendary toughness. Nevertheless, Benjamin had freed himself of his mother's filthy lifestyle.

Just as he'd expected, his aunt had stepped up to the plate and claimed him as a relative. But in Germany things were never easy, especially when it comes to bureaucracy involving minors. They had been interviewed by social workers and judges for weeks before he'd been allowed to permanently live with his aunt.

He'd continued at Helene-Lange-Gymnasium and eventually had been able to get his Abitur. Due to the fact that his father had been an American, he had held dual citizenship since birth. He'd figured that there were only two ways for him to go. Kill his aunt and go to jail for an undetermined amount of time, or move to the US. His aunt had been a royal pain, constantly talking about the husband that had left her. Benjamin had no problem seeing why. What had troubled him had been his urge to put an end to her constant complaints. Jan had never done the dishes, Jan had never done the laundry, he'd never swept the floors, never cleaned the windows, and never cleaned the bathroom, hadn't even made enough money to give her the life she'd deserved. One of her biggest complaints had been Jan's inability to put the toilet seat and lid down after completing his business! If he'd had to listen to her complaints another day, he just might have killed her.

He'd decided to move to the United States of America, the land of his father. He'd figured that he shouldn't have too much of a problem because his English had been almost perfect. Benjamin and his dad had never communicated in German – it had always been English between the two of them.

Between the insurance money and what he'd saved from washing and polishing cars at a small used car dealer's lot, he had enough for the plane ticket and to get started. Somehow he'd find an apartment and a job in his country of choice. While his dad was from the Midwest, Benjamin had always been enthralled by the pictures showing the rich and famous in Miami and Miami Beach. The weather seemed to always be pleasant and the girls looked beautiful. Maybe he could even enroll at the University in Miami.

While his future had been uncertain, anything had been better than staying in Hamburg with his degenerate aunt.

He'd gone to the American Consulate in Hamburg to find out about obtaining a US Passport. The personnel had been rather unfriendly and some of them downright rude. While it had not been a pleasant experience, it had provided him with the information he'd needed, and he'd returned a couple of weeks later with the required paperwork. It took the Consulate 'only' three months to issue his passport.

The loud honking of the semi truck behind him jolted him out of his daydream. He quickly rolled down his window, extended his middle finger out of the window in response to the rather rude reminder of where he was, and stepped on the gas.

Chapter Eight

Sandra Restrepo, Miami (Friday, January 30th, 2015)

Columbia woke up with her right ankle shackled to a heavy metal chain which in turn was attached to an eyehook embedded in the concrete floor of her prison. She rubbed her puffy eyes trying to remember what had happened. The beach, the stranger with the Clinton mask, the blood; it all came back to her and she doubled over on the mattress she was sitting on - naked. There had been so much blood and Kevin never even made a sound, just the strange noise of the blood gushing out of him. She rolled to her side, threw up and fainted.

The next time she came out of it, she noticed that there was hardly any light in the place. Looking around she noticed a light bulb right under the ceiling that emitted a faint glow of light. She was sitting on a mattress that had been stained by her vomit. Not caring about the stench she rolled over and closed her eyes. Who was the beast that had killed Kevin and abducted her?

Before she was able to further ponder her situation, a door swung open and a masked man appeared. He carefully closed the door behind him and walked over to her.

"How are you doing sweetheart?" he whispered in a strange voice. His face was hidden behind a weird looking leather mask that had small openings for his eyes and mouth.

Was he out of his mind? How was she doing? Had there been anything left in her stomach she would have vomited again. As it was she was overcome by dry retching that lasted for a couple of minutes. When she looked up again the man was gone.

Only minutes later he was back with a bucket of warm soapy water, a sponge and a towel. Kneeling next to her he started to tenderly clean her face and neck. He moved down to her armpits, breast and back. Gingerly toweled her dry and started to clean her legs, coming around to her private area before she snapped out of her shock. Kicking at him with all her strength she sent him falling onto his back. Visibly stunned and angry he gathered himself up and approached her again. When she raised her arms to push him away he surprised her by slapping her hard across the face. Falling back she hurt her neck when it hit the edge of the mattress.

He calmly leaned forward and grabbed her right leg with one hand. Pulling her towards him he simultaneously reached for the sponge, dipped it into the bucket and shoved the sponge into her privates. When satisfied with his work, he twisted her leg, forcing her to roll onto her stomach. He dipped the sponge into the bucket again and proceeded to clean her butt, legs and feet. Dumping the sponge he toweled her dry and stepped back. Still lying on her stomach she was glad he had stopped, but was wondering what would come next, when she turned her head she saw him pulling his Polo-shirt over his masked head, kicking off his shoes and pulling down his pants and underwear, revealing his erection.

Columbia started screaming hysterically until he knelt down next to her, slapped her again hard across her face, rolled her over and forced her legs apart. When she struggled again he hit her with his fist. The blow was hard enough to make her feel dizzy. When she found her bearings, he had already started to penetrate her. The lack of any moisture in her vagina made it harder for him, but he just spread her legs further and continued to push until he painfully entered her. To her surprise it was over rather quickly. After a few thrusts he unloaded inside of her. Grunting he pulled out of her and got up.

"Hijo de puta!" she yelled at him, before she rolled over and covered her head with her arms.

"I love you too. Don't get dirty again. I'll be back soon!" he whispered before he put on his cloths and left quietly.

She rolled up into a fetal position and started sobbing uncontrollably. After a while she opened her eyes and scanned the room again. Getting up from the mattress she looked at the chain securing her to the floor. Walking towards the wall that was covered by a tool bench she quickly realized that the chain restricted her movements to only slightly more than a three foot radius. She was going to die in this place. Having seen her boyfriend being killed by this animal, having been raped by this monster, she was convinced she would die by the hands of this freak as well.

Chapter Nine

Benjamin Walker,
Florida Keys (Monday, March 2nd, 2015)

The drive over the Seven-Mile-Bridge was spectacular. The sun had started to edge closer to the water on the gulf side of the road, reflecting off the surface that was smooth and almost mirror like. Pelicans were accompanying part of his trip over the bridge, sailing alongside his car, floating effortlessly at an incredible speed. To his right the old bridge was visible. Once he crossed the peak of the bridge he noticed a small island in the distance on the Atlantic Ocean side of the bridge. When he got closer, he saw a few boats anchored close to the shore, people enjoying themselves. The next island even had a small white beach and people were having a picnic or just hanging out on their boats. To his right he noticed an Australian pine growing on top of the old seven-mile bridge. How bizarre, growing to what looked like at least twenty five feet, out of concrete!

He'd lowered all of his windows and enjoyed the wind blowing through the car. He'd held his left hand out the window playing airplane – lowering and raising the angle of his hand – mimicking the position of the wings on an airplane.

He arrived in Key West Monday evening. Upon entering Key West he maneuvered the triangle, as he found out later it was called by the locals, eventually found the 'Spinnaker' and turned into the parking lot. It wasn't fancy by any stretch of the imagination, but at this time of year the rates were decidedly too high at all the swanky places. Checking in with his fake driver's license had been surprisingly easy. Well, after all, he'd spent enough on the fake to be allowed to enjoy peace of mind.

As soon as he had dropped off his belongings in the room he decided to explore the island. Not being in the habit of wasting money he decided to walk down North Roosevelt Boulevard towards the center of the town. Walking through the first shopping center he didn't find a real bar, so he continued down the street. The second center had a pool billiard bar tucked into the corner of it. The bar was pretty empty and he managed to get a pool table, ordered some chicken fingers and fries, and practice some shots. When the crowd started to arrive a pretty girl asked him if she could join and he played a couple of rounds with her until her boyfriend arrived and informed him that he should get lost. Trying to stay out of trouble he immediately complied with the gentleman's request, knocked down his beer and left. He picked up a bottle of Jack Daniels on his way out. Conveniently the place had a liquor store attached to it.

Walking on the bay side of North Roosevelt Boulevard, he took in the smell of decaying seaweed and mangrove leaves. He also ingested a couple of swigs of Whiskey for good measure. A homeless person nestled between the roots of a clutter of mangroves startled him when he suddenly started moving. The man's bicycle was just below the seawall, draped with full plastic bags, a blanket, and an assortment of plastic canisters. There seemed to be plenty of free spirits on this island. Back at the hotel he finished the better part of the bottle with the help of a few Coca Colas he got from the soda machine down the hallway on the upstairs landing of the hotel.

Maybe he should have done what most vacationers did, hit the usual spot, Duval Street – party row! During the day – according to his friend - they were cruising up and down the street, looking for T-shirts and other tourist trinkets in the many stores. Not to mention a good time in the numerous bars lining Duval Street. Hemingway was supposed to have hung out and gotten hammered at Sloppy Joe's, however, the live music was much better at the Hog Breath Saloon. There were, according to one of his co-workers, a few establishments that offered not only beautiful women dancing on stage, but women performing additional services for a fee. Somehow Key West had gotten a reputation as a heaven for wild spring breakers, gays, party-animals and homeless people. Who would have thought that the small pirate town of the 1800's would transform itself into party city? Maybe it was the weather or the laid back atmosphere. Most of the locals seemed to be carefree and not arrested by the shackles hindering mainstream citizens from enjoying life. There were lots of girls and guys with long hair and cut-off jeans.

Well, tomorrow was another day and he just might try to find out what the party was really all about.

He spent Tuesday relaxed and solitary on Smathers beach. After receiving, what he figured to be the right amount of rays, he retreated to his hotel room, took a shower and then a trolley tour of the island. He learned that Key West was also called Bone Island, after Cayo Hueso, or Bone Key, due to the large number of sun bleached bones found there in the past. Local lore had it that the incoming settlers couldn't pronounce the name Cayo Hueso correctly – and it had changed to Key West.

Later on he followed the vacationer's trail; Turtle Kraals over to Duval Street. He recalled having read an article in a newspaper were a guy had woken up in an alley feeling 'violated'. Later at the hospital it turned out someone had slipped him a rohypnol or roofie and had his way with him! No sir, he was going to be careful.

He visited quite a few bars and got his fill. Somehow he ended up in a strip club on the second floor of a building off Duval Street.

"Next up on stage is Melanie." announced the DJ over the P.A. system.

She was a beauty. Long brown hair, legs up to her neck and the face of an angel sent straight from heaven. After her performance, which must have netted her at least fifty dollars in singles, he intercepted her at the bar where she was making her round.

"Nice seeing the star of the establishment." he opened.

"Thank you." she responded without much interest.

"Can I buy you a drink?"

"What kind of a drink?"

"Champagne?"

"Sure, why not" she sounded a little more enthused.

They got their champagne flutes, after he paid a king's ransom for them, and moved on to a 'private table'. He really liked the way she moved – almost cat like. She was still wearing only a string bikini bottom and no top. Her breast looked firm; the nipples were centered, slightly on top of where gravity took over. She must have been sunbathing recently; they looked tanned and just really delicious.

He felt foolish staring at her breast, but was unable to control his focus! They looked like they had been sculptured by Rubens. No, not Rubens scratch that, they weren't heavy like the typical Rubens breast. She wasn't heavy or anything. To the contrary, her waist was slim, her rear end almost petite, yet full. Her shoulders were well formed, not quite muscular, but definitely more than just natural.

He wasn't able to control himself. She reminded him of his mother.

"I have two hundred bucks that say 'Let's get out of here!'" he informed her.

"Make it three hundred, I'll put on my cloths and be right back."

"You got it."

She went backstage to gather her clothes and other belongings. The DJ announced Sarah up on stage. Not bad. Slightly too heavy for his taste, but she did have nice tits.

When Melanie reappeared she was wearing jean shorts a blue T-Shirt and high heels. If possible, she looked hotter than in the g-string and no bra!

"Where are we going?" she inquired.

"Spinnaker."

She started texting on her phone. He figured it was her boyfriend or pimp she was keeping in the loop.

He had called a cab while she was getting dressed and surprisingly the pink cab was there when they got downstairs.

"Spinnaker." he told the driver.

At least she wasn't pretending to be in love with him like some of the other girls he'd had. Just sitting there staring out into the night.

Business, that's what it was, just another transaction she had to complete to get to where she wanted to go. He didn't care; actually appreciated her honesty, he wanted to get something himself. He wanted to blow off some steam. And she would definitely be a nice vessel to use for his purposes. Just thinking about her got him excited. She was fine. Heck, more than just fine. Looking at her in profile he wasn't able to help but be reminded, again, of his mother.

"Why don't you take a shower?" he asked her once they got to the hotel room.

"What?"

"Take a shower!" he told her.

"Why, do I smell?"

"That's not the point. Please, just take a shower."

"Alright." he was paying her, so she went to the bathroom.

It wasn't that he was overly concerned with germs, but he wanted her to smell good. He didn't want his olfactory system to get attacked by an unpleasant odor that would ruin his mood. And yeah, he was in the mood!

He turned on the TV and started watching the news. What passed as news anyway: Someone had been shot in Overtown … a woman had been raped and left for dead next to the Turnpike … a baby had been found buried in the back yard… a drive-by-shooting had claimed the life of a five year old…

When she came out of the bathroom she looked ravishing. Her hair was damp, toweled dry to the point where she looked as perfect as those girls on TV commercials for shampoo. Oh, he was going to have a good time.

"Why don't you relax while I take a shower?" he wasn't really asking but rather instructing her.

"Sure."

He went to the bathroom. Slob, she had left the soap wrapper on the floor, discarded the shampoo and conditioner bottles in the sink.

No worries, he wasn't going to let it spoil his mood. He turned on the shower, lathered himself from top to bottom. He enjoyed being real clean. He was making sure there wasn't a spot on his body that wasn't getting scrubbed and sanitized.

What was he going to do with her? There were options. He could be the nice guy. He could be the brute. He could pretend to be the sensitive guy – or he could just be himself. Decisions, decisions! He was going to be himself, she deserved that, even though she was a slob, she was pretty – hell, she was gorgeous. He was going to treat her right!

When he came out of the bathroom she was standing by the TV trying to change channels. He glanced over at his small gym bag, that contained his spare cloths and his accessories, making sure it hadn't been moved or tampered with.

"Why don't you lie down?" he asked her politely.

"Sure".

He admired her rear end. Her buttocks were just perfect. He almost started salivating. How could a two bit whore look so good? Then again – his mother had looked very good. Not to him, but apparently to every Dick-and-Harry in the neighborhood. She'd been so popular that his dad had lost his mind.

Well, he wasn't going to follow down that road! She was just a whore. Nothing to it, he would just use her and be done.

Chapter Ten

Sandra Restrepo, Miami (Saturday, January 31st, 2015)

He had stripped Columbia of all of her jewelry and her watch so she had no idea how much time had elapsed when he reentered her room. Wearing a Zorro-like mask that only covered his eyes and the upper part of his nose he walked over to her and looked down.

"Let's try this again." he whispered. "Be nice – and I'll be nice!" he continued before he stripped.

Lying down next to her he started to hold her in an almost gentle way. She tried to pull away, but he just pulled her close again. Leaning in he tried to kiss her, but again she pulled her head away quickly. Another hard slap to her face and a pull on her neck allowed him to start kissing her. He started fondling her breast and stomach. When his hand moved down her body she started to gag. He immediately pushed her back and jumped up. Hastily dressing he faced her for a couple of seconds before he left the room.

She did have some power over him after all. He was squeamish when she retched. He had placed a couple of sandwiches from McDonalds and a soft drink close to where he had undressed. A plan started forming in her head and she ate both sandwiches and drank the soda. It was only a matter of time now until she'd be able to strike back.

Not having eaten meat in over a year, she knew her stomach was bound to object violently within a rather short period of time. When she felt the need to relieve herself, she ignored the camping toilet that was within her range of chain restricted movement. Instead she braced herself to do something she hadn't done since leaving infancy behind – she defecated onto the mattress she was lying on. Disgusted by her own action she waited for the monster to come back.

She didn't have to wait long. She noticed his hesitation when he entered the room. Even though he was wearing the Zorro-mask, she could see his anger when he saw the soiled mattress. Without a word he turned around and left the room leaving the door open. When he returned he had a garden hose in his hands. He walked over to her and punched her hard enough in the face to make her black out. When she came to he was standing over her hosing her down like a wild animal in a zoo exhibit.

As soon as he was done he dragged the hose back outside, returned, closed the door and shed his cloths again. In her desperation she crawled off the mattress away from him. He wouldn't have any of that and pulled the chain hard enough to make her scream in agony and struggle back onto the wet mattress. Before she was able to recover, he had pinned her down again, forcing himself inside of her. She twisted and turned as hard as she was able to. However, all of her efforts were in vain until she decided to reach between her legs and squeeze his testicles as hard as she could. The result was stunning even to her. She jumped up and move as far away from him as the chain allowed, when he started howling like a wounded animal. "Big mistake!" he hissed when he had recovered and then started beating her with a vengeance. Columbia felt her nose break and felt her knees getting weak.

When she started to go down she suddenly saw the straight punch coming again for the center of her face. She lost consciousness before her head made violent contact with the concrete floor.

Chapter Eleven

Jerome Water, Miami (Thursday, March 5th, 2015)

During the morning briefing at the station Captain Santiago put up some rather disturbing pictures depicting a dead girl on the large whiteboard. He explained that the victim had been found floating next to a pier at the Dinner Key Marina close to Miami City Hall. Apparently her body had somehow gotten entangled in some mooring ropes next to a multi-million Dollar yacht. Unfortunately she had been in the water long enough to allow some fish to take rather large portions of her flesh. Since the body had been naked, bloated and somewhat chewed up, the Medical Examiner had to work hard to obtain fingerprints for identification. Her prints were in the Homeland Security system since she was Columbian.

The M.E. had ruled it a homicide. She had been severely beaten and died of blunt force trauma to the back of her head. Even the older detectives averted their eyes after a while. What deranged animal would do something like this to a young girl?

Sandra Restrepo, twenty-one-years old, originally from Cali, Columbia, and according to her passport picture quite beautiful, had been a FIU-student before her untimely demise. Her last known address was close to FIU and the Sweetwater PD would have to be notified and could potentially assist later on in interviewing neighbors, fellow students and faculty.

"Wasn't there another dead FIU student, male, a few weeks ago on Key Biscayne?" Jerome chimed in.

"Indeed Detective..." Captain Santiago trailed off and looked at Detective Poole, who was sitting next to Jerome for help.

"Water." Poole helped.

"...Water. I am glad that someone is following the news from other departments. Det. Water, maybe you should take an active role in this case. Poole, is he ready?"

"Don't know, but I'll keep an eye on him, and my shoes." Poole replied and laughter ripped through the room.

"Alright then, pick up the file, get the file on the kid on Key Biscayne from Key Biscayne PD, contact Miami PD and get going." Capt. Santiago dismissed the group.

"How come we're even catching this case? Shouldn't Miami PD handle this since she was found in Miami?" Water wondered.

"Technically yes, but since she's a floater she may have gone in anywhere, plus she's connected to FIU. If she was killed on Key Biscayne, we will most likely take over officially – with our colleagues in Miami being more than happy to pass on the case." Poole grunted.

"So where do we start?" Water asked Poole on the way out of the room.

"It's your case. Where do you think we should start?" Poole liked the kid and figured he'd let him run with it.

"Well, we have Sandra's address and can get the class schedules for her and the guy that was found on the beach. Maybe we could cross reference their classes, talk to other students and faculty. Interview the neighbors and friends. See if she knew the kid on Key Biscayne." Waters stopped dead in his tracks, "Maybe he killed her and dumped her body in the water?" he said excitedly before it hit him.

"Never mind, he's dead." Water felt foolish for going off like that.

"Sounds like a plan. Let's take a look at the files and formulate a plan of attack." Poole smiled to himself. The kid had some fire in him, reminded him of his younger self.

Poole and Water were going over the files when Water observed that:

"It looks like the detectives hit a dead end with the kid on Key Biscayne. His name was Kevin Miles, twenty-one years old from Lincoln, Nebraska. He had his throat slit in his own car. Too many unknown finger prints; with nothing else standing out."

"Why don't you call the lab and ask them to check the prints against Sandra Restrepo's?" Poole asked. Water could have kicked himself for not coming up with this most obvious idea.

Water called it in and they continued by compiling a list of people to interview, and called the administration office at FIU to schedule a meeting with an administrator who could help them with the class schedules and class mates before heading out.

Chapter Twelve

Thomas Sander, Miami (Saturday, February 28th, 2015)

His flight on the Airbus A380 had been pleasant and uneventful. The huge airplane was truly amazing. Not only did it make you feel like you were moving in your own living room, it was also extremely quiet. He was looking forward to a break from the subpar weather in Hamburg, anticipating sun filled days and serious late night conversations with his sister.

Miami International Airport had been a very pleasant surprise. Getting through customs and clearing the luggage hassle was a breeze. The new terminal for international flights was not only beautiful but also very functional. According to the travel website he'd visited, MIA ranked in the top five to ten percent of US airports when looking at passenger, international passenger and cargo volume. Miami had also recently completed a new leg to its Metro Rail System connecting the existing rail to the airport.

Naturally he wasn't able to verify it's functionality since Sabine was there to pick him up. After a few minutes of intense hugging they walked out of the terminal to her car, parked in the very Miami – Dolphin garage.

He hadn't seen his little sister in a few months and while they kept in touch through frequent phone calls, he had felt somewhat disconnected from her. Especially lately Sabine had gotten somewhat evasive regarding her life in Miami.

Sabine was born on July 4th, 1994. His parents, Tobias and Manuela Sander, had considered this a special day. Not only had they conceived their daughter at a very late time in their lives, but they had always loved the movie "Born on the 4th of July". While Tom Cruise was basically a persona non grata in Germany due to his affiliation with the Church of Scientology, his movies were still pretty good. It also happened to be the Independence Day of the USA. In short, the day was special – mostly because of their daughter's birth! While they hadn't planned for Sabine, they had been ecstatic. Thomas had already been nine years old, but Sabine just completed them.

Thomas loved being the older brother. He had spent hours with her on the playground, got her to the movies, screened her first boyfriend in kindergarten, helped her over her disappointment when she had found out that Santa wasn't real, and helped her with her homework in school.

He remembered his parent's relief when he had helped her over the break-up with her first real boyfriend. Sabine had been fourteen and he had just finished his stint with the German Bundeswehr, the German Army, after completing his apprenticeship to become a Real Estate Broker. While he had moved out three years prior, he nevertheless had made the time to come home to comfort his little sister after her break-up. He had spent the entire weekend talking to her, explaining the short-comings of the male species, taking her on long walks around the 'Alster' followed by dinners at his favorite restaurants. Ah, good old days. Now his little sister was all grown up – or so she thought.

He was very proud of her for having finished her Abitur with a 3.71 GPA, good enough to allow her to apply to - and be accepted by the Florida International University in Miami, Florida. She'd dreamt about going to a school abroad to complete her education. German employers always looked favorably upon applicants that spoke perfect English and had completed their studies abroad. Sabine had wanted to fill that bill. She aspired to become a lawyer for a multinational corporation. Their dad had always been a Law-and-Order-Justice-Junkie! Not only had he read every John Grisham novel, and watched essentially every episode of "Law & Order", he'd actually contemplated going back to school to get his law degree! Alas, he never had. As the principal of a High School with two children making time had been a problem. Their mom had been a teacher and first rate homemaker. She had been the one to keep the family together. Both of them had been extremely excited when she'd been accepted to study abroad.

From conversations with his parents Thomas knew that having to pay for tuition and housing was going to put a serious dent into their retirement plan, but so what? Sabine's future was what their focus was on. Thomas was doing all right selling Real Estate in Hamburg and surrounding areas. Well, really more than just all right. After a couple of tough years working for the man, he had gone out on his own and become quite successful. His specialty was 'Altbau' condominiums. While large parts of Hamburg had been destroyed either during the 'Great Fire' in 1842 or during the Allied bombings in WWII, there were plenty of old buildings left in Hamburg. Thomas had specialized in helping owners to buy-out tenants, renovate and modernize the units and then re-rent the condominiums at a much higher rate, or to sell them. This was no easy task due to German laws that heavily favor the renters. Many owners preferred to have an expert handle this. Thomas had a knack for convincing the – mostly elderly renters – that they could live comfortably with the offered buy-out in a smaller apartment. Thomas' partner and best friend Alex, a general contractor, handled the renovations and Thomas then rented or sold the units under an exclusive listing agreement.

Chapter Thirteen

Benjamin Walker,
Key West (Wednesday, March 4th, 2015)

It was not even 7 a.m.; the sun hadn't started to rise, when he put the small gym bag and the garbage bag into the trunk of his black Mustang and got into the driver's seat. He had mentally gone over every step he had taken in the past two days. He had paid the room at the hotel in cash. He'd used a counterfeit driver's license he'd purchased a year ago. There was no camera in the hotel lobby. Before he'd left the room he had cleaned the bathtub and sink, removed all the hair from the drains, though some of it may not even have been his. He had wiped down every surface in the room, the TV remote control and the door knobs with a small towel. He'd packed all the towels into the garbage bag he had pulled from the trash can outside of the hotel room by the vending machines. He felt good. He started the engine and backed out of the parking space, glanced at the hotel one last time and stepped on the gas.

There was no traffic on South Roosevelt Boulevard as he exited the hotel's parking lot, turned right at the triangle and was on his way back to Miami. On his way to solving his problems, on his way to tying up the loose ends he had left behind. Problem solving had always been his strong suit.

Should he get some gas on his way out of Key West? There was a gas station conveniently located on the right side of the road. He checked his fuel gauge, but figured that he had enough to make it to Marathon without a problem. He wanted to put some distance between Key West and himself.

Finally he got past the businesses and had the open road in front of him. Accelerating to fifty-five mph and letting the wind come in through the open windows, he tried to keep a low profile and stayed within the speed limit. Approaching East Rockland Key, where the two lanes merged into one, he started to speed up. No way was he going to get stuck behind that slow-poke! It wasn't by much, but he made it. He wasn't too concerned about the driver leaning on his horn in anger.

The sign in front of the Fire Department on Sugarloaf Key announced that they were looking for volunteer fire fighters – they even offered free training! There were always some people who believed in the greater good – just like his dad. Well, it hadn't worked out that great for him.

Chapter Fourteen

Franco Tamargo, Miami (Sept. 2004)

Franco's dream as a little boy had been to become filthy rich. He had dreamt about being the CEO of his own company. A company that would buy distressed and failing corporations, turn them around, then sell them and move on to the next one. Not like Michael Douglas in "Wall Street", which he'd watched at least ten times as a boy, more humane, more like Richard Gere in 'Pretty Woman'. He had ended up as a Detective with the Miami Dade County Police Department and then a private investigator. It hadn't been for lack of trying. After finishing at Southwest Miami High he'd taken a break for a couple of months, working at various restaurants in Coconut Grove. Eventually he'd gotten back on track to chase his dream of becoming a millionaire. He'd enrolled at Florida International University to pursue a double major in Finance and Marketing. He'd been a junior living in an apartment complex close to the intersection of US 1 and Kendall Drive. In September of 2004 his life took an unexpected turn when he went to buy some beer at a 7-Eleven on Kendall Drive. After picking up a six-pack of Bud from the refrigerated section he'd walked over to the counter where a young woman with her infant, slung around her front in a scarf, had been checking out with some milk.

He'd noticed a guy walking through the aisles pretending to look at various items without taking any. The dude had been wearing a black shirt, a Dolphins cap, beige shorts, sneakers, and gloves. Really – gloves in Miami in September? Franco had known there was something wrong with the picture.

However, he hadn't really been concerned with shoplifters or other weirdos of society at that time. He'd just wanted to get his beer, walk back to his apartment and relax. That hadn't happened!

The guy had been standing right next to the lady in front of Franco, and then without any preamble the guy pulled a big gun out of his fanny pack and pointed it at the poor Indian clerk. For a moment Franco had thought that he may have an involuntary bowl movement! Luckily he didn't experience that embarrassment. The clerk hadn't been that fortunate judging by the growling sound coming from behind the counter. It had taken Franco a couple of seconds to recover from his initial shock, but he found his bearings and jumped the guy. He'd tried to wrestle the gun from the thug but had been unable to get full control of the guy's wrist. The gun had slowly but surely come around – until it had pointed at his right shoulder – and gone off!

The sound of the gun, fired at close range, had jolted him. Miraculously the bullet went through his shoulder without severing any major artery, or shattering any bone. As he'd found out later, it did manage to chip a small piece off his collarbone.

The thug had jumped up and pointed his gun at where the clerk was standing – presumably to demand the cash out of the register. However, the clerk and the lady had run from the store when Franco started to struggle with the thug. Franco eventually managed to come back up to his feet. Later on he wasn't able to explain how, and why, he just had gotten up. Nevertheless, he had – and he'd charged the thug again. Before he was able to get his hands on the guy he got shot again – this time in his leg. Thug 2 : Franco 0.

Black T-shirt had proceeded to take the cash out of the register and disappear into the night. The clerk, having seen the perpetrator leave the store, had come back and had wrapped Franco's wounds with paper towels as good as he'd been able to. He had already called 911 to report the robbery in progress while hiding in the parking lot. The police officers had beaten the ambulance to the scene and had helped the clerk stop the blood flow from Franco's wounds. While Franco had been very grateful for the clerks help, he'd been glad when the EMT guys carried him out. The smell of the man's feces had started to bother him... They'd taken him to Baptist Hospital which was only two miles from the store. While he'd lost a lot of blood, Franco had been discharged from the hospital after only four days. So much for Southern hospitality, well, technically Florida wasn't considered a Southern State.

Having gotten away with a whopping $357.00, the thug had never been apprehended. The second bullet had done a real number on his femur. After a few weeks of intense physical therapy he'd been able to walk again.

He probably wouldn't have recovered as well without his family's support. His whole family had been – still was – just the best. His parents had fled Cuba. His older siblings had been born in Cuba where his parents had been considerably well off. They'd left with just the clothes on their backs. One of Franco's older sisters had been handed over to a stranger for the flight to Miami. They'd been joking ever since that she'd been mixed up with some other little infants, but the joke always died quickly when people looked at her. She was a dead ringer for their mother.

Settling in the US hadn't been easy. They'd attempted to make a living in Pahokee, Florida, living in a rat infested barn on a farm. After having fought off rats for a few months the excitement had given way to frustration and they had relocated to Milwaukee, Wisconsin. With the help of a wonderful family there, they'd gotten their footing. Franco's dad had worked three jobs to keep his family of six fed! Later on his parents had decided that they'd had enough of the cold weather and moved to Miami. They'd made the trip in a retired and repainted school bus. He hadn't been born at that time so he always felt left out when they reminiscent about the trip. No matter how many times during family gatherings his siblings had told the stories. The furniture had been loaded into the back of the bus; the coolers were distributed throughout. The singing, the laughter, the easiness of life had kept them happy. Good old days.

His crazy sisters had been the driving force behind his recovery. Not a day had gone by without them bugging him to go for walks, to do his stretching exercises. He'd loved them for pestering him. His mother had insisted on cooking him some good Cuban food almost every day. Born in Miami, he had been raised on Cuban food. However, being a second generation Cuban, he eventually had gravitated towards the American cuisine. He preferred a good old burger and fries. Nevertheless, he'd eaten the food his mom had cooked. Black beans, rice, pulled pork or chicken, and plantains. Maybe she'd been right in announcing that only some good Cuban food would bring him back to health – after all, he'd recovered rather quickly. His spirits however hadn't. He hadn't been afraid of life or people per se, he'd just felt uneasy. He hadn't been able to put his finger on it and explain what exactly had been going on in his mind. It wasn't until his dad had taken him aside and explained a few things to him. "Son" he'd said, "a life lived in fear is not worth living. Life sometimes throws you a curveball. Your mother and I had it all figured out, and then Fidel took over. We left everything behind, but we still had each other and you guys. You have a choice to make: Live in fear for the rest of your life, hiding from people; or getting back up and making the best of it"

Who was he to blow his little brush with destiny out of proportion and let it dictate his life, when his parents had gone through so much? Nah, his dad had been right, suck it up and move on. And he had.

He'd switched majors and started studying criminal justice and received his bachelor's degree two years later, followed by six months in the Police Academy in North Dade.

Chapter Fifteen

Jerome Water and Eric Poole,
Miami (Thursday, March 5th, 2015)

Water's and Poole's first stop was Sandra's apartment. The resident manager gave them access to her apartment after a quick look at the search warrant and an even shorter look at her picture taken at the M.E.'s office. Once inside her one bedroom apartment Water looked at the few pictures adorning her living room. Sandra looking happy while horsing around with a couple of girlfriends on Miami Beach. Sandra standing next to her parents, with a Christmas tree in the background, while flashing a huge smile. Sandra and her parents in Paris - with the Eiffel Tower visible in the distance - raising her arms in triumph.

They found her diary in the nightstand next to her bed. Water understood enough Spanish to realize that it revealed no more than ordinary girly confessions of nothing. While that was to be expected, it was nevertheless somewhat disappointing. Her laptop, which wasn't password protected, revealed a ten day old email to a friend named Maria Delgardo in which Sandra announced that she had a date with Kevin Miles, the dead student on Key Biscayne.

So there was the connection between the two victims. They took the laptop with them for further inspection at the station. On their way out they asked the manager if he knew any of Sandra's friends, but didn't gain any more insight since he had never really interacted with Sandra after her move-in. They started to drive over to the university to talk to some of her professors. Since they were early for their first meeting they stopped at a small sandwich store for some lunch.

"So what do you think happened to them?" Water asked while chewing on a big bite of his Ruben sandwich.

"Damned if I know. Unless you believe that Kevin beat her up on their date, dumped her in the water and committed suicide with a knife he was able to throw away before bleeding out – I'd say there was a third party involved." Poole replied.

Water almost choked, swallowed hard and gave Poole a pained look: "Jealous ex-boyfriend then?" he asked.

"Don't know, but it's a possibility."

"We should contact Maria, ah…" Water consulted his notes between bites "…Delgado and see if she knows more. Maybe we get lucky and we can locate some other friends of hers at FIU. There must be someone who can shed some light on her social life." Water added.

Poole nodded while finishing off his sandwich. "Done? Let's go and find out."

Poole was closing the passenger door of their cruiser when his cell phone went off.

"Poole." he answered. Water started the car and began heading over to FIU when Poole tapped him on his arm and indicated for him to turn around. "Station" he mouthed to Water, who shot him a puzzled look but hung a U-turn nevertheless.

"There may be another missing female student." Poole informed him after he hung up. "Also, big surprise, Sandra's fingerprints were in her boyfriend's car." he added.

Chapter Sixteen

Franco Tamargo and Thomas Sander,
Miami (Tuesday, March 3rd, 2015)

His visitor from Germany, Thomas Sander, stood at six feet three inches, broad shouldered; dressed in blue jeans, light blue dress shirt hanging over his pants, and black Nike sneakers. His handshake was strong, but not overpowering. Clearly Thomas had been putting in a fair amount of time at some gym.

Franco tried to exchange some pleasantries, but his visitor seemed anxious to get to the point. Franco obliged.

"When you called you said that your sister is missing."

"Yes, she was kidnapped yesterday!" Thomas responded.

"You're sure about that? Please don't take this the wrong way, but are you sure she's really missing? She might be out with her boyfriend, or have decided to take a vacation." Franco inquired.

"Impossible, I just arrived on Saturday to visit her." An indignant Thomas snorted.

"Why don't you start by telling me everything from the beginning?"

"Alright, I came in Saturday afternoon, from Germany; Sabine picked me up from the airport and we went to her apartment. We ordered pizza, talked and went to bed. The next day she gave me a tour of Miami. We went Downtown, to Bayside, we visited Vizcaya, Coral Gables, the Biltmore Hotel and so on. Yesterday she went to school, came home for lunch, spent the afternoon with me at the pool and went back to school. She was supposed to be back after her last class which ended sometime around 11:00 p.m." Thomas was clearly agitated, though his English held up under duress and was surprisingly good.

"But she didn't?" Franco interjected.

"No, I waited until 3:00 a.m., and then I called the police."

"And you got nowhere."

"What? How do you know?" he asked surprised.

"Never mind, I am sorry for interrupting you."

"Well, I explained everything to them. They asked me the same questions, like does Sabine have a boyfriend, did she have a vacation planned. So very frustrating, and they showed no apparent interest in my sister's case."

"Okay, you have to understand that the police – and I am quite certain this is not much different in Germany – don't investigate missing adults before at least thirty-six hours have elapsed. It's not that they don't want to, they just cannot." Franco explained to Thomas, trying to be tactful.

"You're defending them?"

"Thomas, they don't have the manpower to jump on every case. And frankly, a lot of them turn out to be domestic spats and pranks. No, I am not suggesting that this is the case with Sabine; just trying to explain why they cannot do anything – yet."

"Well, that's why I am here. I've spent the whole morning at the police station and while they are scoring high on making you wait for hours, they have no interest in Sabine." Thomas replied.

"Here are your options: One, you can wait the required period of time and file a missing person report with the police. Two, you can engage me to start looking into this. By the way, how'd you find me?" Franco wanted to know.

"Google, you were the closest private investigator." Thomas replied honestly.

"How flattering." Franco deadpanned.

"What?" Thomas asked with a questioning look on his face.

"Oh I get it, I am sorry, it's just that I don't know my way around Miami, and since Sabine's apartment is not far from your office, I figured you would be the easiest guy to get to. I want to hire you." Thomas continued while looking apologetic.

Franco's office was located in the Datran Center next to the southernmost station of the Metro-Rail, which was indeed fairly close to Sabine's apartment.

Franco handed Thomas a client agreement and waited while Thomas quickly scanned and signed it. Thomas handed Franco Travelers checks for the deposit on the retainer and told him he'd have his bank wire the balance. With that formality out of the way Franco continued with additional questions, obtained a picture of Sabine and the address to her apartment.

Thomas continued to fill Franco in on some other small details.

According to Thomas, his sister had come to Miami to study at FIU and had, rather suddenly, started to be a little evasive when talk touched on her personal life.

Thomas was very close to his sister Sabine. She'd been calling him regularly, at least once a week. A few months after she'd left; her calls had gotten less frequent. He'd scolded her, but she laughed it off, telling him that she had a boyfriend. Her boyfriend was not only cute and funny, but also a player on the FIU football team. Thomas had tried to find out more about this guy, but Sabine had not been forthcoming with any additional information. Why – he couldn't understand.

After a few weeks Thomas had gotten curious enough to decide to take a vacation in Miami. Their parents, who also had picked up on her being a little too tight lipped about her life, had wanted to come as well. Both of them had wanted to fly to Miami to check on their baby girl. Thomas had convinced them to stay in Hamburg for the remaining weeks of the school year. His dad was the principal at a High School in Hamburg and his mom was teaching English at a Hoehere Handelsschule not too far from his dad's school. He'd left his assistant in charge of his business to find out what exactly was going on in Miami. When Thomas, immediately upon his arrival, had started to question his sister about the boyfriend and her life, she'd told him to be patient, that she would explain everything. As a matter of fact, they were supposed to have dinner on Tuesday with the mysterious boyfriend.

Franco and Thomas exchanged cell phone numbers and Franco asked for permission to come to Sabine's apartment to look for additional clues. They agreed for Franco to come to the apartment in an hour.

Chapter Seventeen

Franco Tamargo,
Miami (Tuesday, March 3rd, 2015, 3:30 pm)

Franco had quit the MDPD, but he wasn't beyond using his old contacts within the law enforcement community to obtain information for his cases. Luckily his former colleagues liked him well enough to provide him with information that would have otherwise been inaccessible to him. After Thomas had left his office he called an old friend who'd moved on to Homeland Security. Thomas' and Sabine's stories checked out as far as arrival dates went. He also called FIU to confirm Sabine's enrollment, but the lady who answered the phone was not forthcoming with any information about students, past or present. He googled Thomas, his business, his family and Sabine. They seemed to be a real nice family. Decent and hard working, father had received a reward as an outstanding principal in 2008, Sabine's facebook page testified to her love for her parents and Thomas. Too much information to put on an open channel if you'd asked Franco. But hey, that's what they did nowadays.

Not only had Franco taken Thomas', well really Sabine's case, but he was actually starting to believe that there was something to it. Just his gut feeling and the fact that her up and leaving contradicted everything he'd picked up about her in the information he'd gathered on her. He figured that Thomas had a point in suspecting that something had happened to Sabine...

Chapter Eighteen

Sabine Sander,
Miami (Tuesday, March 3rd, 2015, 1:30 a.m.)

Not knowing how much time had elapsed and disoriented by the darkness, she was startled by the noise of the metal door being opened. A dim light above her head came on and the door swung open; the masked man stepped inside her prison, placed a plastic tray with some food and a cup of water on the ground, stared at her for a minute and disappeared. The heavy metal of the lock on the door unnerved her. At least the lights remained on. She'd never been afraid of the dark, but the darkness, coupled with the circumstances of her being here had utterly shaken her.

She crawled over to the tray that was placed barely within her reach and pulled it closer and inspected it. A red Dixie cup filled with milk and some chocolate chip cookies on a thin paper plate. Surprised by the growling of her stomach she wolfed down the food and drank the milk. Feeling a little better, she looked around her prison space, now that she was able to see. The chain that he had attached to her ankle was solidly embedded in the concrete floor. She could see that this must have been done recently, since a roughly two by two feet area of concrete surrounding the chain in the floor looked much newer. There were no windows visible in the space that was approximately twenty by twenty feet. The walls were covered with some plastic sheeting. She knocked on them with her fist and noticed that they seemed to be very solid, there was hardly any noise from the impact and the plastic sheeting had not budged. Scanning the walls she saw hundreds of screws holding the sheeting in place. She reached out to touch one of them. The screw had a square hole instead of the typical Phillips or flat opening in the middle of it. A rubber washer separated it from the sheeting. Using her nails she tried to get between the screw and the covering but only managed to rip a finger nail. Looking at the wall again she realized that trying to get the screws out was unrealistic. There were just too many of them in neat lines, only inches apart from each other.

The ceiling was covered with the same material. The door looked to be solid metal and was out of her reach. Apart from the king sized mattress, and what looked like a work bench made out of solid wood, a camping toilet – presumably left to accommodate her bodily functions - and the tray, the place was empty. The floor was concrete with a fading gray paint on it, except for where it had been disturbed to anchor the chain. Upon closer inspection she saw that the toilet was bolted to the floor. The removable insert was attached to the contraption and she couldn't pry it loose. Absent, however, was toilet paper. Even though there was no garage door, she couldn't help but think that her prison used to be a garage.

If it was indeed a garage, maybe she could alert a neighbor. She started screaming at the top of her lungs. Her prison seemed to absorb every sound she made. She banged her fists on the wall. No one came to her rescue. If her brother knew where she was, he'd come and rescue her like he'd done before. Well, not from a situation like this, but he was the one person she'd always been able to count on. The knowledge of him being in Miami made her feel a little bit better. She knew he'd be looking for her. Thomas wasn't going to just write her off. He was however unfamiliar with Miami. Heck, she didn't even know where she was. Against her will she started crying again.

Then the already dim light became dimmer, the metal door was opened and her captor reappeared. He was wearing some weird leather headdress and a black satin bathrobe. He closed the door and calmly walked over to where she was sitting on the mattress. Pushing her down he shoved some lubricant he must have already had on his fingers into her vagina, threw his bathrobe open and without saying a word raped her!

When he was done he got up slowly, tied his bathrobe and left without saying a word. Rolled up into the fetal position Sabine cried quietly and wondered again how her life could have ended up here? Her life which had been going according to plan had changed so drastically in such a short period of time. She could feel his fluids oozing out of her.

Chapter Nineteen

The key to Sabine's apartment had been on her keychain. He'd decided to get some of her belongings. Make it look like she'd gone on vacation. He drove over to her place and walked up to her apartment. It was early in the morning, the night after he had brought his visitor to his place. While he was tired from a night that hadn't afforded him any sleep, he was also rejuvenated by the exiting encounter he'd had with his new guest.

When he approached the front door he noticed that the lights were on inside of the apartment. He casually walked by and peered into the window next to the front door. Sure enough, a rather large man was sitting at the dining table in front of a laptop computer. He thought about his next move on his way back to the parking lot. He needed to get her stuff, make it look like she left on a trip. This guy complicated matters. He was blocking his access to the apartment, and was an unknown factor he hadn't been aware of, correct that – should have been aware of.

He decided to wait in his car that was parked in a spot that provided him an unobstructed view of the entire parking lot. Shit, this would cost him time and expose him to attention from neighbors.

Luckily it only took a couple of hours before he spotted the large man hurriedly walking through the lot. Where was the guy going on foot? He got out of his car and followed him out onto the street. The man turned left towards US-1, maybe to catch the Metro-Rail? Bingo, he went straight for the station.

He hurried back to the apartment complex to pack up his guest's belongings. Just to be on the safe side he put on some latex gloves before he entered the apartment, where he quickly found and retrieved the two suitcases from under her bed and filled them. Some of her underwear, a number of socks, three shorts, five shirts, two bras and her toiletry items. He checked the apartment one last time, going mentally over items an average girl would pack for a trip. Bikini - can't leave that behind on a trip in Florida.

He opened the door and his heart almost stopped beating. Right next to him a maintenance worker was entering the next door apartment. Shit, he lowered his head glad to know that the bill of the baseball cap he was wearing was covering his face from the man's glance. He quickly walked away. Close call, but he should be good. Back to his car and away from this place.

Chapter Twenty

Franco Tamargo and Thomas Sander,
Miami (Tuesday, March 3rd, 2015, 4:15 pm)

"Someone broke into my sister's apartment!" Thomas screamed into the phone as soon as Franco answered the call.

"What?"

"Verdammte Scheisse – her apartment is ausgeraeumt, empty, everything is gone!" Thomas was screaming, switching between German and English, without making much sense.

"Thomas, I am on my way." Franco assured him.

Franco almost ran to the garage. As soon as he got out of the garage he floored it, propelling his car towards the apartment complex less than a mile away.

He quickly made his way to Sabine's apartment on the second floor of the third building. The front door was ajar. Franco pushed it open and saw Thomas slumped on the sofa.

A cursory inspection of the door revealed no damage.

"Thomas." Franco announced himself, "What happened?"

"They took her stuff, her clothes, and her personal stuff." Thomas informed him in an angry voice.

Franco noticed that what looked to be all of her furniture, her TV and a small boom box, were still in the apartment. He walked over into the small open kitchen. Opening some cabinets and drawers he found all her plates and silverware still in place. The refrigerator was still stocked with some bread, water, milk and cold cuts. Thomas was beside himself, a strong, tall man shaking in frustration.

"Thomas, calm down. Let's see if we can make some sense of this – okay?" Franco tried to calm him down.

"Sure." Spoken like a true trooper by the obviously upset brother.

Franco walked over to the bedroom, checked the walk-in closet and then checked the bathroom.

"Okay, from the appearance of the apartment, your sister packed her belongings for a vacation, but there are…"

"She didn't go on vacation!" exploded Thomas, "I am on vacation visiting her!"

"Thomas, I am not stating facts, but doing an inventory of what things look like." Franco paused for a few seconds.

"Can we do that?"

"Mmmhh" was Thomas' non-descript reply.

"She obviously did not move out, since her furniture and more valuable belongings are still here. She didn't take all of her clothes either." Franco stopped and went back to the bedroom, rechecking the closet and then went down to his knees to look under the bed. Satisfied he went back to the living room and kitchen.

"There is no suitcase in this place." he announced.

"She didn't go on vacation. Someone broke in here."

"I am not disputing that. However, if we call the police, that's what they will tell you. No sign of forced entry on the door. No sign of forced entry here." Franco had walked over to the sliding glass door in the living room.

"Franco, listen to me – she did not go on vacation!" Thomas said forcefully, emphasizing every word.

"And I am not saying she did. Why don't we see if we can find the manager of this place? Maybe he noticed something weird." There was no way to discuss things calmly with his German client at this time.

It took Franco and Thomas a few minutes, following the signs to the rental office, to locate the middle aged manager of the apartment complex. The man was in the middle of instructing a maintenance worker on what he wanted him to do, and they waited patiently. Franco did, Thomas tried to anyway.

"Good afternoon sir, my name is Franco Tamargo, I am a private investigator and this is my client Mr. Sander from Germany." Franco opened.

"Sabine's brother?" the manager replied.

"Yes sir. You know her? He's visiting her."

"Yes of course I know her; she's a resident of mine.

And yeah, she actually mentioned the other day that her brother was coming. What brings you to me? Everything okay in the apartment? Private investigator? I guess something is wrong?"

"My sister has been kidnapped and her apartment has been broken into!" Thomas couldn't contain himself any longer.

"Whoa, when did that happen? She got kidnapped from here? Did you call the police?" the manager looked something akin to a deer caught in the headlights of an oncoming truck.

"Thomas, please let me try to explain this." Franco implored his client.

Franco gave the manager an abbreviated version of Thomas' story and his own observations in the apartment.

"Have you called the cops about the suspected break in? You want me to call?" the manager inquired.

"That won't help us. What are they gonna do? Dust for fingerprints?" Franco deadpanned.

"Yes, they could do that – no?" Thomas sounded hopeful. Franco chalked it up to Thomas having seen too many CSI shows, the jetlag, the stress of the missing sister, or lack of knowledge of police work. Anyway, he knew that the police wouldn't do anything about a young college student that had – to the unsuspecting eye – packed her bags and gone on vacation.

"Thomas, they would not. They will not even spend a minute on investigating this. Sorry, but that's reality." Franco hated to burst his client's bubble.

"I am sorry sir, what was your name?" Franco addressed the manager again.

"Guillermo, and don't be sorry. I was rude enough not to introduce myself." The man had recovered from his initial shock, and extended his hand to Franco and then Thomas.

"Have you noticed anything suspicious today? Anyone hanging around that doesn't belong here?"

"Wish I had, but I was mostly in the office today, and I can't see Sabine's apartment from here. Wait, we did have a service request in that building today" He called one of his maintenance men on his cell phone.

"Tony, when you did that a/c leak in C-209 earlier today, did you notice anything unusual in C-205?" he listened to the response. "Do you know the guy? Do me a favor, come to the office. Yes, right now." He hung up the phone.

"Tony saw a guy carrying two suitcases from Sabine's apartment. He's coming over here now."

"Thanks, by the way, do you have any surveillance cameras on your property?" Franco asked.

"Nah, we really don't have a need for any. This isn't a high crime neighborhood." the manager replied.

"Tony, can you describe the man that came from the apartment, what was it, C-205?"

Tony glanced at the manager who nodded in approval.

"No, never seen him before."

"What did he look like?" Franco followed up.

"Well, I didn't really stare at him. Let me see, he was wearing shorts – beige, some dark T-shirt and a baseball hat. The hat was covering his face when I saw him. There wasn't really anything else remarkable about him. Other than that he wouldn't look at me or say anything."

"Thank you very much. Here's my card, if you remember anything else, please call me. Oh, did you see where he went?" Franco handed Tony his card.

"No, I went into C-209."

"Thanks Tony, please make sure you finish up in A-107 before the resident get's back." The manager dismissed his guy.

"Now we have proof that Sabine didn't go on vacation. Let's call the police again!" Thomas almost shouted.

"They will still think that it could be her boyfriend who carried out the luggage for her. Sorry Thomas, I honestly believe that would be a waste of time." Franco answered him.

"Can you have the lock changed in my sister's apartment?" a resigned Thomas wanted to know.

"Yes, but then you won't be able to get in." Guillermo answered, and Franco knew where the manager was coming from.

"You could give me a key."

"No, I couldn't, because you're not on the lease. However, I understand the circumstances here. So just hypothetically: If you were to change the lock yourself – and drop off a duplicate key in an envelope – I sure wouldn't know who dropped it off – as long as I have access to the apartment." The manager winked at Franco.

"Thank you for all your help Guillermo, if there's anything else you remember, hear from the tenants or see in the future related to Sabine – please give me a call." Franco handed the manager one of his cards and shook the man's hand firmly.

Thomas stopped Franco outside of the manager's office. "Sabine has a diary. Maybe we can find it and learn something."

"How would you know about her diary?" Franco inquired. "She's had it since she was little."

Franco and Thomas went back to Sabine's apartment to look for her diary, which according to Thomas; she'd been keeping since she was eleven years old. They found it under her mattress, another indication that her apartment had been cleared out by an intruder and not Sabine. Thomas started going through Sabine's diary sharing some passages with Franco. She had been happy in Miami. She had loved going to FIU, her professors had been nice, and classmates had been pleasant. She had met a few boys that had hit on her, but nothing serious. She had gone out with a couple of them but it hadn't developed into anything more. She mentioned a Professor Martin, who according to her diary had his own investment company, that was teaching her finance class and who made it very interesting. Then she had met a football player that had taken her breath away! According to her journal there had also been a math professor who'd been hitting on her. However, what was painfully absent from her journal were any additional names. It was only "he" or "she" did this, that, or the other.

The entries to her journal had started to become less frequent a few months ago, and her mood had become decidedly more somber. A guy had started to stalk her. First she had noticed him around the hallways when she had gone to and from classes. He'd followed her leaving classes. He'd never talked to her, always wore a baseball cap. But he'd been there way too often for it to be coincidental. He looked oddly familiar to her, but she never got a clear look at his face. Then, just as sudden, her mood was back to normal. The stalker was gone, her classes were fun.

They weren't getting anywhere. Sabine had not described the guy. They had no idea what the dude looked like. Franco decided that he would have to see if he could locate any of Sabine's friends at FIU. Maybe one of them had seen the creep. Franco figured he shouldn't have a hard time figuring out where to find Prof. Martin, the Finance professor, and the Math professor.

Franco convinced Thomas to stay at the apartment and promised to be back with a new lock the next morning. As far as Franco could tell; his client was going to be alright. No imminent danger and he had calmed down considerably. On his way back to the parking lot Franco stopped again at the manager's office.

"Guillermo, did you ever see any of Sabine's friends? Do you know any of them?"

"No, I can't say I do. Well, there's one girl that lives here that I've seen a couple of times talking to Sabine."

"Who is she?" Franco wanted to know.

"Man, we don't really give out information about any of our residents unless you can provide a judge's order."

"Listen, I think we can move past that – can't we?" Franco made sure to put a most pleasant tone in his voice.

"I don't really want to dig my own grave here – but let's just say if I was a gambling man, C-103 would be a great number to play in the upcoming lottery…" The guy had a sense of humor, that was almost downright funny.

"Thanks a lot!"

Franco trotted back to the building and knocked on the downstairs apartment C-103. No answer. He decided to come back later in the evening, went to his car and drove to the Publix supermarket next to his office for some dinner, before he went back to his office to finish up some paperwork on another case he had to close out.

Chapter Twenty One

Roberto Suarez, Miami (Spring Semester 2015)

She met him in her Finance Class at FIU. During the part where professors made the students introduce themselves to the rest of the class – she always hated it when professors did that to the students – she found out that Roberto was a jock. Though in his defense, he introduced himself rather conservatively. No brouhaha about his on field accomplishments, being the top rated wide receiver on the team, but some insight into what he wanted to do after his hopefully professional career as a football player. He wanted to become a certified public accountant after his football career. How refreshing – a jock with ambitions.

Prof. Martin encouraged all of his students to really get to know each other. According to him, relationships built in college had the potential of lasting a lifetime – and tended to be extremely beneficial to the students. Sabine thought that he might have a point.

It took only a couple of weeks for Roberto to find the courage to ask Sabine out. She was so pretty, foreign and well spoken. He felt that his communication skills were inferior to hers and that she might just laugh at him, and it therefore took him a while to gather all of his courage.

He was surprisingly refined about his approach – considering he was only a jock. Granted, his come-on-line wasn't the most original: "Could I interest you in a football game?" However, the way he delivered it, the softness in his voice, his insecurity audible, was kind of cute. He wasn't puffing himself up, he wasn't posing as a star athlete - which he was - but just being himself. He was taking a risk, asking her out to a football game, in a refreshingly innocent way.

She agreed to come to the next game.

Roberto had pleaded with her to wait after the game so they could go and get some pizza. Somewhat reluctantly, because she wasn't even sure that she liked the guy all that much, though her first gut instinct was pointing her towards liking him, she had agreed.

Over a pizza in a small pizza joint not far from the stadium they really hit it off. The place had started to empty out early and the proprietor didn't mind them staying well into the night without ordering anything else after their meal. He'd been young once and thought it cute to have these two lovebirds tell each other everything about their families and themselves.

Chapter Twenty Two

Sabine Sander and Roberto Suarez,
Miami (Spring Semester 2015)

Roberto's parents had escaped from Cuba during the 1980's Mariel boat lift. They'd spent weeks in the camp that had been built close to and under the I-95 Expressway. They'd been subjected to listening to the traffic passing by next to them – and overhead – almost nonstop. Roberto had been well aware growing up, that quite a few people were looking at the balseros as mostly drug dealers and mental patients. Before the boat-lift his dad had worked as a carpenter and his mom had served in a hotel catering to American tourists. His dad was now working hard as a custodian for the Miami-Dade-School-Board, to allow his only son to go to college. His mom was also working part-time as a babysitter. She'd had a second part-time job cutting hair at a barber shop for as long as he could remember.

Luckily Miami had a very diverse population. Sixty-Five percent of the population was Hispanic, twenty percent Black, fifteen percent Anglo and the remainder fell into the broad category of 'Other'.

Technically, Roberto fell into the Hispanic as well as the Black or Other category. He was, by all counts, somewhat black. But not really, especially since he was also Cuban, which made him something of an 'Other'. The classifications in the statistical charts could be vexing...

Sabine didn't know if her family would ever approve of her dating such a 'diverse' guy.

Sabine was surprised to realize that she was really falling for this guy. He wasn't necessarily her type. Sabine stood at 5"11' and he only had a maximum of two inches on her, not exactly a giant by German standards.

She had gotten used to guys looking at her, hitting on her. She'd had many conversations with her older brother about guys in general, about their M.O., what they were after, what they wanted. She considered herself somewhat of an expert on boys, not because she'd had that many boyfriends, as a matter of fact Roberto could have been considered her first real boyfriend, but because of her brother

Thomas. He had been very protective and had tried to prepare her for the "real world" as he'd like to call it.

Sabine was, at twenty, still a virgin. It wasn't as much a conscientious decision to remain pure until she married, as it had been a lack of a boy who really sparked her interest and made her fall head-over-heels. But now it had happened and she wasn't sure if Thomas was going to approve. Her brother's approval had always meant a lot to her. He'd been her hero as far back as she could remember. It wasn't that she hadn't adored her parents, but Thomas had always been her go-to person. He loved her unconditionally, and had always been there for her. Was he going to be okay with a guy who played football and was black? She had tried to convince herself that Thomas wouldn't have a problem looking past the fact that Roberto was black. Then again, Germans weren't really known for being that open minded towards other ethnic groups.

In the end she'd decided to wait until she herself was sure that Roberto was the guy she'd wanted to be serious about before she sprung the news onto her family, especially Thomas.

Chapter Twenty Three

Benjamin Walker,
Florida Keys (Thursday, March 4th, 2015)

All Benjamin had ever wanted was what everyone else seemed to already have. A functional, caring family that once in a while would utter some affectionate words directed towards him. Was that asking for too much?

His dad had been a great guy and he surely did not prefer to remember his mother. All he wanted was to find the woman that he could love, cherish, and please. Working hard every day to make her happy and for her to love him back. They would have children; sit at the dinner table and exchange stories about their day. He would never raise his voice; his wife would never turn tricks, take drugs or abandon his children.

Deep down inside of him he probably subconsciously realized that other people could perceive him as a stalker or weirdo, but he knew that that was not the case. He was only being extra careful, extra vigilant in identifying 'The Perfect One'.

"Are you a student here?" one of the roaming security guards at Florida International University had asked him in a professional, yet stern voice. She had picked up on the fact that he had been snapping pictures of girls walking by his table on the second floor lobby-like area of the library. Maybe he should have sat in the little Starbucks shop downstairs by the main entrance. Surely that location would have allowed him to not only see everyone who'd entered or exited the Green Library through the front entrance, but hide his picture safari.

He silently chastised himself for having been so obvious. "Yes, just taking a few pictures for my mom home in Pennsylvania while I am waiting for a friend of mine." he'd said pleasantly. She'd nodded and after shooting him another glance moved on. Attention was the last thing he'd wanted to attract.

Maybe he should go back to the Graham Center, the student center. There was much more activity, but people were passing through too fast. He wasn't able to see them interact, express themselves, disclose any of their traits. In short he wouldn't have an opportunity to really study them. He was running out of time.

He would soon turn twenty-four and he needed to find the perfect mother for his children. Two to be exact, a boy and a girl. The order didn't really matter. If the boy came first, he could keep an eye on his little sister. Should, Sharon be born first, he already had the name for her but was struggling with a name for the boy, well; she could baby her little brother.

Don't worry Sharon and yet to be named son, I'll find her. I'll find her soon.

He still clearly remembered when he had first spotted her. When he'd seen her walking through the Graham Center, he'd immediately recognized her as 'The Perfect One'. Since his father's untimely death he'd known that he would have to approach life differently than his dad had. He wasn't going to fall for some floozy. He wasn't going to leave it up to chance. Planning things tended to yield better results than chance. He was determined to find the girl of his dreams. Determined to identify and meet the girl that was the perfect match for him – in short 'The Perfect One'.

She had blonde medium long hair, blue eyes, and a slim figure with long legs and well developed breasts. After having looked at girls passing through the Center for more than four weeks her looks had registered as an 11 on his

1 through 10 scale. But that didn't mean anything if her personality didn't match her looks. He had to observe her interacting with other people. He was going to find out about her background, her likes and dislikes, in short; he was about to study her.

From their first encounter, which hadn't really been an encounter, he'd followed her. She had left the building, and walked to the parking garage next to the Graham Center. Almost running, he'd managed to ride the elevator with her. She had pushed the button for the 3rd floor and he'd pushed for the 4th floor. She hadn't made eye contact with him, but he'd been able to inhale her scent. Not being an expert on women's perfume, he'd been unable to determine the name, but it sure had been intoxicating. After she'd left the elevator, and he'd reached the 4th floor he'd hustled to run down the ramp to see her get into an older model Civic. He was, however, unable to get the license plate number.

He had to wait until next week, same place - same time, to be in a position to watch her getting into her car. It had been a gamble to wait in the same garage. He had been looking over the wall towards the Graham Center in hopes of seeing her walk towards the garage. Bingo, she had walked to the elevator by herself. He had watched the lights light up on the display over the elevators. 4th floor. He'd been on the 5th floor. He scrambled to run down the staircase to see her. Yup, good fortune had been smiling upon him. She had been parked far away from the elevator which had allowed him to catch up with her. He wrote down the license plate number on the back of his hand as she pulled out of her parking space.

After that it had been easy. The following week he'd followed her to her apartment building and observed which apartment she'd gone into. For good measure he'd repeated his surveillance a couple more times to make sure she hadn't visited a friend.

Chapter Twenty Four

Sabine Sander's friend Nadine,
Miami (Tuesday, March 3rd, 2015, 7:30 pm)

Franco went back to the building and again knocked on the door to C-103, which again went unanswered. It was close to 7:30 p.m. so there was a chance that the girl was still at work or school. Unhappy about his lack of success at this end, he figured he should try his luck at FIU, which was only about ten miles from his current location. Maybe he could find this Prof. Martin, or get some more information about the players on the football team.

Traffic was light and he made it there in less than twenty minutes. He turned off 107th Avenue onto the Campus and into the visitor parking area close to the Graham Center. He looked for the information desk, which unsurprisingly at this time was unstaffed. Off to the Green Library, where there were some computer terminals. He took the escalator to the second floor and found an unoccupied computer.

He figured since Prof. Martin had his own company he'd be teaching in the evenings. It only took him a few minutes to find information on Prof. Robert Martin, and to look up Martin's office telephone number and email address.

He called the number but only got the voicemail. He left a message. He also sent an email to Martin explaining who he was, asking him to give him a call.

He wasn't as successful in locating Roberto the team's jock, but was able to determine the time and place of the teams next practice. He'd be there tomorrow, 9:00 a.m. sharp at the FIU-Stadium.

It was 9:30 p.m. and Franco was back at Sabine's friend's apartment. He knocked – still no answer. He decided to sit in the pool area which had a clear view of the apartment's front door.

Finally at around 10:00 p.m. she showed up. She was a small girl, probably no taller than 5'3", dyed blonde hair, cut off jeans, sneakers, and with a tight shirt. She disappeared into the apartment. He gave her a couple of minutes then knocked on the door with his PI credentials in his hand, ready to convince her that she should talk to him. She opened the door almost immediately.

"Hi, my name is Franco Tamargo, I'm a private investigator trying to locate Sabine Sander." he introduced himself.

"Yeah, I know Sabine." she answered.

"Could I please ask you a few questions about Sabine?"

"Sure, please come in."

He was surprised and somewhat disappointed that she was so trusting and friendly. It was dark outside; he was a total stranger – what was wrong with girls nowadays?

They settled in the small living room. He sat on the sofa while she took the lazy-chair.

"Thanks for letting me in. What's your name?" Franco inquired.

"Nadine".

"Nadine, my client, Sabine's brother, has reported Sabine missing. Do you have any idea where she might be?"

"What do you mean missing? I saw her just the other day by the pool. I was coming home and she was by the pool with some really tall guy. What's going on? Did that guy kidnap her?"

"No, that was probably her brother you saw with her by the pool."

"Okay, so what happened?"

"I don't know; that's why I need your help!"

"Well, the last time I really spoke to her was, let me see, maybe two weeks ago. Maybe less, anyway, we were just hanging for a bit at the pool. She told me that she and Roberto, her boyfriend, were planning a weekend in the Keys."

"What's Roberto's last name?"

"I don't know his last name, but he's on the football team at FIU."

"Did she mention any problems with Roberto, or anyone else?"

"No, I think she really likes Roberto, but Sabine was a little concerned about the creep being back."

"What creep?"

"Well, according to her there is this guy who'd started to always be around. He would be in front of her classroom when no one else was there. He would be parked next to her in his old black Mustang. She had been freaked out about it. Then he was gone for a while. Last time I spoke to her, she'd told me that he had reappeared."

"Have you ever seen the guy?"

"No, I'm sorry. But my friend Melissa saw him once. Actually, she lives only two apartments over. You want me to see if she's home? She works part time at Quizno's, but I think she's off today."

"Yes, please"

Chapter Twenty Five

Sabine Sander's friend Melissa,
Miami (Tuesday, March 3rd, 2015, 10:20 pm)

Nadine knocked on the front door – and luckily - Melissa was home.

"Hi Melissa, this is Franco, he's checking into Sabine's disappearance."

"Into what?" Melissa was clearly lost and just stood in the open door.

"Rude, aren't you gonna ask us in?" Nadine joked.

"I'm sorry, come on in." Melissa offered.

"Thank you Melissa." The group settled around the small dining table. "My client, Sabine's brother, told me that Sabine disappeared Monday night. Also someone broke into her apartment. I am a private investigator trying to find out what happened and of course trying to find her."

"Yeah, well, I haven't seen her for a while."

"When was the last time you saw her" Franco inquired.

"Don't know, maybe two weeks ago."

"Do you know anything about the guy that was following her?"

"Over at FIU?"

"Yeah, did you see him?"

"Sure, he was real creepy. He was just sitting there in his car - watching."

"Is there anything specific that you remember about him or his car?"

"Sure, I remember that plate on his front bumper."

"Really, what'd it say?"

"It was one of those plates you can have custom made – Terminator II – I'm sure about it. It kind of freaked me out when I saw the guy sitting in his car. He even had sunglasses on. In the middle of the night!" she looked at Nadine with big eyes waiting for some confirmation as to how weird it was. "I sure remember that. I was parked in front of him. Sabine was parked next to him two cars over."

"Can you describe the guy?"

"No not really," she paused to concentrate "I kind of got stuck on the sunglasses, and then we just wanted to get away from there."

"Did you see his face?"

Melissa again thought for a few seconds.

"No, I think he had longish hair, but I am not even really sure about that. Sorry, it was way too dark."

"That's alright; did you happen to see his rear license plate?" Franco was hoping.

"Uh, not really."

"Shit – sorry." Franco apologized quickly.

"What about his car?" Franco continued. "Anything that stood out?"

"It was black, but not shiny – you know - that flat finish. It was an old Ford Mustang."

"What do you think happened?" Nadine inquired.

"I don't know, but hopefully I'll find out, and hopefully it's all good! Would you happen to know what year the car was?"

"No, I don't know much about cars. It wasn't the last model, or the model before that, I think I know that."

"Is there anything else you recall about him or the car?"

"No, not really. I wish there was more, but I really just wanted to get away from him."

"Thank you very much for your time – both of you. Here's my card, please give me a call if you remember anything else."

Franco handed his cards to Melissa and Nadine and left.

Franco headed home to his house near Tropical Park, appreciating the fact that it was a short drive. He was dead tired. Tomorrow was another day and he needed some sleep.

Chapter Twenty Six

Benjamin Walker,
Florida Keys (Wednesday, March 4th, 2015)

Having filled up his tank at a gas station in Marathon, Benjamin continued towards Miami; once again lost in his thoughts. It almost felt like yesterday. He recalled stepping onto the sidewalk right outside of the Miami International Airport. The humid air had hit him as if he had stepped into a sauna. The heat coupled with an insane degree of humidity had almost suffocated him. But more than anything, the realization that he was completely on his own, in a foreign country, had suddenly dawned on him. He was instantly terrified. What was he going to do? He didn't have a degree, had no special skills – besides killing his mother. He was, so he'd been told, a good looking guy. One hundred and seventy five pounds spread over a frame of six feet and one inch, with handsome soft features probably qualified as good looking – but was that going to be enough to make it in a foreign country?

Finding a place to stay had proven to be his first challenge. For starters, the fact that he was only eighteen years old had precluded him from renting a car – as he'd found out as soon as he approached the first car rental counter, so he'd walked up to a yellow cab parked right by the curb. He'd asked the cabbie to drive him to the nearest used car dealership. Benjamin was sure that the chatty driver had taken the scenic route to the 'closest' dealership. After buying an old clunker of a car on 27th Avenue, he drove around trying to find an apartment. None of the halfway decent places would accept him. Even his offer to prepay the first six months of rent didn't sway any of the managers. He crashed in a cheap hotel off Flagler Street, where some of the rooms were apparently rented by the hour judging by some of the noises that kept waking him up. After a restless night, a quick breakfast consisting of a stale muffin and some lukewarm coffee, he'd continued his search. While the complex looked a little run down, he'd finally been successful in securing an apartment in a somewhat suspect neighborhood. Even though he had money, he needed to find a job soon if he wasn't going to deplete his funds quickly and start living under some bridge.

He'd spent the rest of the day visiting a variety of stores to make his new place livable. A mattress that he tied to the roof of his car had almost gotten airborne before he'd made it back to his apartment. He'd only bought the most pressing necessities, since securing a job had been foremost on his mind. While still in Germany he'd read up on Miami, its different neighborhoods, tourist centers, sports and cultural activities. Based on his research, he drove to Coconut Grove in hopes of getting a job as a waiter in one of the many restaurants or bars. He struck out the first four times, but eventually got a job as a busboy in a restaurant in the Coco Walk Center. Not exactly what he'd hoped for, but better than nothing. After a few weeks he was promoted to a waiting position. The money wasn't bad, but far from good. The girls were getting substantially more in tips than he. No tits – no tip. Once he figured that out, he changed up his game. He'd started acting gay. Not a very sophisticated move, but it had in fact allowed him to double his tips.

Preserving his funds had been important to him. While he had money, he'd figured that starting out at Miami Dade College would be a lot less expensive than going straight to FIU. So he took his first 60 credits at MDC before transferring to FIU to complete his studies in hospitality management.

Chapter Twenty Seven

Franco Tamargo and Roberto Suarez,
Miami (Wednesday, March 4th, 2015, 8:00 am)

Franco called Thomas the next morning at 8:00 am, asking if he wanted him to bring some breakfast. Thomas thanked him but declined, saying he'd found some cereal and milk in the fridge. Franco grabbed a granola bar and an apple from his own fridge and a screwdriver from his toolbox before heading over to Sabine's apartment to update Thomas. On his way he stopped at an ACE Hardware store to pick up a new deadbolt.

Thomas looked like shit. It could have been leftover jet lag, but Franco's money was on him being worried about his sister. While quickly installing the deadbolt, he told Thomas about the stalker in a Ford Mustang with the Terminator II plate who may or may not be a student at FIU, and about Roberto, Sabine's boyfriend. He told him that he was about to question Roberto, and Thomas pressed Franco to come along. While it wasn't easy, he was eventually able to convince Thomas that he was way too emotional to have a rational conversation, and it was therefore counterproductive for him to participate. He promised Thomas to inform him immediately about any new developments. On his way to the parking lot he put the second key to the lock in an envelope he had brought and put it in the manager's mailbox outside of the office.

Franco decided to run down the boyfriend first since finding a black Ford Mustang among the thousands of black Mustangs in Miami sounded a bit more daunting.

Roberto was on the FIU football team - well, Franco was going to start there. He knew they were going to start practice at 9:00 a.m. How many players could there be with the given name Roberto.

While driving over to the campus, he called the Admissions Office again and spoke to a very nice girl that also politely declined to give out any information about any of the students. So much for that. He still had one ace up his sleeve. He'd call an old friend at FIU after his meeting with Roberto.

Franco found the head coach on the field and asked him about a player by the name of

Roberto. The coach wasn't rude, but basically ignored Franco until he explained the circumstances to him. Coach mellowed and agreed to get Roberto. It turned out that there were four players by that name. Welcome to Miami. The wide receiver Roberto Suarez was Sabine's boyfriend.

"Roberto, my name is Franco Tamargo. I am a private investigator checking into the disappearance of Sabine." Franco informed Roberto.

"Finally someone is coming! What the fuck took you guys so long? I reported her disappearance yesterday morning!" Roberto exclaimed.

"I assume you reported it to the Miami Dade Police Department? Well, I am not with them, Sabine's brother hired me." Franco was a little surprised by the outburst of his prime suspect.

"Where is she?" Roberto inquired.

"It's why I'm here. Trying to figure out what happened to her."

"Have you guys even been looking?"

"Again, I am not with the MDPD. You also have to understand that Sabine is an adult; they don't really have the manpower to investigate cases like that. They probably figure she just went on an unscheduled vacation. Or she wanted to get away from you. Cool it; I am not saying she did. How about I ask you a few questions?"

"Bullshit, she'd never just dump me! We were going to have dinner with her brother, who's visiting from Germany, tonight. We were going to surprise him." Roberto exclaimed.

"Maybe she changed her mind, was embarrassed to introduce you?" Franco was purposely pushing the guy's buttons.

"I'm her boyfriend! I love her, she loves me! End of story! Where is she?"

"Pretty much the same question I was going to ask you Roberto! Where is she?"

"What's wrong with you? Are you really asking me this question? Are you really this stupid?"

"Buddy, while I am not with the MDPD anymore – I promise you that if I walk away from here without some answers, you will meet my ex-colleagues very soon." Franco had just about had it with this guy's machismo behavior.

"So you are part of them – the cops!"

"Not anymore – let's focus!"

"I called the police yesterday morning when she didn't come to class. We were supposed to meet for breakfast, but she never showed. Maybe her brother had something to do with it." Roberto volunteered.

"Her brother is the one who hired me." Franco wondered what Sabine, an A-student, saw in Roberto.

"Anyway, the cops told me that they'd check into Sabine's disappearance. I haven't heard anything since! I've called them four times – got the runaround – but no answers!"

"How long have you known Sabine?" Franco wanted to know.

"Pretty much since the first week of this semester, so for about five weeks."

"Has she ever mentioned someone following her?" At this time Franco had basically ruled Roberto out as a suspect.

"Yeah, she mentioned it a few times. I told her to call me immediately if she saw him again. That I would take care of the guy!"

"So you never saw the guy?"

"No, he wouldn't have bothered her again had I seen him." Roberto slipped back into the macho boyfriend routine.

Franco handed him his card with the usual line to please call him if he thought of anything else. Roberto came right back at him by asking him for a pen and a piece of paper. He scribbled down his own cell phone number and demanded that Franco call him with anything he discovered. Young love.

Chapter Twenty Eight

Franco Tamargo,
Miami (Wednesday, March 4th, 2015, 10:00 am)

Franco's old friend Carlos Mendez, who'd been unable to land a job with the MDPD after finishing the Academy, and who had subsequently ended up taking a job with the Campus Police Department at FIU was Franco's first stop. Franco had decided that a face to face was going to yield a better result than a phone call.

"Hey Carlos, what's up?" Franco had caught up with Carlos in his office.

"Who are you?" Carlos inquired half jokingly.

"Funny, I am the guy who's gotten you through most of your tests when you were still trying to become a real cop!"

"Fuck you Franco – I am a real cop!"

They both knew that being a FIU cop hadn't been high on their list of potential employers.

"Listen Carlos, I know I am not a cop anymore, but I really need your help on this one." Franco opened.

"Sure man, after all the BBQ's you've invited me to, all the toys you've sent to my children, why not – actually – NOT!" Carlos replied.

"Okay, so I haven't been in touch with you for a while."

"Five years."

"Has it been that long?"

"Fuck you! What do you need?" Carlos wanted to know. He'd always been a good sport.

"I have a client whose sister is a student here at FIU. She's been missing and we believe something may have happened to her. Any chance your video surveillance cameras in the parking areas go back more than four weeks?" Franco inquired.

"Are you kidding me? You have a client who's been missing for what? Two hours? Even I can tell you that this is BS!"

"Math was never your strong suit! She's been missing now for..." Franco glanced at his watch "Thirty-Four hours. Man, this is different. She is really missing. Someone cleared out her apartment, made it look like she went on vacation."

"Maybe she did! Did that ever occur to you – hotshot?"

"Listen to me! I know you don't owe me anything – but I am asking you to please take this seriously! I honestly believe she's missing – most likely kidnapped from YOUR CAMPUS! So – please – help me!"

Franco surprised himself at having lost his cool. He immediately regretted it and stepped closer to Carlos.

"I'm sorry man. That was uncalled for. My only excuse is that I truly believe that there is something amiss in this case. Can you please help me?" Franco laid it on the line.

Carlos took a couple of seconds before he responded. "Wow, got some fire left in you, hey? And yes, as a matter of fact, we keep two months of surveillance video on file." Carlos informed him proudly.

It took Franco four hours of going through surveillance tape. But he finally struck gold. A black Ford Mustang with a front plate reading Terminator II! He continued watching the tape, but the next camera that had picked him up from the rear hadn't revealed the license plate. Equally disappointing, there wasn't a clear shot of the driver's face. He made a note of the exact time the driver exited before getting up and stretching his back.

Back to square one. He thanked Carlos promising him to be in touch before the next five years went by. Carlos just snorted.

Franco was straining his brain – who could help him out? Eduardo, in Traffic, had been on the crime suppression unit with him years ago.

He drove over to the brains of the MDPD traffic unit. Eduardo Vargas remembered the good old days after all and allowed Franco to view the traffic cameras installed along 107th Avenue. It took Franco another two hours of going through traffic surveillance tape. Bingo, three weeks ago a black Ford Mustang had run the red light at the intersection of SW 107th Avenue and Tamiami Trail. The license plate was clearly visible. Wham – here was his smoking gun. This would get him a name and an address!

"Eduardo, man I really owe you one. This has the potential of breaking my case wide open! Can you throw in the name and address?" Franco was definitely exited.

"Sure thing – just don't forget you owe me a lunch at Shorty's and a dinner at Outback…"

"I am poor, not like you cops that get overtime, tickets to the Dolphins, the Heat and all the Clubs on the Beach – but when this is done – I'll pick you up for lunch." Franco promised.

On the way back to his car in the visitor parking area, Franco called Thomas, willing to share some good news. The call went straight to voicemail. Franco left him a detailed message asking him to call back.

Chapter Twenty Nine

Graciela Manciani,
Miami (Monday, February 9th, 2015)

Columbia's death had been very unfortunate. He'd had great plans for her, alas, nothing ever seems to works out the way one draws it up. It saddened him that she had triggered his dark side. She had been an 11 on his scale of 10. While he wasn't back to square one, he had his work cut out. He also would have to control his emotions to prevent another unscheduled 'departure'. There were going to be additional departures, but they would happen on his schedule – not because he lost his cool!

He went through his mental file of possible candidates, and to his surprise quickly came up with a replacement for Columbia. Graciela Manciani had actually come in a close second to Columbia on his original search. How could he have forgotten about her? Well, it was her turn. He'd scout her comings and goings, and then he'd sweep in and take her to their nest!

He was getting excited about the future and noticed an erection developing. Yes – his gut was feeling it – his focus was right on!

During his next class he checked her out again. She was kind of short, and her bottom half was maybe a tad bit on the chunky side, but she had that certain look to her. There was no way he would ever be able to articulate what this look was, but it was there.

He quickly reviewed her personal information on her facebook page using his laptop, while the students were reviewing an article that had been distributed earlier. He found her home address, age, country of origin, etc. She was born in Miami to an Italian father and a Cuban mother. From what he had observed, she was on the quiet, shy side. Columbia had been outspoken and popular. Her disposition and shyness might work better for his purposes. Hopefully she'd be able to follow his demands and not act rebellious and obstinate.

He knew that she had a class that ended at 10:50 p.m. Since this was his last class for the day, he followed her around for a while to see if she had a boyfriend. He wasn't concerned about that, but wanted to avoid any complications.

After following her to the food court, the library and the bookstore it became apparent, that she wasn't meeting anyone. Graciela's late class on Mondays and Wednesdays was taught in the Business Center, so he presumed that she'd be parking her car somewhere on that side of the campus. Most people were creatures of habit and he reasoned that if he found where she parked today, that's where she'd be parking on Wednesday.

He found a parking spot close to the Business Center and at 10:40 p.m. walked towards the main entrance to wait for her class to end. When he saw her exiting the building he leisurely followed her. She walked past the Engineering Department and crossed the perimeter street to the small parking lot across the street. He observed her getting into her red VW Beetle and quickly wrote down her license plate number on the palm of his hand.

Two days later he pulled into the same parking lot at around 9:00 p.m. and could hardly believe his good fortune. An old Camry parked right next to the red Beetle pulled out when he got close. He backed into the spot and walked over to the food court for a celebratory dinner. While munching on some chicken fingers and fries, he went over his plan. When he saw her crossing the street he would get out of his car, open his trunk for cover and then get her when she was opening her door. Shouldn't be a problem – and it wasn't.

As Graciela unlocked her car he popped up next to her his face covered by his Bill Clinton mask. He showed her his gun, waived her towards his trunk, and quickly duct taped her mouth and hands. Graciela was in utter shock and disbelief. It didn't even occur to her to scream or resist.

"Get in the trunk." He instructed her calmly.

She awkwardly climbed in and he duct taped her ankles together.

The whole process had taken less than two minutes and he was on his way to his nest. Ah, they would have fun.

Chapter Thirty

Franco Tamargo,
Miami (Wednesday, March 4th, 2015, 4:30 p.m.)

There was no sense in wasting any time. The TV-Show "The first 48 Hours" had it right. The longer someone was missing, the lesser the chance of finding the person alive. He went straight to the apartment building, where, according to Eduardo's information, one Benjamin Walker resided. The address revealed a small apartment complex with fading yellowish paint and dirty brown doors, off Bird Road. He parked his car in one of the two visitor's spaces and quickly found apartment A-23 on the second floor. Not knowing what to expect, Franco reached for the gun in his hip holster, which had been covered by the light blue shirt he wore loosely over his beige pants, making sure he was ready for any surprise. He knocked loudly on the front door. Franco looked around while waiting for the occupant to answer the door.

Typical low-income small apartment complex; ripped screens on the windows, stickers on most of the front doors, laundry drying on the balconies and draped over some of the banisters in front of the apartments. Not exactly the classiest place.

No movement on the inside of the apartment that he could detect. He knocked again, louder.

"Mr. Walker." Franco called out.

No answer. Well, that would have been easy, alas, no such luck.

Franco looked for the manager's office and found it close to where he'd parked his car. He knocked on the door and struck out again – no answer. Come on, the day had started out so promising. The manager couldn't even leave a note – like 'back in five minutes'? Franco walked around the complex, looking for the black Mustang. Lots of older cars, some of them were up on blocks and in various states of disrepair. No Mustang.

Franco walked back to his car, resolved to wait for the manger to come back, when he noticed an elderly woman walk towards the office door. He hustled over to the office to intercept her.

"Excuse me Madam, are you the manager here?"

The lady turned around eying him curiously.

"Como?"

"Disculpe, usted es el gerente aqui?" Franco's Spanish wasn't really up to par.

"No, why? I am looking for him as well. Where is he?" The old lady replied now in English.

"I don't know."

"That lazy S.O.B. never works. You'll be looking for him forever! He never comes to the office. Never fixes any of my problems. Just the other day my toilet was overflowing – I called him twice, went to the office four times. He's never there, never anywhere. S.O.B.!" she exclaimed.

"Do you know where he lives?"

"S.O.B. probably lives in some mansion overlooking the Ocean. He charges us an arm and a leg for rent! Never fixes any problems! Just collects the rent. He's a bloodsucker that doesn't give a shit about us!"

"Thank you." Franco tried to get away from her.

"Martha in B-15 had an electrical problem the other day. Her apartment could have burned down! She called him – and he actually answered his phone and promised to take care of the problem. But that was it! He never showed up. Martha ended up calling FPL and they came out telling her it was one of the breakers in the apartment that was causing the problem. SOB never showed up to fix the problem. Martha's been staying with me. It's a crime. Is that black car yours? Are you with the Police? Are you here to arrest him?"

"No Madam, I am just looking for the manager." Franco was almost dizzy from listening to her.

Franco left the very irritating lady and his car in front of the office and walked to the corner of Bird Road which was only a hundred yards away where he had seen a Cuban restaurant that offered him somewhat of a view of the apartment complex and settled down for an early dinner.

He ordered a Bistec Empanisado with rice, black beans, a coke and a glass of water from the matronly waitress that called him corazon. Ten minutes later, while his waitress was walking up to his table with his order, he spotted an elderly, well dressed man walking towards the apartment office's door with a key in his hand. Franco asked the waitress to just leave the food, dropped a twenty on the table and ran across the street.

"Hi, how are you?" Franco opened still breathing hard from his sprint to the office.

"May I help you?" the gentleman replied.

"Yes sir, my name is Franco Tamargo, I am a private investigator trying to locate a Mr. Benjamin Walker."

"What for?"

"He may have inherited some money from an aunt." Franco lied.

"May have? Son, you're gonna have to do better than that!" the manager responded.

"Alright, my sister is pregnant. I just want to talk to him" Franco continued lying.

"Really, that's your best?"

"Happens to be the truth. I've never seen the guy, but my little sister is pregnant and she's been seeing the guy. No, I am not here to kill him, just to talk to him. However, he seems to be absent from his apartment and I was wondering if you've seen him lately."

"Still don't believe a word you're saying, but no, I haven't seen him lately. His rent is paid up though. And this will end our little Q & A session – have a good day." This guy was a real peach.

"Is there any way I can sweet-talk you into giving me a call when you see him? I'd be happy to make a donation to the charity of your choice."

"Bribing me now?" he laughed. "Just pushing your buttons, I assume you have a good reason wanting to talk to him. You promise me though that there won't be a sudden vacancy due to death – right? I'll call you – no donation necessary." the manager said.

"Thanks a lot, really appreciate it. Sorry, what was your name again?" Franco pulled a card from his wallet and handed it to the man.

"Higinio."

For now this was a dead end. Franco walked back to the restaurant to eat his food. His matronly girlfriend had kept it hot on the stove and brought it over when he sat down.

"Muchas gracias guapa." Franco thanked her.

Over his hot food he started to contemplate what his next move was going to be. He figured Benjamin to be pivotal to this case.

Hopefully Higinio would follow through on his promise. Maybe he should try to track down some of Sabine's fellow students. How to go about that? Well, maybe he could abuse Carlos again. If Carlos introduced him to the people in the office of Student Affairs, he just might be able to get somewhere. His mind made up he enjoyed his food, and on his way out left an extra five bucks on the table for his newfound girlfriend.

It was close to 6:00 p.m. and Franco decided to just camp out in his car at the apartment complex.

Back in the comfort of his car, sleepy from his meal, his mind started drifting back to the old days.

Chapter Thirty One

Franco Tamargo, Miami (early days)

Six years in the Miami Dade Police Department had thoroughly disillusioned Franco. He'd become a law enforcement officer to help people, prevent crime and uphold the law. Such noble intentions, yet reality had caught up with him after a few years. In the beginning, while patrolling various neighborhoods, he'd felt good, connected to the people he had been serving. Later after he became a member of a crime suppression unit, he'd had high hopes of doing something even more meaningful. Weed out criminals before they could strike. However, he'd quickly found that some of the methods his unit had been using varied only in context from those of the street punks they were trying to suppress.

Eventually he'd resigned from the force and obtained his private investigator license. What a joke that had been. Either his degree in criminal justice or his years on the force satisfied the requirements to sit for his Class C License Exam. Needless to say, he'd aced the exam.

Starting out on his own hadn't been easy. He'd first worked out of his apartment – well, worked was a bit of a stretch - since there hadn't been any work. He had contacted what seemed to him like hundreds of law offices, eventually connecting with two that specialized in workmen's compensation disputes, and finally had been able to make some money. He hadn't really aspired to become the next Magnum P.I. when he'd started out, but sitting in his car watching people's houses or some old warehouses had gotten old quickly. Luckily he had been able to use an old contact from the MDPD to secure work at the Miami International Airport. Fuel theft had become rampant, and while investigating these had been only marginally more exciting than watching houses, at least he'd enjoyed watching the planes take off.

After he'd busted a fuel delivery driver and his airport team mate, who signed off on the delivery that never took place, the director of operations had taken an interest in him. He still recalled the first meeting they'd had.

"Mr. Tamargo, outstanding work busting those clowns last week!" the director had opened.

"Just doing my job, sir" had been his modest response.

"Even so, good work. Unfortunately, an operation the size of this airport has myriad problems. Theft by baggage handlers, stealing from elderly or disabled passengers when they are transported in wheelchairs, the list goes on." the director trailed off.

"Sir, I presume you are telling me this, because you think I may be of assistance?" Franco had ventured.

"I've read up on your background. Some college education in business and finance, bachelor's degree in criminal justice, six years with the MDPD, care to elaborate?"

"During my senior year I was involved in a robbery – not as the robber, but the guy who took the bullet – two actually. Anyhow, after that I decided to switch majors and studied criminal justice. Naturally I started out with the MDPD, but found that my objectives scratch that, my idea of police work, differed from that of my employer." Franco had tried to keep it neutral.

"Interesting, what part of your job assignments was so objectionable?"

"Ahh, just the way we approached things." Franco had known better than to throw mud.

"Alright, would you be available to do some work as an inside mole in some of our departments?" the director had inquired.

"Sir, if I may ask: why don't you have the Office of the Inspector General or the MDPD investigate this?"

"Good question. By the way, call me John. See, if I get the IG or the MDPD involved and they bust the cases wide open, then it turns into the 'scandal at the airport' story. If we investigate ourselves and solve the problem, we look like we know what we're doing" the director of operations, John Knoll offered.

"Why don't you have your department heads check into this?" Franco had wondered.

"Well, at this point I have no clue who's involved in what. I therefore believe it may be wiser to get an outsider to do the snooping. You would get introduced as a temporary employee in the respective departments. Don't bust anyone until you get through all the departments. I don't want the news of an undercover operation to spread and spoil the harvest – if you know what I mean... Think you're up to the job?" the director had fixed his eyes on Franco.

"Yes sir – aahh, John. I'd be happy to help." Franco knew he'd be up to the challenge and was certainly interested in additional paychecks.

A car door slamming right next to him brought him back to the present. His muscles felt stiff and knotted, checking his watch he realized he must have dozed off. It was 6:56 p.m. Though he would have loved to call it a night, he convinced himself to stay. Forcing his stiff body out of the car he went up to Mr. Walker's apartment. No lights. He checked the parking lot for the black Mustang and went as far as peeking down the street to see if it had been parked close by. No such luck though. Not wanting to lose his chance to talk to his main suspect he decided to give it a couple more hours. After all, the seat in his car was comfortable enough.

Chapter Thirty Two

Benjamin Walker,
Miami (Wednesday, March 4th, 2015, 7:45 pm)

Why was life so damn complicated? He decided to pull over on Anne's Beach to sort this out. It was still early and the beach was empty. He grabbed a towel, shed his shirt and walked to a somewhat secluded area. Sitting in shallow water he tried to plot his next move. Finally – shortly before the sun started to do some real damage to his exposed face – he made up his mind:

The girl was his, and he was going to keep her in his life. It was time to announce his feelings to her. He decided to go to her apartment, knock on the door and introduce himself. The thought terrified him. Was there a better way? No, he had to grow up and get it done.

While he had made up his mind, he was still extremely nervous about his course of action, which caused him to take a leisurely late lunch at a Burger King. After enjoying a fish sandwich and a chocolate shake he continued his trip towards 'The Perfect One'.

Having decided to take US 1 instead of the Turnpike he stopped at Coral Castle. What could have been a more fitting place to take a short break? A man had built the castle by himself. A man desperately in love with a woman - that had never loved him back. He'd built a small castle for her and the child he'd wanted her to bear? Ultimately a sad story. Maybe he should have stopped somewhere else!

He didn't waste any time and continued up to Kendall Drive, and then headed straight for her place. He knew the way since he'd watched her place before.

Benjamin knocked on the apartment door. No answer, so he knocked a little harder. Still no answer, however a girl two doors over was leaving her apartment.

"Who are you looking for?" the girl inquired.

"Sabine." He replied a little surprised.

"You haven't heard?"

"Heard what?" Benjamin was alarmed.

"She's missing!" the girl exclaimed.

All of a sudden the door to the other side of Sabine's apartment opened and a burly man emerged. "Everything okay here?" he inquired in a loud voice.

Benjamin, who was still standing in front of Sabine's door stumbled back towards the banister of the second floor and almost toppled over, catching himself just before losing his footing. The big guy came towards him: "Who are you? What do you want?" spoken in a somewhat angry tone.

Benjamin was wondering why this man was so loud and angry, but didn't wait around long enough for the guy to say anything else. He bolted from the landing, down towards the parking lot. Glancing back he saw the guy looking surprised and unsure. Who was that guy? Was Sabine in the apartment with him?

Back in his car, speeding away from the complex. He realized that he was shaking. What had happened? Where was Sabine? Sabine was missing!? What did that mean? What had happened while he was in Key West?

He slowed his car down to comply with the speed limit and started to think. If she was indeed missing, who had abducted her? Then he realized that he might know who had taken her. A few weeks ago he had parked in Sabine's apartment complex' parking lot, just to see what she was up to, when he'd noticed another car pulling in. The driver had not exited the car and he'd gotten real curious. His car had been in the blind spot of the other driver's mirrors, so he was reasonably sure to have gone undetected. The driver had left after about an hour and Benjamin had gotten a good look. To his surprise he'd recognized the face: Prof. Martin – his Economics professor.

He decided to go home and do a search on Martin. Maybe he could find his home address, and check to see if Sabine was at his place. While it sounded like a long shot even to him, he wasn't going to sit back and do nothing.

Benjamin headed home to access his computer, and if he could get an address, he might also need some tools. Mainly the baseball bat he'd purchased after his brief encounter with the man who'd wanted to have sex with him! Well, maybe he'd also grab a quick shower after the long drive and get a change of clothes.

Pulling into the parking lot of his apartment complex he immediately noticed a black sedan. Looked like an undercover police car, but upon closer inspection turned out to be a Marauder. The former vehicle of choice for a few select FHP officers, therefore nothing he'd have to worry about. He proceeded to his apartment when he noticed a guy sitting by the small pool area. He was just sitting there looking at his cell phone – maybe a new tenant.

Benjamin walked up the stairs to his apartment and looked back at the pool. No one left in the area. He was putting his key into the deadbolt when he saw a shadow moving towards him.

"Benjamin Walker? My name is Franco Tamargo. May I have a word with you?" was all Benjamin heard before he bolted from his front door. Down the stairs towards his car jumping the four foot fence separating the complex from the parking lot. He reached his car – which he'd left unlocked – scrambled in, jammed the key into the ignition and took off with his tires leaving a fishtail mark on the parking lot pavement.

He scanned his rearview mirror for his pursuer but didn't detect anyone before he careened around the next corner taking him into a residential area. It must have been the guy in the Marauder who was trying to get him. Well, too slow – catch me if you can!

Who was that guy? Had the sexual predator died after their encounter? Had the cops tracked him to his home? Unlikely. Benjamin decided to go to the FIU library to find a computer for his search. If he succeeded, he'd sit on Martin's house, find out if Sabine was inside, or wait until he made a move that would lead him to where Sabine was. The more he thought about it, the better he felt about his hunch. Anything was better than to do nothing.

Surprisingly it took him only a few minutes to find Prof. Martin's home address. Thanks to the Miami Dade County Property Appraiser's website.

Leaving FIU he turned right on 107th Avenue heading due south. Left on Killian and a couple of minutes later he turned onto Martin's street. It was late enough for the guy to be home. He assumed that the professor was home and not somewhere else. He slowed down trying to see the house numbers. Shit, he overshot his target. Not to be obvious, he continued down a block before he hung a U-turn. The house was on his right hand side. Lots of areca palms blocking his view. He'd have to park his car somewhere and come back on foot.

Benjamin was contemplating calling the police. He was by now almost convinced that the guy had her in his house or would lead him to 'The Perfect One'. That he was keeping her prisoner was, to Ben, almost a certainty. The only thing that prevented him from doing so was the unknown outcome of his encounter with Mr. Gay-Asshole. He wasn't sure if the guy had survived their altercation without permanent damage. He wasn't going to find out by talking to the cops and then end up in jail. He'd steer clear of that obstacle.

He was facing another small dilemma, where should he park his car without drawing any suspicion? At Miami Dade College he wouldn't have been noticed, but it was way too far away. There was a high school only a couple of blocks away. Still a risk if the Professor took off, he'd have to scramble to get his car and might lose him. It might also look funky to the neighbors to have a guy hanging around on foot. Fortune smiled upon him. There was a house for sale only three houses down and across the street from the address. That should do nicely. Benjamin turned off his lights and backed into the driveway. The large ficus tree in the middle of the front yard provided enough darkness for him to be almost invisible from the street.

He opened his glove compartment and took out a small can of mixed nuts. He was ready to wait for as long as it would take. On second thought, he dropped the can on his passenger seat, turned off the interior lights and got out of the car for a quick walk by. There were some lights on in the house. It looked like the guy was still home. Back in his car he settled in and started to devour most of the nuts. He was still troubled by the guy at his apartment.

Chapter Thirty Three

Graciela Manciani,
Miami (Wednesday, February 11th, 2015)

Once inside his nest he removed the remaining restraints from Graciela and looked at her appreciatively.

"Get undressed." he ordered her from behind his mask in a muffled voice.

"Please let me go." she responded in a quivery voice.

"Get undressed – now!"

When she didn't move he slapped her hard with his open hand. The force was enough to send her onto the mattress. He held out his hand to help her up and when she again failed to move he grabbed her hair and pulled her to a standing position. She slowly started to unbutton her blouse, dropped it and waited.

"All of it." he demanded with a voice that revealed his excitement.

She continued by taking off her bra and shorts and stopped again.

"Keep going." he demanded.

She complied and took off her underwear, shoes and socks. When she was done he grabbed the pile of clothing and dropped it by the door.

"Lay down on the mattress."

"No, please, just let me go."

"Lay down." he said louder while simultaneously raising his hand.

She sat down sideways, pressing her knees together and covering her breasts as well as she could. It only took him a few seconds to shed his pants and come over to her. She averted her eyes when she saw his erection, knowing full well what would happen next.

Mercifully it had been over rather quickly. 'Bill Clinton' had locked her right ankle to a heavy chain, put on his pants and left her in the space that looked like a converted garage. Sitting up, she noticed his fluids leaking out of her. Disgusted she moved around on the mattress to get them off her.

Desperation and horror swept over her like a tidal wave. She felt like she was about to lose her sanity and connection to reality. How could anyone do this to another human being? Who deserved to be treated like a piece of meat? A sex slave? Would she ever get out of here? Even if he'd ever let her go – what would she have to endure before that moment arrived? Would she get pregnant? Would she ever be able to overcome not only the trauma of the experience, but the stigma of having been a sex slave?

She recalled having seen some report on abducted and raped women and how they struggled with the experience. Many of them had started to take drugs, some of them committing suicide, but all of them living with nightmares. The testimony had obviously not included those of the majority of girls that had been killed by their rapists. She started crying again when she realized that her life was over. It was only a question of how many times she wanted to endure being raped before the inevitable would happen.

When she finally stopped crying and wiped her tears away, she was almost surprised by the clarity of her thoughts.

Her parents weren't exactly 'Old School', but they had instilled certain values in her. No, she hadn't been a virgin before this brutal abduction and rape – but the one time she'd been with a guy – it had been her choice.

She scanned the room for an escape route, but was severely limited in her movement by the heavy chain that tied her down next to the mattress. Okay, he was wearing a mask, which indicated that he was not interested in her identifying him. So there was a chance that he would let her go eventually.

Her eyes focused on the camping toilet. She crawled over and investigated it. There was a removable plastic insert, which she removed. She smashed it hard onto the concrete floor and it broke into three pieces. Grabbing the largest piece she crawled back to the mattress and prayed. She asked God and her parents for forgiveness, took a deep breath and cut her carotid artery in one swift motion. The pain was bearable. She saw her blood running down her bare breast and lowered her back onto the mattress. It only took a few minutes before she lost consciousness.

Chapter Thirty Four

Thomas Sander,
Miami (Thursday, March 5th, 2015)

It wasn't in Thomas' blood to just sit still and wait for something to happen. Not when his baby sister was involved anyway. Franco was a nice enough guy and all, but Thomas wasn't going to sit in Sabine's apartment twirling his thumbs. He thought that there was a chance that the kidnapper would come back to the apartment. There wasn't a doubt in his mind that it had been the kidnapper that had removed Sabine's things from her apartment. What if the guy was armed? Thomas thought that he should be ready for that potential encounter. And, maybe he should level the playing field! He figured that Miami, even though the Cocaine-Cowboys weren't around anymore, warranted some extra tools. He was going to get some additional protection, well, a tool really.

Once he'd finished some research on Sabine's computer, he took a cab to Coconut Grove where, after a quick lunch at a restaurant in a beautiful mall, he'd walked the area. The 'Drunken Pirate' looked like a place where he might be able to find the information he needed.

He played a couple of rounds of pool with some guys. After losing fifty dollars, he felt the time was right to ask for some information.

"By any chance, do you guys know where I could buy a gun for target practice?" he asked them.

"What's your target?" Darius asked.

"Just target shooting at a range."

"Fuck man, you can probably rent a gun there, or any gun store should do." Dwayne told him.

"Yeah right." confirmed Darius.

"Well, I am not a citizen; will they sell it to me?"

"Shit no!" Dwayne informed him.

"Man, it's not like I would go on a crime spree, it's just that in Germany the gun laws are real strict and I'd love to just mess around with a gun a little." he lied.

"Most gun ranges rent guns." Dwayne repeated.

"Man, for all we know you're a cop!"

"Never mind, it's not that important." he said.

Thomas quickly ordered two more pitchers of beer. He beat Darius in the next pool game and reclaimed his fifty Dollars.

"Man, if you really need a gun, we might be able to help you out." Dwayne offered.

"Nah, forget it." he replied.

"No shit, seriously. If you're really hung up on target shooting we can help you out." Dwayne insisted.

"I don't know, now you guys make it sound like it is a big deal to buy a gun." he said.

"You want it – or you don't?" Dwayne inquired.

"I don't know. Yes, I guess." he answered.

They told him they knew a guy who would be able to help him out. He was supposed to meet them in a couple of hours at the Brownsville Metro-Rail station. He was told to bring at least three hundred Dollars.

In order to kill some time until his meeting, he walked around Coconut Grove, looking at the different stores, but really seeing nothing. He was preoccupied with his sister's whereabouts. He was hoping that Franco knew what he was doing. He kind of liked the guy, but didn't know if he was really any good at his job.

He wandered down to the water, passed the old Convention Center towards the Miami City Hall. Not much of a City Hall compared to the Hamburg City Hall, into which about one hundred and fifty of Miami's City Hall would have fit easily. He continued on up to a restaurant and outdoor bar, and then turned around. On his way back to Main Street he stopped at an ATM and withdrew $ 400.00 with his Master Card. He was able to get a cab that was discharging its passengers in front of a restaurant and asked the driver for a ride to the closest Metro Rail Station. The Caribbean driver was clearly upset to have caught such a short fare and told Thomas to get out of the cab. Thomas offered him a twenty Dollar bill and the driver decided to take him to the Metro.

Once inside the station it took Thomas more than ten minutes to figure out how to purchase a ticket. Luckily after his umpteenth attempt a security guard explained the machine to him. He made it through the turnstile and barely up the escalator in time to catch the northbound train that was about to leave. The interior of the train had seen better days, but Thomas was not in the mood to ponder the shortcomings of the public transportation system. Where was his sister? What was she going through? Why had she been kidnapped?

He didn't trust Darius and Dwayne, but he didn't know how to hedge his bet. What the heck, he was going to meet them in broad daylight at the bottom of a very public train station. How bad could it be?

He was about to find out. When he arrived at the Brownsville Station he was surprised by the blight. The landscape had started to look progressively worse on his train ride. Houses with blue tarps, apartment buildings with cars propped up on concrete blocks in the parking lots, derelict bicycles littering the fences along streets – sans their wheels.

Once downstairs he looked around for Darius and Dwayne. No sign of them. He waited for more than twenty minutes until they finally showed.

"Hey Thomas." Darius greeted him.

"You guys had a problem finding the station?" the ever inpatient German wanted to know.

"What?" Dwayne inquired.

"Never mind."

"Alright, let's get going." Dwayne suggested.

They started walking down the main street

towards an increasingly dark sky. Thomas thought this to be a bad omen, but continued anyway. After two blocks they turned left into a smaller alley of run-down apartment buildings. They waited next to a smelly dumpster for about ten minutes before the dealer-guy showed up. Thomas recognized the problem right away. The guy wasn't alone; his posse consisted of two additional dudes. Tough looking dudes. Thomas wasn't prepared for this turn of events. Well, he'd just have to wing it.

"Hi guys." he'd offered.

"So you're interested in a gun?" the leader wanted to know.

"Yeap."

"Well, do you have money to pay for it?" the inquisitive dealer wanted to know.

"Sure."

"Let's see it."

"Let me see the gun." he insisted.

"Money first."

"Come on guys – I'm in the minority here!" he responded. Thomas was starting to realize that his idea may not have been as brilliant as he had thought.

"Let's see the money." the dealer shot back.

"Alright, here it is." Thomas flashed his wad of twenty Dollar bills.

Thomas never had a chance – the baseball bat hit him without any warning.

Wham – his lights had dimmed!

Unfortunately they hadn't stopped!

They continued to kick him. In the stomach, in the head, his back!

When he finally woke up, he was in a room with light green walls, gauze covering his head and large areas of his body. He had no idea how he'd gotten there. The pain was tolerable, but he was totally confused as to what had happened to him. Thank God for morphine.

He remained in a stupor for a few more hours. Then Franco was there, and then Franco was gone. Maybe it was a dream. Thomas wasn't sure about it. When the swellings subsided, they lowered his morphine drip – he found out quickly, that there was pain – real pain – and his nurses would testify to that. His groaning and complaining was keeping them busy.

Chapter Thirty Five

Franco Tamargo,
Miami (Thursday, March 5th, 2015, 7:08 p.m.)

While Franco knew that time was of the essence in solving Sabine's disappearance, he had other obligations, which is why he'd spent the day at the airport. He had just pulled into the driveway of his house when his cell phone started ringing with the 'unknown' tone. Alright, that must be Thomas calling him back.

"Hello, this is Franco Tamargo." he answered.

"Mr. Tamargo, my name is George Garcia I am a nurse at Jackson Memorial Hospital, we found your business card on a person that was in an accident."

"What's the person's name?" Franco was puzzled.

"We don't know." came the response.

"So why do you think I know the person? Never mind – my card."

"The man is about thirty years old. He's about six feet three inches tall; he was wearing blue jeans and a red shirt. Does that help?" Mr. Garcia inquired.

"Yeah, well, maybe. What happened to him?"

"He seems to have been in some altercation." Garcia informed him in a non-committal voice.

"Can you be more specific – please?"

"How about you visit him?" the man suggested before disconnecting the call.

Chapter Thirty Six

Jerome Water and Eric Poole,
Miami (Thursday, March 5th, 2015, 5:45 p.m.)

When they got back to the station they went straight for Captain Santiago's office. His door was open and he was talking to Lieutenant Perez who sat in front of the desk. Santiago motioned them in and handed them a missing person report for a Sabine Sander, international student from Germany, missing for 66 hours.

"For all I know she's just shopping, but when I saw that she's also a FIU student, I figured we should take a look." Santiago told them.

"Who called it in?" Poole inquired.

"It's all in there. Her brother; who's visiting her from Germany."

"Who, according to the fingerprint comparison with the homeland security database, is now at Jackson Memorial with a couple of broken ribs, abrasions, a concussion and God knows what else." Lt. Perez interjected.

"We also have the attorney for Poole's recent arrest here. The guy who knifed his wife. He's waiting at the front desk, wants to ask you a few questions." Perez continued.

"What happened to the brother?" Water asked.

"Here's the report from the patrol officer." Perez handed it to Santiago who scanned it for a few minutes.

"Great timing. Okay Poole, you talk to the vulture, Water you check on the brother. Go." Santiago gave the report to Water and dismissed them with a wave of his hand. Poole snatched the report from Water and looked it over.

"Hey Jerome, from what I read here the guy took a pretty bad beating. So try to keep your food down." Poole just couldn't help himself.

Chapter Thirty Seven

Jerome Water,
Miami (Thursday, March 5th, 2015, 7:01 p.m.)

Taking the unmarked Ford out of the lot he drove over to Jackson Memorial Hospital, cursing at the traffic as he went. The day had been pretty hot, but it had started to cool down, so he rolled down his windows and turned off the a/c. If it hadn't been for air conditioning, only a fraction of the people would be crowding this city, well metropolitan area really. Luckily the hospital had a few parking spaces reserved for police vehicles, so he was spared the arduous deal of searching for a parking space. He parked the cruiser and went over to the information desk, checked in and got directions to the ICU.

On the fifth floor he exited the elevator and went to the nurse' station only a few steps from the elevator. Standing six feet three inches tall, with light brown close cropped hair and a body shaped by years on the swim team in High School, he looked good enough for the nurse behind the counter to pay immediate attention to him.

"How may I help you?" she inquired pleasantly.

"Hi, I am Detective Water. I am here to check on a robbery victim. Name listed as unknown, who was brought in about two hours ago with abrasions, broken ribs and other unpleasant injuries." Water flashed the badge he was carrying around his neck as well as a smile.

"Sure, he's in room 512, but he's heavily sedated, so you will probably not learn much from him." the helpful nurse informed him. "My name is Maria if you need anything." she added.

"Thank you Maria. Which way is the room?"

She pointed down the hallway to her right.

Water found room 512 and entered through the open doorway. Well, Maria did have a point. The guy was wearing quite a few bandages around his head. He walked over to the bed and looked down at the victim. From what he could see, just by the outline under the thin blankets, the guy must be as tall as he was. The victim's eyes were closed and he didn't respond to the noise of Water approaching him.

Not having much experience in talking to hospitalized robbery victims, he just touched the man on the shoulder.

"Hello, sir?" Water started.

No response. He poked the guy a little harder. "Sir, can you hear me?"

"Aaahhhh!" the guy opened his eyes, well, he attempted to anyway.

"I am sorry. My name is Detective Water, what is your name, sir?"

Too late, the guy had closed his eyes again. Uncertain as to what protocol required at this point, Water sat down in the chair next to the bed. He'd wait a little and see if the guy would come around. There was no way he'd go back to Det. Poole empty handed. He looked around the room. Typical hospital room, lots of equipment behind the headboard of the bed. Oxygen lines, plenty of other lines and computer cables. The man's vital signs were displayed on a screen. Heartbeat regular at 60 beats a minute. Blood pressure being taken every so often revealed 128/93.

He decided to take a little break for dinner at the downstairs cafeteria. On his way to the elevator he noticed Maria looking at him.

"He's sleeping. I am going to grab some food downstairs and be back in a little bit." he told her. "Can I get you anything?" he added.

"How sweet, no thank you." Maria answered with a smile.

Before she could notice his face flush, he'd turned towards the elevator. Pretty girls tended to do that to him.

The food in the cafeteria wasn't half bad. He had the tilapia with mashed potatoes and a fruit salad. The prices were reasonable as well. He took his time and enjoyed his meal while checking out the other visitors. Roughly half of them looked to be hospital personnel, with the remainder being visitors and vendors. There were some sad faces among them and Jerome started concentrating on his food. He had enough drama in his life without looking for more while having dinner.

Chapter Thirty Eight

Franco Tamargo,
Miami (Thursday, March 5th, 2015, 7:31 p.m.)

Franco had a good idea who the 'unknown' person was. Thomas Sander!

Once he arrived at Jackson Memorial Hospital it took Franco only the better part of twenty minutes to get to Thomas' room. It hadn't been easy to make it past the nurse in charge of the floor – apparently not the one who'd called him...

"How are you doing?" he asked once he arrived at the room and identified Thomas under the bandages. Such a stupid question, considering he was looking at a guy that was probably unable to see him out of his swollen eyes. Thomas was wrapped like a mummy, with bandages covering almost his entire head making him look quite grotesque. There were small traces of blood penetrating the bandages around his nose and eyes.

"Gohhoodd" was the almost audible answer. Franco had seen a few victims in his career. Thomas, however, was up there – at least when it came to the 'live' ones.

Uttering that single word appeared to have drained all of Thomas' strength, for when Franco looked at him again, he'd fallen asleep – more like lights out.

Franco checked with another one of his contacts. According to the report of the patrol officers, which his source was kind enough to email him, the officers had found Thomas at NW 55th Street and 27th Avenue. The officer had learned that Thomas had attempted to buy a handgun in the wrong neighborhood. A witness who'd observed the deal had come forward after the dust had settled; a rare species in that part of town, and given a statement. According to the man Thomas had tried to procure a handgun. The guys he'd spoken to had asked to see the money. Thomas had agreed and had pulled out, what looked to the witness, like a few hundred bucks. Once his newfound friends saw the money, they'd apparently decided to just take it. Thomas hadn't gone down without a fight. Although, outnumbered three to one, he hadn't fared too well. They had started to beat the living daylights out of him. Once he fell, they proceeded to kick him, in the back, chest and head. By the time the ambulance had arrived he had certainly looked different from just fifteen minutes earlier. They'd taken him to the trauma unit at Jackson Memorial Hospital.

Franco wanted to know what the perpetrators had looked like, but also why Thomas had wanted to buy a handgun in the first place. Unfortunately he'd been unable to get any information at all during his first visit. Having been the victim of a senseless attack himself, Franco felt passionate about Thomas' plight, but at the same time wondered what the hell was wrong with the guy!

Chapter Thirty Nine

Jerome Water and Franco Tamargo
(Thursday, March 5th, 2015, 7:54 p.m.)

He disposed of his garbage, put the tray in its correct place and headed back to the victim's room. When the elevator door opened, he noticed, with a little bit of disappointment, that Maria wasn't behind the station's counter anymore. Instead, a male nurse was manning the post. He started walking past the station when the guy asked: "Can I help you sir?"

"Detective Water, I am going back to room 512 to interview a robbery victim." he replied.

"He already has another visitor. A Mr. Tamargo."

This certainly had the potential to make things easier for Jerome. The visitor, if the victim was still asleep, might be able to answer some questions for him. Water picked up his steps and entered the room again.

"Hi, my name is Detective Water, do you know this man?" Jerome opened.

"Hi, I'm Franco Tamargo, Private Investigator." Franco had risen from the chair and extended a hand.

Jerome shook the hand and asked again: "Do you know this man?"

"Yes, he's a client of mine. His name is Thomas Sander. His sister has been abducted and he hired me to help him find her."

"Yeah, we know. He filed a missing person report." Water responded.

"You guys actually looked at it already? As a matter of fact, I was just going to call an old friend of mine – Detective Poole – to inform him about this case."

"You know Poole?"

"Yes, we worked a few cases together when I was with the MDPD's crime suppression unit." Franco explained.

"What happened to him?" Jerome pointed towards the bed.

"He hasn't really said anything. I found out that he tried to buy a handgun in the wrong neighborhood. Well, you probably know this as well, since I've learned that from a friend in the MDPD."

"Okay, why don't you start at the beginning? Why did he want to buy a gun in the first place?"

Franco explained Thomas' suspicions, his own observations and the events of the past few days with as much detail as he could. Jerome had taken out a pad and took notes throughout Franco's story. When Franco finished, they sat in silence for a few minutes until Jerome offered: "We have two dead FIU students, one male, one female, which is why we jumped on this. Do you want to come to the station with me and run it all by Det. Poole?"

Franco agreed to follow Jerome to the station to brief senior detective Poole.

Chapter Forty

Eric Poole, Jerome Water, and Franco Tamargo
(Thursday, March 5th, 2015, 8:53 p.m.)

"Magnum P.I." Poole exclaimed and grinned when Jerome and Franco walked up to his desk.

"Dirty Harry!" Franco shot back.

"Nah, not anymore, Clint and I will soon retire. Too much action may kill us before we get to enjoy the fruits of our labor." Poole replied. "This kid here" pointing at Franco for Jerome's benefit, "used to be a pretty good cop – until he buckled under the pressure."

Poole and Franco both knew that to be untrue. Franco decided to play along. "Yeah, but only because you somehow always managed to pull out the larger gun."

"At the urinal!" Poole laughed while simultaneously starting to cough.

"No, there was never a competition there, since you always went to the ladies' room!"

Poole was now having serious problems controlling his laughter and coughing.

"You wouldn't dare give me this kind of lip if you were still on the force!"

"Hell no, you were and for all I know still are, the most dangerous cop I've ever been around – and I am not suicidal."

"Franco was a Rookie on my team eight years ago. He didn't know the butt of his gun from his own, but somehow managed to stay alive. Just kidding. There was that one time when half of the MDPD and the FHP chased the killer of an FHP officer into an apartment complex and the perpetrator thought he could shoot his way out of it. Magnum P.I. here was part of that little Showdown at the O.K. Corral." Poole explained to Jerome after having caught his breath.

"How'd it end?" Jerome wanted to know.

"We won." Poole replied dryly.

With Poole and Tamargo done reminiscing about the past, Tamargo filled Poole in on the background of the robbery victim, the past couple of days including Sabine's disappearance, the missing items from her apartment, his interviews with the boyfriend and the friends, his encounter with Benjamin Walker the previous night, and everything else he was able to recall without his notes.

"The guy may have a problem with going into the wrong neighborhood with the wrong intentions, but I honestly believe his concerns about his sister are legit." Tamargo informed them. "She is missing, and I do believe Thomas, the brother, about the break in. Sure there were no sign of forced entry, but there were little things that were just off." Franco insisted.

When Tamargo was done with his narrative, Poole sat still for a while, silently nodding his head.

"Poole, are you guys going to pursue Sabine Sander's disappearance? If you do, I'd really like to stay involved – not only for the money – but I think I can help by doing some of the grunt work that we all like so much." Tamargo offered.

"I don't think the Captain is going to like a civilian trotting along, but I've always appreciated your work, so feel free to do some of the work. Just as long as we understand each other regarding the parameters of how this is going to work. We are not paying you. You will let us know about everything you find out in a timely manner. Agreed?" Poole glanced at Tamargo.

"Sure thing, I always wanted to find out firsthand what it's like to work for a Plantation owner." Tamargo joked.

Poole, all business again, shot him another glance. "Franco, you know this is against policy – so don't push it."

"Thanks Poole." Tamargo knew when to shut up.

"Okay, here's the plan. I am talking to the Captain while you guys follow up on Franco's leads. Benjamin Walker, Prof. Martin and Prof. Rupert.

"Who is following up?" Jerome wanted to know.

"You and Franco, kid. You may actually learn something from Magnum. Franco, be nice to the kid – I kind of like him. First time he threw up he missed my shoes…" Poole waived them away.

Franco suggested driving over to Benjamin Walker's apartment, and Jerome agreed. On their way out of the station Det. Poole caught up with them. "Water, I need for you to log in some evidence and sign the report on the puke incident. Just kidding, but you do have some paperwork before you go out into the world playing cop."

"Don't worry; I'll take the first shift. Why don't you come by at 3:00 a.m.?" Franco offered.

"No shit, you guys barely met an hour ago and are already out on a date?" as soon as he said it, Det. Poole started his usual laughing – cough.

"Have you tried the 'Improv'" Franco inquired while turning to walk away.

"Where's your sense of humor - small gun?" Det. Poole, working on another coughing fit, wanted to know.

"Tired, but laughing on the inside. Jerome, see you later." Franco kept walking while waiving his extended right middle finger at Poole.

"I'll be there." Water called after him.

Chapter Forty One

Benjamin Walker's Apartment,
Miami (Friday, March 6th, 2015, 3:00 a.m.)

Water made it to the parking lot at 3:00 a.m. sharp. When he arrived at Franco's car, Franco told him that there hadn't been any movement.

"How about we meet at the Starbucks on the FIU campus at 8:30 a.m.?" Franco suggested.

"See you." Jerome replied while Franco was starting his car.

Jerome raised his hand and walked back to his car to start his shift.

Chapter Forty Two

Sabine Sander, Miami (Spring Semester 2015)

The fact that he was good looking certainly helped the students in his class to stay focused, well, mostly the female students, and mostly focused on him, not necessarily the lecture. His first lecture was interesting and really inspiring. He talked about how history – in the world of business – kept repeating itself. How greed had essentially negated all forms of the original idea of a positive, working capitalism.

He explained to the class – and made sure to identify these as his own thoughts – that both communism and capitalism – had failed!

She was fascinated by his explanation to both ideologies.

Communism was the ultimate – yet unachievable – form of being. Capitalism was the ultimate – yet not anymore achievable ⁃ perfect form of an advancing society.

Everyone in class had their own opinion!

"What about the achievements of the Russian Revolution? They were able to free themselves from their Masters. They implemented a society that focused on the people! The people were to drive the society, the economy, and their own future."

"Milton Friedman had it right! If we were to determine our own destiny, to take care of ourselves and our surroundings without government influence and supervision – the world would operate without flaw!"

Prof. Robert Martin listened to all of the comments. He never admonished any of the students for any of their remarks. Never made the students feel stupid – no matter how misguided or off color their ideas sounded. And boy had some of them sounded weird!

In short, Prof. Martin was a favorite of almost all of the students. He'd even gotten a "hot" on the "rate my professor" website.

Unfortunately, he was one of those professors that took their job of teaching the students seriously. When, at the end of class, he handed out the syllabus for the class, everyone took a deep breath. The guy was Old school – Midterm and comprehensive Final. One paper on a subject to be picked by the student, minimum of twenty pages! Everyone realized immediately that this was going to be one of those classes where you really had to put in some serious time.

Chapter Forty Three

Their first encounter had been so sweet. She had been a virgin! He couldn't have painted the perfect picture any better than that. Yeah, she'd cried a little and she fought him a little. But wasn't that what real courtship was all about? The male, dominant species taking control, pounding the female into submission, making her his!

In the past he'd gone about this all wrong. Sure, Homo sapiens had evolved – but had it really improved life on this planet? In the past men had made women their servants. Not in a negative way, just so that society could function. There hadn't been any questions, there hadn't been any courtship, and there hadn't been any fancy dinners – just adrenaline and testosterone dictating the outcome that was predetermined by nature. Men had always been destined to be superior.

He was on his way to restore order to what modern society had destroyed. Equal rights, gay rights, shared custody of children, ADA rules, all that crap that the federal government was force-feeding down the throats of law abiding citizens. No more guns, abortions at will; take-it-from-the-rich-and-give-it-to-the-poor-schemes. What had happened to: Help yourself and God will help you?

He was so sick and tired of all the social restraints that had been put on life in general and healthy relationships in particular. Didn't they remember where the wedding band originated? It was the raiders, who took the women from other tribes, who invented it. First they'd tied them up, then they only left a rope around their wrists, then they left a band around their finger as a reminder as to who owned whom. But first had been the raid. The taking of what men had wanted. No excuse, no sorry if I hurt your feelings, no, did I comply with your expectations! What a joke. The divorce rate in the western civilized world was well above fifty percent! You had a better chance of hitting the numbers on a roulette table at any of the Indian tribes casinos! He knew he'd found the right way to restore order in his universe. He'd take what he wanted and needed. When he was done with her, he'd move on. But he wasn't done with Sabine, his third guest, not by a long shot. How sweet she was. A virgin! Like in the novels he'd read about the Spartans. Well, he wasn't going to let her carry his baby and throw the baby – if it was a girl - down a ravine. Nope, it would all be over way before they'd reach that point. How it would end he hadn't really thought about. Heck - that was something he'd neglected to address in all his planning! Well, he'd figure it out in due time.

Chapter Forty Four

Jerome Water, Franco Tamargo, and Prof. Martin
(Friday, March 6th, 2015, 8:30 am)

"What's up?" Franco asked as he sat down heavily on his barstool.

"And Good Morning to you Sir." Jerome responded.

"Another comedian. How long have you been working with Poole?"

"Just started, but I'm a quick study!" Jerome shot back.

"Shit, I am tired and can't catch a break!" Franco used both hands to comb his hair back. "Just kidding, didn't sleep too well."

"Not me – I stopped watching the apartment at 7:00 a.m., went home, took a shower, had a light breakfast, and drove over here…!" Jerome came back.

"Okay, you win." Franco admitted.

"Where do we start?" Jerome inquired.

"How about Prof. Martin, she likes him. She met Roberto in his class. Got to start somewhere – right?" Franco replied.

They walked over to the Admissions Office.

"Good morning Miss… "Jerome was looking down at the name plate on her desk "…Melody. My name is Det. Jerome Water, I am with the Miami Dade Police Department this is my … associate Mr. Franco Tamargo. We need to know where we can find Prof. Robert Martin. Please." Water flashed a smile and produced his badge.

How about that? Jerome Water appeared to be more of a smooth talker than Franco had expected. To be fair Melody was very pretty. Long dark brown hair framing a beautiful face; illuminated by big hazel eyes. Franco shook his head while shooting Jerome an amused glance.

"Is there anything wrong?" Melody had picked up on Franco's headshake.

"Nope, nothing wrong. Prof. Martin?" Franco repeated Jerome's question.

"Let me see." Melody started typing furiously on her keyboard.

"Looks like his regular schedule is for evening classes, but it says here that he's actually filling in for Prof. Buttercup today." She informed them.

"Prof. Buttercup?" Jerome had to stifle a laugh.

"Yes, the class is almost over. You have ten minutes to make it over to the Business Center before the class is out."

"Thank you Melody." Jerome flashed another smile that left Franco wondering if he was out with Casanova. He also realized that he was missing the badge. Oh how much easier it made life.

Walking quickly towards the Business Center, Franco started laughing.

"Are you sure you're in the right line of business? You would be a shoe-in to replace Warren Beatty!"

"Very funny, you don't know me. Did you see me turn purple?

"No, can't say I did."

"Well, only because I am very quick in turning my face away from prying eyes!" Jerome admitted.

"What?"

"Don't laugh – I am actually very shy – and blush when I talk to pretty girls!"

Franco's face broke into a wild grin, but he curbed it as soon as he saw the look on Jerome's face.

At the Business Center they located the class-room where Prof. Martin was teaching in and waited outside. Three minutes later the students exited and Jerome and Franco walked in and introduced themselves to Prof. Martin.

Prof. Martin was accommodating enough. He offered them a seat in the two – very uncomfortable - chairs in front of the desk – and sat down on his own. "I would ask you to come to my fancy office upstairs, but I don't have one." Prof. Martin said by way of an apology.

"No problem. Thank you for taking time to talk with us Prof. Martin." Jerome opened the conversation.

"How may I be of assistance to you officers?" Prof. Martin replied.

"One of your students has been reported missing. We were hoping you could give us a little more background on her." Jerome answered, neglecting to inform the Professor that Franco wasn't with the MDPD.
"What's the student's name?"

"Her name is Sabine Sander." Jerome replied.

"Sander – can't really say I'm recalling that name. Let me think for a minute." Prof. Martin was leaning back in his chair, closing his eyes.

"Maybe we can help you. Here's a picture of her." Jerome held out the picture that Franco had gotten from Thomas.

Prof. Martin snapped forward and took the picture from Jerome. Leaning back into his chair he studied it for a few seconds.

"Yes, sorry, I am terrible with names. Sander, international student from Germany, if I recall correctly from her introduction in class. Good student. She's missing? When did that happen?" Prof. Martin looked concerned.

"When was the last time you saw her?" Jerome replied without answering the professor's question.

"Let me see, today is Friday – she's in my Macroeconomic class which meets on Tuesdays and Thursdays. I don't think she was in class on Tuesday or Thursday. Can't say I recall having seen her in class last week." Prof. Martin seemed to make a real effort trying to remember if Sabine had been present last week.

"Could you check your attendance sheet?" Franco chimed in.

Prof. Martin looked at Franco like he noticed him for the first time.

"I don't take attendance. Guess that's the reason why my class is popular." he cracked a smile that disappeared as quickly as it had sprung up.

Franco couldn't help but think that Prof. Martin was a little full of himself. Did the guy think he was something special? He shot a glance at Jerome who was consulting his notes.

"Prof. Martin, where were you last Monday from 10:00 p.m. until 1:00 a.m.?" Jerome asked.

"Whoa, did I just become a suspect in a missing person case?" he answered with a smile while starting to flip pages in his calendar that had been in front of him.

"Okay, I must have been home grading papers, since I had to turn in the grades the following day to be entered into the computer system. Unfortunately I am a procrastinator who likes to do things last minute. Is that when she went missing?"

"Is there anyone who can verify that?" Water asked.

"I live alone, so no."

"Was there anything you've noticed that was different about Sabine – when you last interacted with her?" Jerome wanted to know.

Prof. Martin leaned back in his chair again. Franco again thought that the guy took himself a little too seriously. Leaning forward in his chair Prof. Martin responded:

"Sabine – now that I'm able to put the name to her face – is a very good student. I actually was very blessed to have such a bright student in my class. The universities, as well as the professors, get graded on how students fare after graduation. Bright and successful students are good for us. When they find good jobs afterwards and make decent money, that looks good on the evaluation of the university."

"She is doing well in class." he continued, "She is an A+ student. If I recall correctly, she did hook up with another student that's in my class. Ah – the football player. Wait."

Prof. Martin flipped open the dark brown satchel on the desk and pulled out a folder, leafed through it, extracted a paper and scanned it. "Roberto Suarez. Yup, if I am not totally mistaken, they are seeing each other."

"Was there anything out of the ordinary going on between them? Fighting? Bad blood?" Franco wanted to know.

"No, nothing that I've ever noticed. Is he a suspect? You think they had a falling out and he did something to her? So when exactly did she go missing? Or maybe they just went on a little trip?"

"Sir, we thank you for your time. You have been very helpful." Franco stated while getting up from the torture chair that had been killing his back. Franco looked at Jerome from the corner of his eyes and saw the confused look on his face. Nevertheless, Jerome also stood and, following Franco's lead, shook hands with Prof. Martin.

"No problem." Prof. Martin seemed a bit surprised by the abrupt end to the conversation, but tried his best to hide it.

"Please keep me in the loop. If there is anything else I can do, any questions you may have, my door is always open." Prof. Martin assured them.

"Here's my card in case you remember anything else." Jerome handed his card over.

Prof. Martin took it and returned his own business card to Jerome.

Jerome played it cool until they reached the exterior door a couple of hundred feet away from Prof. Martin's classroom.

"What's the matter with you? You mind telling me why you cut me off like that?" Jerome was angry and lost at the same time. Sure Franco had more experience than he did, but to cut him off like that – he was after all the only police officer present – well, that didn't sit too well with him.

"Look, I am sorry. I didn't mean to put you on the spot – question your authority. Don't you agree that the guy is a little off? I thought it would be better not to let him know that we don't trust him."

"We don't trust him? You're already speaking for both of us?" Jerome was more than just a little put off by Franco's assessment.

"Man, I am really sorry. Do you trust him? Did you see his facial expression throughout the conversation? The guy is a little too schmuck for my taste. The way he tried to make Roberto a suspect. Notice how he tried to insert himself into the investigation?"

Jerome didn't want to overreact on his first case and swallowed hard.

"Well, I haven't really ruled out Roberto. Okay, his demeanor was a bit odd." Jerome admitted while hitting Franco with a little stinger that Franco might have ruled out Roberto, but that he hadn't.

They walked back towards the visitor parking lot in silence for a few minutes.

"You were right about him!" Jerome informed Franco out of the blue.

"Right about what?" Franco inquired.

"The guy has something to do with Sabine's disappearance!" Jerome replied.

"Okay, I agree, but why do you like him for it now?"

"He questioned when she went missing and suggested that Sabine may have gone on a trip. What concerned Professor would suggest everything is okay instead of asking us to find her?" Jerome came back.

Franco just nodded his head.

"Why don't we meet up with Det. Poole and see if we can obtain a warrant for Martin's house?" Franco finally answered.

"See you at the station." Jerome hurried to his car.

Chapter Forty Five

Prof. Martin, Miami (early days)

He fancied himself a pretty bright guy. He'd finished Harvard in the top 5% of his class. He'd opened his own investment company by the age of twenty-eight, made his first million by twenty-nine, became a part time professor at FIU a couple of years later. He'd published articles in the Journal of Economic Literature, the Quarterly Journal of Economics, and the Journal of Finance by the age of thirty-two. Come on, this wasn't anything to sneeze at. So why wasn't he smart enough to keep a meaningful relationship going? Why had all of his relationships fizzled after only a short few months? He knew it wasn't for his lack of trying. After the sad accident, and subsequent demise of his first wife, he had laid low for a while. They had been vacationing in New Mexico, when his wife of only eight months had lost her footing on a hillside that ended more than fifteen hundred feet lower at the bottom of a gorge. Granted, he might have been able to save her, but after all the insults she'd hurled at him the night before he hadn't really been in Superman mode or mood. He had spent the next few months being interrogated by various police officers from New Mexico, but the district attorney decided not to file charges against him. While he had spent the next few months primarily focused on his business success, he had eventually opened up to the rest of the world again. His first girlfriend, Gloria, had been understanding and sweet when he hadn't been able to restrain himself for more than a minute. They had actually worked on preventing his premature ejaculation problem with tips gathered from the internet, and he'd gotten better. While three minutes would probably not get him into the Guinness book of records, it had been a vast improvement over their previous attempts.

Unfortunately Gloria hadn't shared his enthusiasm over his improved prowess and had left him after only ten months. It had taken him more than four months to even think about another attempt at dating. Eventually it was a senior student in his class that had gotten to him. She'd kept on coming on to him and he had finally asked her out.

Patricia had been extremely interested in him, as far as he could tell, but played hard to get for quite a while. They had intimate dinners at various hotels on Key Biscayne but never stayed. More than once they'd parked next to the Miami Seaquarium on their way back, enjoying the view of the Bay, exchanging stories. After three months of courtship Robert gathered all of his courage and invited her to take a weekend trip to Islamorada. He'd booked a room in the hotel next to the original Tikki bar. Spending a beautiful day jet-skiing, snorkeling and drinking they had gone up to their room to consummate their relationship. It ended in complete disaster – really it had ended within seconds that had left him embarrassed to his bones. The anticipation had proven to be too much. Patricia had been a good sport and had kept up the appearance for a couple more weeks. But eventually it had become clear that they were not dating anymore.

Devastation wouldn't even have come close to describe how Robert had felt. This time it had taken him the better part of half a year to recover from the blow to his self esteem.

Against all hope, and his deep rooted fear of rejection, he'd believed that Amanda was different. They had connected on an intellectual level that ran deeper than pure sexual attraction. Sure, she'd also been a student in his class which ran counter to what FIU's policy dictated, but this had been different. She had been his soul mate. She'd been unlike any girl he'd ever met. Smart, funny, witty and yes – extremely attractive. He'd gone all out. Wining and dining her at the fanciest places Miami had to offer. They'd cruised over to the Bahamas on one of the gambling-boats. Spent a lovely weekend in a beachfront cabin where they had intercourse for the first time. He'd been extremely anxious and fumbled their first encounter, but recovered on the second attempt.

Finally – heaven had descended upon him. He'd found the ying to his yang. They went looking for shells on the sandy white beaches of the Bahamas. Snorkeled around the shallow reefs and took a boat tour to explore the other small islands. Could it be? Was she the answer to all his dreams? He certainly felt that way.

Chapter Forty Six

Sabine Sander, Miami (Tuesday, March 3rd, 2015, 1:55 a.m.)

When she was able to focus again, she noticed that her captor had again left the lights on. The mattress, which didn't have any sheets on it, had absorbed her blood which had also dried on the inside of her legs.

The tears she'd shed had dried on her face. Her eyes felt puffy and were itching. What an animal he was. How could he do this to her? How could he do that to anyone for that matter? Deep down in her soul she feared that she wasn't going to get out of this place alive. But maybe there was still some hope. Her captor was still keeping his face covered. That was a good sign – wasn't it?

Her inside felt raw. She looked down between her legs and tried to wipe away the blood. Without a sheet, a towel or napkin she was reduced to spiting on her hands to loosen up and wipe away the dried blood. What was the sense in cleaning up anyway? He was going to come back. Continue with his torture. Continue to receive his pleasure by raping an innocent girl that was completely defenseless, chained down like an animal.

Chapter Forty Seven

Jerome Water, Eric Poole, and Franco Tamargo,
Miami (Friday, March 6th, 2015, 11:15 am)

Back at the station Water and Tamargo had to wait for Det. Poole to get out of a meeting with the station's Captain.

"Why did you quit the department?" Water wanted to know.

"Ah, just a difference of opinion I guess." Franco responded without much enthusiasm for the topic.

"Come on, spill it."

Franco's face went blank as he sat in total silence for a few minutes reflecting on how he had ended up quitting.

"When I started out as a patrol officer I thought I was making a difference. I mean I like to believe I actually did. Patrolling neighborhoods, talking to people – it was fun."

"What changed?"

"My assignment did. I switched to crime suppression, which I thought would really be the outfit to make a huge difference on the streets."

"But it didn't?" Water pushed.

Tamargo again sat quiet for a minute.

"No, yes it did, mostly – especially in the beginning. We truly did take a large chunk out of crime in certain neighborhoods." Tamargo answered while staring out the dirty window behind Water.

"So what happened?" Water, ever inquisitive, pushed him to continue.

Tamargo came back from his trance and looked at Water as if he'd just woken up from a bad dream.

"We became them. We dressed up like them. We walked like them, talked like them. We hung out at the same places as they did. We infiltrated them on all levels. Eventually there was no difference between us and them. We even committed petty crimes. We dealt some drugs, sold some guns and had a couple of prostitutes working for us. It was all fun and games in the beginning – just like a big joke we were playing on the bad guys. But after a while

I really started to wonder. What the fuck was the difference between us?" Tamargo looked almost exhausted from his little emotional outburst.

Water was surprised by how passionate this guy was after all the years that had passed since his involvement.

At that moment Det. Poole walked back into the room. Judging by the frown on his face he wasn't happy with whatever conversation he'd just had.

"Give me something good guys. Just had my ass handed to me for allowing a civilian to be part of the investigation." Poole sat down heavily in his swivel chair.

"Franco, sorry man, you're out."

"What are you talking about?" Tamargo looked more frustrated than angry.

"Come on, you knew it was a long shot for the Captain to agree with my half-baked idea of letting you be part of any official investigation." Poole tried to make his raspy voice sound pleasant – but failed miserably.

"However" he added in a quite tone "there is nothing anyone can do to stop a Private Investigator from following an officer – as long as he doesn't interfere with the investigation…

and who knows, maybe sometimes the officer leaves some crumbs behind … and vice versa …" Poole looked at Water and then Tamargo.

"Okay, what did you guys find out?" Poole wanted to know.

Water filled him in on their conversation with Prof. Martin and their suspicion that he knew more than he admitted. He told him about their idea to get a search warrant for Martin's house.

"Sounds good, but its way to thin for a search warrant. I need more than that. Let me know when you have something solid."

Poole got off his chair in a swift and sudden move and proceeded to walk out of the room.

Tamargo and Water exchanged glances before they exited the room and subsequently the station altogether. Across the street they reconvened at a diner and ordered lunch.

"Okay Tamargo, while I hate to admit this, you may have a little more experience investigating cases! So why don't you suggest our next step?" Water understated the situation.

"Listen Jerome – I don't want to jeopardize your career. It's your butt on the line. No hard feelings if you don't want me around. Sure I've spent a few more years on the force than you have – but heck, I've been out for just as many years! It's up to you." Tamargo stated his case, but wasn't going to make it easy for Water.

"Okay, so I am an idiot for listening to you. I was thinking about having a little chat with the other professor that you said Sabine mentioned in her diary. You're up for it?"

"As soon as we're done here." Franco replied.

Chapter Forty Eight

Amanda, Miami (early days)

Back in Miami they kept dating and their romance kept getting more serious. He eventually invited her to move into his Brickell Avenue apartment overlooking the bay. To his delight she agreed without hesitation. The furniture in her apartment had been rented and there hadn't been a problem fitting her cloths into his oversized walk-in-closet. They went jogging from his apartment to the bridge over the Miami River almost every day. They spent evenings at many of the restaurants in Downtown and on Brickell Avenue. His "problem" had somehow reappeared after a couple of weeks and he started to watch porn on the internet to steel himself from getting too exited too quickly. He was actually getting better at controlling his premature ejaculation problem. Had it back up to three minutes!

It was on a Friday evening when Amanda had come home earlier than expected. Catching him "training" in front of his computer. The embarrassment almost made him throw up, but eventually he had snapped out of it and explained to her why he was watching porn on the internet. It took a couple of hours of explaining, but Amanda eventually understood what he was trying to accomplish. While she didn't particularly agree with his method, she calmed down.

They agreed that he would limit his 'training' to times when he was assured that she wouldn't walk in on him.

Seeing that Amanda was amiable to different things, he suggested a few new and different positions which could potentially improve matters. Alas, they didn't. What was wrong with him? What kind of stimuli or, in his case non-stimuli did he need? He started surfing the internet and found his answer. Amanda was reluctant to give his new ideas a try, but eventually agreed. After a couple of sessions Amanda announced that she didn't like the way they were 'connecting'! Two days later he came home to an empty closet and bed.

He wasn't going to beat himself up over his latest misfortune. So he was a little different, deal with it. Maybe he needed to focus on a different kind of girl. No, nothing wrong with the girls, he needed to change the sort of relationship he was having. No sense in long courtship and expensive dinners. He'd tried a couple of hookers, but found that experience too impersonal.

He needed to figure out a better way ....

Chapter Forty Nine

Captor, Miami (early days)

He'd finally figured out the solution to his dilemma, the key to his paradise. He wasn't living in a perfect world. He had to accept his short comings and move on. On that note he'd decided to compartmentalize his life. He was going to be the first guy to have his cake and eat it too!

Finding the right location to implement his plan had been a challenge. What he needed was an isolated location, minimal if no traffic at all, no busybody neighbors, secluded, yet accessible to him. No small feat in a bustling metropolitan area of more than two million people. He'd started out by driving around aimlessly. After several days he decided on a more scientific approach. He purchased a street map of Miami, drew a penciled grid on the map and started exploring. He'd ruled out approximately ninety percent of the map as too congested. But there was still a lot of ground to cover.

He'd concentrated on the edges of the map first. Krome Avenue and Homestead had been his first choices. After spending more than three weeks of driving through rural areas and immigrant dominated residential neighborhoods, he'd realized that he wasn't going to find what he was looking for. The areas around Krome Avenue, while deserted and mostly devoid of any traffic had produced a surprising number of really suspicious neighbors. Every time he'd driven down a small dirt road there'd been some dog barking or some light turned on in some godforsaken small little home.

Homestead had been equally disappointing. There had been just too many people that enjoyed sitting out in front of their yards or on tiny porches. He'd never realized that Hispanics were such nocturnal animals.

He'd gone back to the drawing board and tried to identify a better suited area. Eventually it had been an article in the Miami Herald that had gotten him on the right track. According to the story there were still a number of developments next to the Florida Turnpike and around Florida City that were mired in litigation. Developments with only a few residents, but plenty of vacant or half finished homes; and no Home Owners Association. The next day, a Saturday, he'd set out to investigate his potential El Dorado.

He'd taken the Turnpike down towards Florida City and had realized that he'd had no idea where to exit. Shortly before he'd reached the second toll booth, he'd noticed a development. Some of the homes were clearly occupied, as evidenced by cars in the driveways, but the majority of the homes he saw were unfinished. He passed through the toll booth and had continued to the next exit. It had taken him the better part of an hour to double back and find his way to the development.

He'd parked his car in a vacant lot and started to walk around. Unfortunately it took only ten minutes before he was confronted by a security guard who wanted to know if he could be of assistance. He'd declined politely telling the man he was just checking out different neighborhoods for their 'feel'. The guard had given him a somewhat suspicious look and left on his golf cart.

He'd struck out again.

Chapter Fifty

Prof. Steve Rupert, Miami (Spring Semester 2015)

He'd been teaching at FIU for more than ten years now. Had listened to, interacted with and looked at thousands of students. Well, he'd looked mostly at the female students and had listened to the male students who seemed to have a better grasp on math.

Lately he'd been distracted by one of the international students who had warranted not only a second but a third look. Yeah, he knew too well that none of them were looking back. He had developed a little bit of a life preserver in his mid-section, and yes, he was south of forty. But hey, he could look - no harm in that. Well, correction – his sensitivity class, a mandatory class at FIU for all its professors, had actually indicated that too long a look was dangerously close to harassment. Screw them; she was worth the extra time he spent looking at her. All he had to do was figure out a way to get to know her. Interact with her away from the classroom. Okay, so she could be his daughter – but she wasn't!

Chapter Fifty One

Jerome Water, Franco Tamargo, Melody Rodriguez, and Prof. Rupert, Miami (Friday, March 6th, 2015, 1:05 pm)

Water and Tamargo decided to take Water's cruiser for the ride back to FIU. Back at the campus they visited Melody again.

"Back so soon?" she smiled up at Water.

"Yes, we need to ask you another favor." This time Tamargo did see how Water blushed. Nice deep color too.

"How may I help you Detective?" Melody swept her long hair back out of her face.

"Please, call me Jerome. Could you find out which Math professor Sabine Sander has this semester?"

"Do you have her student ID?"

"No, sorry we don't."

"Doesn't matter, I'll find her." Melody started to work the keyboard again.

Franco looked around the office. He sneaked a partial view of a photograph on Melody's desk. It appeared to be of her with a large Labrador on some beach. Looking at her hands he noticed the absence of a ring on her left ring finger. Good news for Casanova.

"She is currently taking two math classes. She's taking MAT 2010 with Prof. Rupert and MAC 1120 with Prof. Garcia." Melody announced.

"Do you know either or both of the professors?" Water inquired.

"I know Prof. Garcia, she's pretty cool. This is actually her first semester teaching here."

"Where would we find the other Prof. Rupert?"

A quick smile, directed at Water, and a couple of seconds of typing later they had the answer.

"It must be your lucky day today. He's in class over in the Diuxieme Maison Building. Room 305. The class should be over in half an hour."

"Thank you so much Melody, you have been very helpful. Could we come back if we need more information?" Water wanted to know.

"Anytime, please do."

Jesus Christ, Franco thought; get a room already.

On their short walk over to the DM Building Franco couldn't help but rip Water a little.

"It appears you found a solution to your problem." Franco started.

"What problem?" Water responded.

"Your blushing issue, doesn't seem to stop you – nor her for that matter."

"Shut up!"

Chapter Fifty Two

Jerome Water, Franco Tamargo, and Prof. Rupert
(Friday, March 6th, 2015, 1:15 pm)

In front of Prof. Rupert's class room they did what all Detectives do best – wait. When the class room door finally opened they stepped aside to let a bunch of zombie like students escape from the room. Peeking inside they saw Prof. Rupert engaged in conversation with a very pretty student, who appeared to be flirting with the professor. Tamargo looked at Water and shrugged his shoulders. Tough break for the professor, they went inside and stood behind the girl posing for Rupert.

She must have been totally focused on the professor, since she continued her conversation. "So if I get an A on the next test, would that allow me to pass the class? Is there any extra credit work that I could do? I mean, really, I would do any…" she must have noticed the look on the professor's face and turned around.

"Oh, ahem, I guess I'll talk to you later. Okay?"

"Okay Stacey." Prof. Rupert answered.

"May I help you?" the flustered Professor asked.

Water did the usual introduction while Tamargo checked out Rupert. Late forties, approximately five feet eight inches, two hundred twenty pounds of mass, thinning light blond hair, blue shirt somehow tucked into beige pants with no belt.

"May we ask you a few questions Professor?" Water inquired.

"Fire away."

"We are investigating the disappearance of one of your students -Sabine Sander. When was the last time you saw her?"

"Sabine, the German student? She was supposed to be here in this class." Prof. Rupert answered.

"But she wasn't. When was she in your class last?"

"Let me check." he flipped open the big binder on the desk next to him. "Friday last week."

"Did you notice anything unusual about her during that class?" "Or before or after that class?" Tamargo threw in.

"Unusual? No, I don't really know her all that well." Water and Tamargo noticed a slight change in color in Prof. Rupert's face.

"Not as well as this student?" Tamargo pointed towards the door that the flirting girl had used to exit the class.

"What are you insinuating?" Prof. Rupert had straightened up behind the desk.

"Nothing." Tamargo calmed him. "So you didn't have much … interaction with her?"

"I really don't appreciate your line of questioning Detective!" a now clearly uncomfortable Prof. Rupert responded.

"Where were you on Monday night between 10:00 p.m. and 1:00 a.m.?" Water interjected.

"Are you out of your mind? Are you suggesting that I had something to do with Sabine not being in class today?" Prof. Rupert's eyes had widened, and he started to click the mechanism on the pen he'd been holding in his left hand.

"We're just covering all the bases." Water came back.

"I didn't have any late classes, so I was home with my family. You can ask my wife."

"We may have to."

Prof. Rupert had started to perspire heavily. There were droplets of sweat easing down his forehead. One larger drop fell from his right ear onto his collar.

"Do you have many female students asking for extra credit work?" Tamargo asked.

"I think this is enough now. Do I really have to answer these questions? Do I need a lawyer?" there was fear in his voice.

"You are not under arrest Sir. No, you don't have to answer any questions, but we may have more questions later on. If it is more comfortable for you, we can ask them at the station." Water informed him.

"No, that's okay. But I don't think I have anything else that I can contribute that will help you." Prof. Rupert was shoving the binder and a textbook into his briefcase.

"We'll be in touch. Thank you for your time Prof. Rupert." Water added before the professor managed a hasty exit from the class room without another word.

Water glanced at Tamargo before he took a seat in the first row of the class.

"Don't know. He was nervous as hell and I don't think the girl would have come on to him the way she did, if he doesn't have a reputation for accepting 'extra credit' work." Tamargo stated.

"Yeah, he's definitely leaning towards the perv end of the spectrum."

Tamargo checked his watch. "I have a couple of errands to run. How about I take the first watch on Walker's apartment again? Unless you want to? If nothing breaks we could meet tomorrow for breakfast? Do you have to check in with Poole?"

"Don't really know. I'll give him a call later and let you know. Denny's okay with you?"

"Sure. The one on Bird?"

"Yup, eight thirty?"

"See you tonight. Shoot, I forgot, we came in your car." Tamargo remembered.

They walked back to the parking lot silently when Tamargo informed Water:

"She's not married – you know."

"What? Who?"

"Melody, she's not married. Hope you like dogs though."

"What do I care?" Water replied.

"Bullshit."

"Okay, I bite – how would you know?" Water couldn't help himself. She was cute.

"I used to be a Detective – remember? They used to call me Holmes. Well - Watson, for starters, there is that picture on her desk with her and a beautiful Labrador on the beach, and no ring on her left or right ring finger."

"You know, if anyone qualifies as a bona fide comedian, it's you!" Water tried hard not to chuckle while processing the information. Truth be told, he did find Melody very attractive and pleasant. Maybe they would need more information from her in the future...

Chapter Fifty Three

Captor, Miami (early days)

Back to square one! Maybe he should just find a house that was somewhat secluded and away from the neighbors. There was a neighborhood that would satisfy those requirements. Horse Country. Why hadn't he thought about this before? Located roughly between Bird Road and Sunset Drive on the northern and southern edges and 117th Avenue and 127th Avenue as the east and west border. He was going to find his El Dorado there. Not far from his own house which was located off Killian Drive.

He immediately drove over to Horse Country and systematically covered most of the streets looking for homes for sale situated on large lots. He wrote down the address to three properties that had potential and headed home.

After his breakup with Amanda he had bought a house in a side street off Killian Drive west of US-1. A block before he was going to turn off Killian onto his street, traffic came to a standstill due to a large vacuum truck that was apparently cleaning out a storm sewer on Killian. He hung a quick right to avoid wasting time and took the back road to approach his home. Driving down the street perpendicular to his own street, he noticed a house for sale. Could it be? Was this house directly behind his home? It was for sale. He slowed down and started to shake his head, rubbed his eyes and started laughing out loud like a slap-happy little child. He'd wasted weeks on his quest to find his El Dorado, when it had been in his backyard all along. Even though the house was on the smaller side, it did have a detached two-car-garage in the back yard. He wrote down the Realtor's phone number and continued home.

Chapter Fifty Four

Prof. Martin, Miami (early days)

He was giddy with delight! He offered the Realtor the full asking price and the owner signed the contract two days later.

Just to make it a little harder for prying eyes, he established a corporation and purchased the house under that name. After the closing he took stock of his new property. A detached garage in the rear of the property was what really had clinched the deal for him. Concrete floor, block walls, solid roof – he was excited. While the house itself would have offered much more comfortable accommodations, he didn't think that occupying the house was a good idea. He was afraid that neighbors walking their dogs, the mailman or some delivery driver mistaking an address would become alert to anything out of the ordinary in the house. Sure, he could have insulated it as well as the garage, but it was that much closer to the street and public observation.

No, he decided to spiff up the house and landscaping just a little bit, just enough to portray the picture of an occupied home. He didn't need anyone to nose around the property just to see if it was for sale, or if they could steal something. He made sure the chain link fence and the gate were in working order and installed a padlock on the front gate and the gate guarding the driveway.

Since his company had always been a one-man-show, he was able to work on his own schedule. The few large investors he had knew to leave him to do his job without the need for much interaction. He had chosen not to have a glitzy office and the other trappings that went with the typical investment company. This semester he'd only been teaching one class on Tuesdays and Thursdays in the evening. He'd been able to dedicate some serious time to the build-out of his little nest.

He would have to soundproof the garage. He'd spent a couple of hours on the internet locating a supplier of recording studio grade insulation material. Fortunately one was located in Ft. Lauderdale. He placed an order for heavy duty insulation and four days later rented a U-Haul truck to pick up the material. On his way back from Ft. Lauderdale he stopped at a Home Depot to purchase vinyl siding as well as a load of wood to install the insulation and siding.

He installed a grid of 2 x 6's under the ceiling and every wall in the garage, including the inside of the roll-up garage door. Next he fitted the insulation and then covered it with the siding. He used a jackhammer, which he rented, to open up a hole in the center of the garage. Once done chipping he installed a substantial eye-hook and cemented it into the floor. The heavy metal chain he attached to the hook was equally substantial.

While he would have appreciated a full bathroom for his guest, she was going to have to make do with a camping toilet and a bucket of water. Not exactly his style – but one had to compromise in order to achieve the ultimate goal.

No frills, just the bare necessities. A king sized mattress (no box spring or frame). The metal cage that he installed over the two overhead lights would prevent any tampering with the fixtures. He rewired them so that the only way to operate them was by opening a locked box next to the door, or from the outside. He would have loved to put sheets on the bed, but had been afraid that she'd use it as a weapon or to harm herself. Maybe he could change the mattress once in a while to keep it clean and inviting.

Chuckling he'd thought of his little place as Fort Sex. Screw all the gold at Fort Knox; he was going to strike gold right here! However, all this would be for naught if it didn't pass the 'sound test'. He'd gotten a boom box and put a hip hop CD into the drive. He checked the noise level on the outside with the door closed. Nothing. He went back inside and increased the volume to the highest level and also put the base to its highest setting – still the noise barely registered outside of the garage.

Finally, all the pieces had been in place. All his hard work over the past month was about to pay off. All that had been left to do was to find his "guest". He'd been sure that was only going to be a matter of time. The new semester was about to start. He'd find a worthy candidate!

The garage side door opened to the outside, which would make it easy for his guest to try to bust it open. However, the fact that she would be chained to the floor should prevent any unforeseen incidents. Just to be on the safe side he installed a 180 degree peephole in the door leading into the garage, as well as a heavy duty padlock on the outside.

Chapter Fifty Five

Sabine Sander, Miami (Tuesday, March 4th, 2015)

With the lights on and no natural light coming in; she was still unable to determine how much time had passed. She had to somehow get out of here. By now she was convinced that her prison used to be a garage, she'd even spotted a couple of tire marks close to one wall. That's probably where the garage door was. Was the door only covered with the same material as on the interior walls? Or had he built a concrete wall to further muffle all sound from the inside? Crawling towards the wall she was painfully stopped by the shackle around her ankle.

Back on the mattress she stared up at the ceiling, which looked to be at least ten feet high and covered with that same plastic sheeting that decorated the walls. She looked up at the lights in the ceiling. Clearly out of her reach. She didn't even bother trying to jump up to reach them.

Frustration, shame and fear hit her again. She was being kept like an animal. She hadn't been kidnapped for ransom. She was being kept as a sex slave! The realization hit her like a ton of bricks! The hopelessness of her situation made her cry again. Oh how she hated to be weak! Crying wasn't going to change anything. Think! Sabine – come on – you're a smart girl. Try to figure something out. Try to find an angle. Try to find a way to get out of this prison. Analyze the situation, explore the possibilities, evaluate your options, and then act decisively!

Since there were the two lights in this place, there was electricity. Where there was electricity, there were wires and conduits. So there were openings in the plastic lining to allow for the light fixture and the light switch. She started looking for a switch but couldn't find one. Okay, so concentrate on the light fixtures. How was she going to get to the fixtures or the hidden garage door? Sitting down on the mattress she closely inspected the shackle and chain.

She scanned the place for anything that would allow her to manipulate the chain links or the bolt on the shackle. There were no tools on the work bench which was out of her reach anyway.

She eyed the camping toilet and wondered if she could somehow get it loose and break it apart so she could use a piece to scrape the concrete out from next to the embedded eyehook; when the door opened and her captor demanded her attention.

Chapter Fifty Six

Jerome Water and Franco Tamargo,
Miami (Friday, March 6th, 2015, 2:24 pm)

When they pulled into the parking area of the station Water broke the silence: "Somehow we're not really getting anywhere."

"I was thinking the same thing. But remember, Rome wasn't built in a day either, and we have to bring something solid. So we are kind of the underdogs here."

"That won't help Sabine much – wherever she may be." Water came back.

"Okay, let's proceed as planned. See you at 3:00 a.m."

"Let's have breakfast at 9:00 a.m. so I can grab a shower before breakfast."

"Please do…" Tamargo shot back. "Also, why don't you try to talk Poole into issuing a BOLO on Mr. Walker?"

"I'll try." Water responded while Tamargo was extracting himself from the cruiser.

Walking up to his car Tamargo realized that he was getting paid for his efforts, while this was most likely not the case for Water. He was probably not even going to put in for the overtime. Well, he'd pick up the tab for breakfast tomorrow, maybe even lunch, depending on how Water behaved.

He was actually starting to like the guy. He kind of reminded him of himself in his previous life. Except that he had never been as flirtatious and prone to blushing.

Chapter Fifty Seven

Sabine Sander,
Miami (Wednesday, March 4th, 2015)

She knew she was in trouble as soon as she looked at him. He was dressed in his usual attire: A leather headdress and black satin bathrobe. This time he had a bunch of clothes wrapped over his arm.

He stepped inside and laid the clothes on the mattress. He retrieved a schoolgirl's skirt and a white smallish looking blouse and tossed them towards her. She opted not to catch the items but to let them drop to the floor. He shook his head and closed in on her. Stepping back she tripped over the metal chain and fell down hard next to the mattress. Before she was able to get into an upright position he was over her slapping her hard across her face. She fell back and her head hit the edge of the mattress and bounced to the left straining her neck.

Before she was able to regain any kind of composure, he'd thrown her on the mattress, forced her legs apart and entered her without the benefit of any lubricant.

After he'd finished, she rolled to her side and cried softly. To her surprise he spoke to her:

"Next time follow my orders" he said in a raspy voice.

Chapter Fifty Eight

Jerome Water and Franco Tamargo,
Miami (Saturday, March 7th, 2015, 9:00 am)

The previous night had been uneventful and both Tamargo and Water had seen better days. Tired and a little frustrated they silently ate their breakfast until Water's phone rang.

"Yeah, Water." he answered and then listened for a couple of minutes. Disconnecting the call he waived for their waitress before turning to Tamargo.

"That was Poole – they found another girl. Washed ashore by the old Marine Stadium. Some kids spotted her. Poole wants me over there asap."

The waitress had dropped off their check; Tamargo quickly picked it up, left a few dollar bills on the table, and went to the cashier.

"Did he mention me?" Tamargo wanted to know.

"Nope."

"Well, I guess I'll trot along and see if he's still cool with me shadowing you." Franco quickly paid their bill and walked out.

They took both of their cars since they didn't know if they would be allowed to continue their investigation together. Traffic wasn't too bad on Bird and US 1, but it took them almost half an hour to get to the Marine Stadium that had been abandoned long ago, but was now supposedly going to be refurbished by the City of Miami and the County in cooperation with some private investors.

Det. Poole and the medical examiner were standing over the naked corpse of a young girl that had, obvious even to the untrained eye, died of a rough cut to her carotid artery.

A couple of teenagers fishing had discovered the body on the shore. The two boys looked like they've been through hell and back and were talking to a paramedic who was trying to calm them down. As soon as Water stepped closer he thanked his lucky stars for not losing his breakfast. The sight of the young woman that had been in the water for quite some time was – to put it mildly - unpleasant.

"She's been dead for at least a few weeks, no clothing, and no purse." Poole informed them solemnly.

"She could be another student." Water ventured.

"We'll find out." Poole replied. "Okay, I guess you can take her." Poole nodded to the medical examiner.

"My gut says your right Water. I just got off the phone with the director. The case is now a priority. If she turns out to be a student, he wants to assemble a Task Force. We may have a serial killer on our hands. What did you guys get?" Poole looked expectantly at them before lighting a Marlboro followed by some coughing.

"We have a perverted Professor that is most likely not involved, another Professor who is somewhat suspect but we're thin on proof, and a stalker who is our number one. We sat on his place last night, but he hasn't shown." Water reported to Poole.

"Okay, I'll get a BOLO out on him. I'll get back to you regarding the last victim as soon as I get her name and background. In the meantime you guys continue shaking trees. I'll send reinforcement over to FIU to interview students about the Columbian girl on Monday. The shit is going to hit the fan if our latest victim turns out to be another FIU student. Tamargo, keep your head low, I don't need any additional pressure from the director for having you tag along." Poole instructed them before walking over to his car.

"Make sure to fill me in on any new developments. The press is going to be all over this." he called back to them.

As if on cue, the first TV-station van pulled up at the Stadium.

Tamargo and Water walked back to their cars parked a couple of hundred yards away.

"Back to FIU? I don't know if the offices are open on a Saturday? But I'll call in an unmarked unit to sit on Walker's place 24/7." Water told Tamargo.

"Meet you over at the campus?"

"Yeah, let's see if anyone is there. Meet you at the Graham Center."

"Yeah."

Chapter Fifty Nine

Prof. Martin,
Miami (Thursday, February 12th, 2015)

"What the hell?" Martin couldn't believe his eyes. The bitch lay in a huge pool of blood on the mattress. He didn't have to check her pulse to know she was dead. Unbelievable she had taken her own life.

Frustration and anger washed over him and he walked over to the mattress and kicked Graciela hard. Now he would have to dispose of her as well and find another – hopefully more durable - candidate. On second thought; he enjoyed the challenge, the selection process, the capture and the first encounter. So maybe it was all good. He would need a new mattress as well. He took a large folded heavy gauge plastic drop cloth out of a metal cabinet and proceeded to roll Graciela into it. Going back to the cabinet he retrieved a rope and tied up his bundle.

Using duct tape he secured all seams to make sure no blood would exit. Nice job, he could have started as a worker with any moving company, he chuckled to himself while dragging the package over to the door. Walking over to the house to bring his car around, he was contemplating where to dump her.

Chapter Sixty

Jerome Water and Franco Tamargo,
Miami (Saturday, March 7th, 2015, 10:45 am)

What was wrong with the traffic in Miami? No matter what time of day – there was always way too much traffic for his taste. Tamargo was already in front of the Graham Center by the time he got there.

"What took you so long?" Tamargo inquired.

"Traffic."

"You're a cop, don't they let you through?" Tamargo kept needling him.

"You're a funny guy – too many years with Poole." Water shot back. "Let's go, we may have a serial killer."

Water had just finished his sentence when his phone rang.

"Water" he quickly answered after looking at the number displayed on the screen.

"That was fast." he replied to the caller.

"Got it, thank you." He finished the call after having listened for a while. He quickly pulled out a small notebook and wrote down an address. Putting the book and pen away he said:

"That was Poole, they ID'd the girl. Graciela Manciani, twenty-one years old, FIU freshman. The Director has briefed the Mayors of Miami and Miami-Dade. A Task Force is being assembled as we speak and Poole would like for us to find the killer before the day is over…"

"Wow that was quick!" Tamargo interjected.

"I have the honor of breaking the good news to the family." Water looked clearly distraught over this new development.

"Ever done that before? Notification?" Tamargo wanted to know.

"No and I can't say I'm looking forward to it either." Water replied. His face looked like he just bit into a lemon.

"Want me to tag along?" Tamargo offered.

"You better not; Poole may not like it much. Why don't you start by getting Graciela's class schedule and a list of her class mates?"

"Wanna loan me your badge? Might get things done a bit faster." Tamargo wanted to know.

"Just talk to Melody – she knows we're investigating together." Water responded as his facial complexion changed slightly.

Tamargo didn't harp on it this time. "Sure thing." he mumbled while trotting off.

Water headed back to his car. Luigi and Carmen Manciani, were living only a couple of miles away from campus. Yet, their daughter, as it turned out only daughter, who had studied so close by, would never return home. Some twisted freak had seen to that. Anger started to boil up inside of Jerome, who felt a wave of nausea meeting the acid reflux in his gut.

Chapter Sixty One

Franco Tamargo and Melody Rodriguez's desk
Saturday, March 7th, 2015, 11:05 am)

"Hi Melody – it's me again." Tamargo opened.

Melody, who'd been focused on her computer screen looked up. "Hey there. Where's your partner?"

"He had the misfortune to lose the draw – he's on his way to notify the family of a victim. But what are you doing here on a Saturday?" Tamargo didn't believe in disclosing more details than necessary.

"Oh how awful! Poor Jerome! How is he doing?" she answered without taking a breath.

"Yeah, he wasn't too happy about the assignment." Tamargo responded with the understatement of the year.

"However, would you be willing to help us again?" he continued.

"Sure, what can I do?"

"I need a list of all of Graciela Manciani's classes, professors, and classmates. Is that difficult for you to get?" he inquired.

"No Silly, that will only take me a couple of minutes." she told him.

Melody started hacking away in her usual high speed fashion, when all of a sudden her typing slowed down a bit. Without looking up the said: "How long have you known Jerome? Detective Water I mean?" she corrected quickly.

Tamargo hesitated for a couple of seconds before responding: "I don't want to say that we are old friends, but he's a good guy – if that's what you're asking me."

"Oh, good!" she said while increasing the speed of her vicious typing. "Is he – you know, is he engaged or attached?"

Tamargo noticed that Melody's complexion had turned decidedly darker even though she had tried to keep her face down over the computer screen. A match made in heaven he thought trying to suppress a smile.

"He is unattached and though I will probably

get in trouble for saying this – I think he was wondering the same thing about you – being attached or engaged." There he said it. Water would thank him later.

"Oh, well, ahem, tell him I am not. Engaged or anything. Only if he should ask of course. You know." Melody had actually stopped typing when she said this, but quickly resumed her attack on the keyboard.

"Sure." was all Tamargo said.

The printer started humming and Melody swiveled around in her chair to retrieve the pages.

"Here you go. Classes, professors and classmates."

"Thank you very much Melody – you've been – again – a great help. I'll tell Jerome you said 'hi'".

"Yes, please do!" Melody looked straight at him without flushing.

This girl was serious. He might have to warn Water instead of playing Cupid.

Sitting down on a bench outside of Melody's office he scanned the pages for names that would look familiar. Starting with the professors he noticed Prof. Martin and Prof.

Rupert. She had taken Math with Sabine and while he couldn't really recall many of the students' names on the list with Sabine's classes, he did notice Sabine's boyfriend on the list. Graciela and Roberto had taken some Accounting class together. Had he been wrong about the guy? He didn't think so, but would bring it up with Water anyway.

Chapter Sixty Two

Jerome Water and Graciela Manciani's parents
(Saturday, March 7th, 2015, 11:20 am)

Luigi Manciani, a middle aged, short, broad shouldered man opened the door a couple of minutes after Water rang the doorbell.

"Can I help you?" a clearly exhausted father with red rimmed eyes asked Water.

"Good afternoon Sir, my name is Detective Jerome Water with the MDPD. May I come in?"

"She's dead!" Luigi exclaimed while stepping back into the small but well maintained house.

"Luigi! What happened to Graciela?" a voice screamed from the back of the house – which Water presumed was Mrs. Manciani.

"Come in." Luigi gestured.

Stepping inside Water noticed a number of religious figurines. He recognized St. Patrick and St. Francis of Assisi, but there were many more displayed.

"What happened?" a now teary Luigi asked Waters.

"Sir, I am very sorry to inform you that we have found your daughter. Deceased." Water regretted his words as soon as they had left his lips.

"Deceased! You mean she's dead!" Luigi almost screamed before he dropped to his knees. Carmen rushed into the room and fell down next to her husband.

"What happened to our baby?" she wailed.

Luigi and Carmen found and hugged each other on the floor. Water didn't know what to say, or where to look. He retreated a few steps towards the front door.

It took the Mancianis a while to recover enough to pull themselves off the floor and face him.

"Where is she? What happened? Who harmed her?" Carmen sobbed barely audible.

Water wasn't prepared for this kind of emotional response. Sure he'd received some training, but this was different. It was real. These were the parents of a dead girl. She'd been killed by some freaking asshole. He took a deep breath before turning around to face them.

"I wish I had all the answers for you, but we don't – yet. There are hundreds of police officers investigating this case. Your daughter's case, and I hope that we have answers very soon." He replied feeling inadequate and miserable.

"Can we see her? Where is she?" Carmen wanted to know while Luigi just stared at him with a blank face.

"Yes Mrs. Manciani, you can see her at the morgue tomorrow." Again feeling like he was flying by the seat of his pants. He didn't even know when they would be able to see their daughter.

"Where is she now?" Luigi asked in a voice that sounded like gravel.

"Sir, I honestly don't know."

"Okay." was the weak response from a man broken by the news of his only daughter having been taken from him.

After gently placing his business card on the coffee table nearest him he quietly left the house. Once safely in his car he took a few breaths and rubbed his face. Realizing that this was part of the job, he briefly wondered if he'd picked the right line of work.

Shaking his head he turned the engine over and headed back to the campus. He called Tamargo and then met up with him at the Green Library where they ordered coffee at the Starbucks downstairs. Having secured a small table they went over the list.

"How did it go?" Tamargo asked looking at Water's pained expression.

"Not good, but I guess that was to be expected."

"You want a piece of advice? Don't let their pain bring you down, use it as your fuel and your motivation to get the person who caused their pain."

Water sat in silence for a minute.

"Okay, any connection between the two as far as professors and students go?"

"Yeah, I don't have Sabine's list with me, but both Prof. Rupert and Martin are on the list. Also Sabine's boyfriend. Even though I still don't think he's involved."

"Prof. Rupert, who has an alibi for Sabine's disappearance, but may not have one for Sandra's or Graciela's. So on the off chance that the cases are unrelated we should check him again – and with his wife for the night of Sabine's disappearance." Water suggested before holding his hand up when his phone rang.

"Water." He listened for a minute and disconnected the call. "Poole – he wants me to come in. You're not invited to the party, but I can fill you in afterwards if you want?"

Tamargo didn't hesitate "Yes, call me when you're done and we can meet up. Jerome, do we have a timeline for Graciela's disappearance, we need to find out before we're checking Rupert's alibi."

"Damn, your right. Okay, see you later." Jerome replied while walking away shaking his head over his own stupidity.

Chapter Sixty Three

Police Station,
Miami (Saturday, March 7th, 2015, 1:30 p.m.)

Back at the station on 117th Avenue he was flagged down by the desk sergeant. "Poole asked me to send you to the conference room – full house." He said before turning to pick up a ringing phone.

Water stepped into the room and discovered that the Sergeant hadn't exaggerated. Det. Poole, Captain Santiago, Lieutenant Perez, three detectives from his station, the MDPD Director, Captains from the Miami PD, Key Biscayne PD and the Sweetwater PD were seated around the large table.

Having noticed Water the Director stopped in midsentence and looked questioning towards Poole.

"Det. Water has been on this case from the get go and will give us an update later." Poole ignored Water's incredulous stare and nodded to the Director.

Water sat down and listened as the Director continued to address the troops.

"As I was saying" he threw a quick glance at Water, "While we don't know if we have a serial killer on our hands, we will treat this case as such! Some of you may remember the 8th Street Killer or the infamous Mr. Cunnanan! We don't need another outbreak of citizens looking over their shoulders. For the time being we will NOT talk about a serial killer. However, if there is credible evidence that there is a connection between these girls, I will inform the public accordingly. Questions?" The Director looked at the assembled troops.

"Sir." Water stopped, realizing that he should probably just have stayed quite. "All of the girls were going to the same campus, had some of the same professors and classmates."

"And this leads us to Det. Water's update on the case." Poole jumped in to save Water the embarrassment of having directly challenged the Director.

"Yes, both dead girls, the boyfriend plus the missing girl – Sabine Sander – went to FIU. They all shared a couple of classes. We are currently cross referencing students and professors. Thus far we have discovered they all lived in different neighborhoods. They all come from different backgrounds, and the only thing they have in common is their college. At this point we believe that it is someone connected to the college. We think it may be a student, a professor, a classmate, a maintenance worker or anyone else who frequents the campus." Water, who had risen for his little speech sat back down.

"Thank you for your insight Det. Water. The MDPD has the lead on this investigation. Captain Santiago has the lead on the case and will coordinate our efforts with Key Biscayne, Miami and Sweetwater. I expect full cooperation gentlemen – no turf wars over jurisdiction and egos! Jorge, I want to be briefed on this no later than 10 a.m. every morning until we catch this S.O.B.! Gentlemen, that's all – let's get the perp!"

Once finished with the pep talk the Director and Captain Santiago left the room.

"You heard the man. Sweetwater should check surveillance cameras around the campus – including traffic lights. Key Biscayne should question regulars on the Beach and check the cameras on the toll station. We will check with the ME to get an approximation of how long the victim's have been in the water. After that we'll check with the guys over at NOAA and the Coast Guard to see what current would have taken them to where they were found. Once we have that established we may be able to narrow down the dumping ground and time. If the perp lives on Key Biscayne, Charles, your guys should check with the businesses lining the island. See if they have cameras. Am I forgetting anything?" Lieutenant Perez connected with every participant of the meeting by making eye contact.

"Alright guys, let's exchange numbers and get going. We don't want this to get out of hand! Water join me in my office."

"Have a seat." Lieutenant Perez instructed.

"I realize you're a rookie on the detective squad, but you were the first one on the case. Hang on; let me get Poole in here." Perez picked up the phone and instructed the desk sergeant to get Poole.

"Do you think we have a serial killer?" he continued after hanging up.

"Sir, as you correctly stated, I am a rookie. But I do feel that the cases – including Sabine Sander – are connected."

"Poole, sit with us." Lieutenant Perez invited Det. Poole through the halfway opened door.

Poole settled into the vacant second chair in the Lieutenant small office.

"I assume that Det. Water has kept you abreast of his investigation?"

"Certainly." Poole replied.

"Good. Do you think Det. Water is up to the task? Sorry, no offense Water – but you are a little green."

"Yes, I have a lot of confidence in Det. Water. Especially – and this is at the same time something of a problem – he is supported by former Det. Tamargo."

"Who is Tamargo?"

"Former Det. Tamargo was one of our finest until he quit the department. I have agreed for him to tag along with the investigation, since he has been retained as an investigator by the missing girl's brother."

"Hold it right there Poole! You allowed a civilian to 'tag along' on a police investigation!?"

"Sir, Tamargo used to be one of our best. Besides, he was already investigating for the brother. I thought it would be best to have him contained instead of potentially contacting the press." Poole didn't sound defensive.

Perez sat quiet for a minute before he responded. "Good thinking – I guess. You're sure there is no liability that can be pinned on us? And that you can contain any information he obtains due to his 'tagging along'?"

"He was a great cop. He was at the OK Corral shoot-out."

"Alright. Poole I trust you – don't mess this up. The Director is – as you know – all over this case! Okay then – get to work."

Outside of the Lieutenant's room Poole stopped Water. "Jerome, I just put my neck on the block for you and Tamargo. You guys better come up with something good. Don't make me have to retire before I am ready to go!"

"Yes Sir!"

"Fuck you – get it done!"

Chapter Sixty Four

Jerome Water and Franco Tamargo,
Miami (Saturday, March 7th, 2015)

"You're still awake?" Water opened.

"If I wasn't - now I am. Just kidding, I am not that old! What happened?" Tamargo answered.

Water gave him the low down on the meeting.

"So the Director took over, but doesn't want the wrong answers".

"Sounds about right; Poole agreed to keep you in the loop – low profile though!"

"Man, I'm bushed – wanna meet for breakfast at Allan's?"

"Sure, Nine?"

"See you tomorrow."

Chapter Sixty Five

Jerome Water and Franco Tamargo,
Miami (Sunday, March 8th, 2015, 9:00 am)

"Hey!" Tamargo offered.

"Yeah! Is it always like this working a case? No or little sleep and working with weirdos?"

"Nah, only when working with you!"

"Okay, so we're back to Comedy Central!" Water responded with a weak smile.

"You started it!"

"You wanna get serious? "

"Sure" Tamargo put on a contrite face.

Water and Tamargo kicked around what little they knew and agreed that their main suspects were Benjamin Walker, Professor Martin, or anyone else for that matter in the Greater Miami area that was male and maybe over the age of fifteen.

"Did you guys ever find Sabine's car?" Tamargo suddenly wanted to know.

"Don't even know if we ever looked for it to be honest. I guess we could search the parking lot at FIU."

"Might be a good idea. If it isn't there, maybe she was abducted in it. You could put out a BOLO on it." Tamargo suggested.

"Great idea!" Water responded before continuing: "What day is today?" Tamargo shot him a questioning look. "Sunday." "Right, I don't think Prof. Martin teaches on Sundays." he answered while loading his fork with part of the spinach omelet he'd ordered.

"I don't think anyone does. Want to try and see if he's home?"

"We may as well, since Benjamin Walker seems to be in the wind." Water agreed and waived for the waitress. When the waitress brought the check Tamargo quickly took the slip from her, dropped five dollars on the table and walked to the cashier's counter by the exit. Water joined him:"Feeling generous today?" he wanted to know. "Nah, I just figured it's my turn." he replied.

"Don't get me wrong – I am not objecting, but next time let me know before we order, so that I can go for the good stuff." Water grinned at Tamargo. "There won't be a next time!" Tamargo grinned back.

They decided to leave Tamargo's car at the diner and took off in Water's unmarked cruiser. Water got onto Bird Road and headed west. "Turn left on 72nd Avenue." Tamargo told him. "Why?" Water looked at his passenger.

"I hate riding on Bird Road – just too many nut-jobs around here." came the short reply. "Thought you were a hardened cop?" Water laughed.

"Whatever."

Water turned on 72nd Avenue and headed down to Miller Road, turned right and continued until he got to 87th Avenue where he turned left. "See how much smoother the traffic is here?" Tamargo asked. "Sure old man. Less drama for the faint hearted." Water smiled.

Shortly before they reached Kendall Drive Tamargo instructed: "Slow down and get into the right lane!"

"What?" Water jolted upright in his seat. He scanned the cars behind and next to him.

"Three cars ahead - in the left lane. Matte black older Mustang." Tamargo had started to flip through the pages of his little notebook. "7X9 K12 – that's Benjamin Walker's car!"

Tamargo had raised his voice in clear excitement. "Don't get too close man, stay back, give him plenty of room."

"I got this!" Water noticed the adrenaline rising in his system. Finally they might be able to talk to Walker.

They followed him leaving at least two cars between them and Walker. He continued south on Galloway before turning right on Killian Drive. Water looked over at Tamargo.

"Where the hell is he going? Miami Dade College, Turnpike or Professor Martin's?"

"If he turns into Martin's street, don't slow down, just go past him, we'll double back."

"As I said – I've got this!" Water noticed he was getting a little annoyed with Tamargo, but redirected his focus on Walker's car that had slowed down and turned left onto the

Professor's street. He continued at the speed limit and glanced down the street Walker had turned onto. Yup, there he was, cruising by Martin's house. They turned left at the next corner and slowed down. "How do you want to play this? If he just drives by, he might come back up this street. Do you want to continue and roll up the Professor's street? He might spot us?"

"Go down the block and stop two houses from the corner. I'll take a quick walk over to the next block and see where he's at." Tamargo offered.

Tamargo jumped out of the car and quickly walked over to the next block, making sure he stayed as close as possible to the fences and hedges of the houses he passed. Shortly before he got to the corner he stepped into a hole in the grass, twisted his ankle and fell forward hitting the ground semi hard. Cursing under his breath he got up and peeked around the corner. There was no Mustang in sight. Did Walker just drive by and leave? Tamargo dialed Water's number on his cell phone while walking up the street.

"Yeah." Water answered.

"Yeah, I turned the corner, but can't see the Mustang from here. Don't know if he's gone or parked in front of Martin's house. I'm walking up the street to get a better look."

Walking on the opposite side of the street where Martin's house was located, he saw a man standing in front of Martin's house, banging on the front door with his fist. There was a pretty little BMW parked in the driveway, but no answer at the front door.

He speed dialed Water again. "He's in front of the house. Looks like Martin is home but not answering the door. Shit!" Tamargo said before bending down to pretend tying his shoe laces.

Benjamin Walker had turned to look at him. "What's going on?" Tamargo could hear Water over the phone that was lying next to his shoes. Tamargo finished 'tying' his shoe and stood up in time to see Benjamin walk away from Martin's door. Turning slowly and walking back down the street like a neighbor having checked on something in his front yard he raised his cell phone: "Get ready! He's probably gonna drive down this street towards your corner. I'll let you know." Tamargo instructed. "Okay, he's going south. I am coming down the street. He's turning left. Come and get me – I'm pretty sure he made me!" Tamargo disconnected the call and limped down the street.

He was still three houses away from the corner when Water's cruiser appeared at the end of the block. Gritting his teeth Tamargo started running towards the car.

"Are you okay?" Water inquired. "Twisted my ankle in some stupid hole." Tamargo answered while Water gunned the car effectively slamming the passenger door a nanosecond after Tamargo had gotten his foot in. "Easy now, we don't want to get there before he does…" Water accelerated to sixty mph. chasing after the Mustang east on the street parallel to Killian. "Where did he turn?" Water shouted. "How would I know? Slow down for the intersections so we can take a look!" Tamargo shot back.

"There he is!" Water exclaimed turning the steering wheel hard enough to send the car fishtailing around the corner and taking out a small tree on the right side's right-of-way. "Don't lose him!" Tamargo suggested while Water hit the gas hard. "Shut up!" Walker - or whoever the driver was – had obviously spotted them. He took corners without slowing down, leaving plenty of rubber on the road.

"This is Det. Water requesting backup. We're chasing a potential suspect in the killing of the College-Girl case. We're headed west on 112th

Street towards the Don Shula Extension. Black Mustang. License plate 7X9 K12." Tamargo, impersonating Water, told the dispatcher. "We'll dispatch units." came the calm answer from dispatch." "Looks like he's turning onto the Turnpike Extension southbound." Tamargo informed her.

The driver of the black Mustang turned onto the Extension and accelerated to over 100 miles per hour. Water followed him but refrained from getting too close in order to prevent the driver from acting stupid and potentially endangering innocent civilians. "He just passed the first toll plaza." Tamargo informed the dispatcher. "They are ready for him at the Eureka exit." replied the ever calm voice of the dispatcher. "Thanks."

The driver was smart enough to pull over onto the shoulder when he saw the spike strips on the road. Stopping his car he rolled down his windows, placed his hands on the steering wheel and waited. Tamargo and Water having followed him were the first ones to get to him. Approaching from the rear with their guns drawn they walked up to him.

"Hands out of the window!" Water shouted while walking up. "Don't move!" he added for good measure.

The driver sat motionless in his car until Water was next to him. "Slowly step out of your car! No sudden moves!" Water instructed while opening the driver's door with his left hand while keeping the gun leveled at the driver's face.

Tamargo had assumed a position close to the passenger's side door. The driver slowly and very carefully exited the car.

"On the ground, face down and interlock your hands behind your head!" Water continued his instructions.

Tamargo had walked around the front of the car to have a clear shot.

Water walked up to the driver, who had fully complied with his instructions, and grabbed the man's hands with his left hand pressing the fingers of the suspect's hands together.

"Wow, that hurts!" winced the man. Water quickly holstered his gun in its hip holster and cuffed the man's hands behind his back. Pulling the guy by his left armpit he instructed: "Turn sideways, bend your knees and get up slowly. What is your name?"

Tamargo had kept his gun leveled at the man to suppress any thought of attempting any funny moves, but had to admit to himself that Water had taken down the suspect expertly. Way to go rookie he thought. The MDPD and FHP officers had already removed the spike strips and were directing traffic around the two stopped cars. Four of them had come over to assist them with the suspect. What a difference a few years made Tamargo was thinking. In his time the cops didn't give a damn about traffic backing up for hours. Now – they actually alleviated the problem by clearing the scene quickly!

"Benjamin Walker." the driver had responded. Water nodded at Tamargo. "Great, we've been looking for you." Water answered. "What for?" Walker wanted to know. "We'll explain it at the station." Tamargo offered before they escorted him to the cruiser.

Chapter Sixty Six

Jerome Water and Benjamin Walker,
Miami (Sunday, March 8th, 2015, 10:58 am)

Benjamin had seen enough 'Law & Order' episodes to know that he should keep quiet. They would most likely play the 'good cop – bad cop' game with him. He didn't know any attorney – let alone a criminal attorney. He was almost certain that this was about the gay guy. There was no way they could connect him to Key West – was there? He'd be best off to just play dumb.

"Mr. Walker – my name is Detective Jerome Water, I am with the Miami Dade Police Department. We want to question you regarding the disappearance of a college girl. I will read you your Miranda Rights now." Water did just that and continued: "Would you like to tell us your side of the story, or would you like to invoke your right to counsel?" Water finished. Tamargo, Lt. Perez and Det Poole flinched on the other side of the window.

"Really Poole? He's up to it?" Lt. Perez wanted to know. "Just wait; he's using the soft approach." Poole didn't sound too convincing. "Sure!" Perez fired back. "You go in there and talk to the punk!" he finished.

"Mr. Walker, I am Detective Poole." Poole introduced himself before Walker had a chance to invoke his rights. "We just want to rule you out as the suspect in the disappearance of a couple of girls. If you have nothing to do with it, you'll be out of here in no time!" Poole placed a sympathetic smile on his face. "What girls are you talking about? I don't know any girls." Walker felt like a ton of bricks had been removed from his shoulders. That left, however, an even greater fear lodged in his gut. This was about Sabine. She was missing and the cops were seriously interested in her whereabouts. So he'd been right about Prof. Martin! Alas, they would never listen to his allegations – or would they?

"Hypothetically – if there are some girls that disappeared from a campus, doesn't it seem likely that someone very familiar with the comings and goings of that place may be involved?" Benjamin inquired.

"You mean such as yourself?" Poole questioned.

"Okay – bad cop! I am done talking!" Walker was clearly upset over Poole's response.

"What exactly do you mean by that?" Water inquired.

"It means I would like to talk to a lawyer."

Water and Poole exited the room.

"Great job guys!" Lt. Perez commented.

"Sorry I took the kid-gloves off!" Poole responded in a much louder tone than normal – before he started to cough.

"Yeah, well, he invoked his rights." Perez observed.

"I don't think he's the guy!" Water threw in.

"Based on your vast experience with serial killers?" Lt. Perez looked at Water like a cobra about to strike.

"Yeah, that works! The rookie doesn't know." Water regretted his words as soon as they had left his mouth.

"Careful! I have a few extra years of experience on you punk!" Perez snorted. "Having said that – I like your fire. What is your take?" Water realized that he needed to cool it, tune it down a notch or two. He took a deep breath, trying to relax and get a grip on the tension that had held him tight ever since they started chasing Walker.

"Did you notice how he suddenly relaxed when we asked him about the girls?" Water asked.

"Sure, but it only lasted about fifteen seconds and he was as tight as a drum again!" Poole interjected.

"Okay, do you guys have any other suspects?" Lt. Perez wanted to know. "Couple of weird professors; one that we like better than the other." Water informed him while staring through the glass at Benjamin who sat motionless at the table with his hands propping up his chin. "Okay, follow up on that. Get the guy an attorney. Poole you do the interview. Call me when you have something. Keep checking into Walker as well." Lt. Perez finished while walking away in a gait that resembled a soldier on the parade ground.

"How does he get his legs up that high with the extra fifty pounds he's carrying with him?" Water mumbled under his breath. Poole had an incredulous look on his face when he stared at Water, then smiled, started to laugh, and eventually started coughing again. "You really should quit those smokes Detective."

Poole and Water headed into the squad room and sat at their respective desks.

"Alright kiddo, I'll keep down the Fort and check into everything available on Benjamin Walker and your professors, by the way let me have the names again. Once the assistant public defender's office sends over a vulture I'll see if Mr. Walker opens up a little more. I got the feeling he wanted to tell us something before he clamped up." Poole informed Water.

"You're right; he was starting to open up. I really think he's not the guy. Maybe he saw something on campus, or knows about other incidents where girls were stalked." Water agreed. "I think I'm gonna go back to the campus, talk to some more students and professors that know the victims and the somewhat suspect professors." He finished.

"Sounds like a plan. Don't forget to talk to the maintenance personnel, landscapers and cleaning crews. They oftentimes see stuff but don't report anything." Poole advised.

"Good idea, I had forgotten about those potential sources!" Water admitted.

"That's why they pay me the big bucks." Poole confirmed. "Actually not – come to think about it." Poole continued with a sour expression on his face.

"Stop crying Poole, you've got to be pulling three times what they're handing out to little guys like me."

"Okay, maybe even a little more than that, since I started under a slightly different contract..." Poole trailed off.

"Fine, now that you have moved me close to tears over my miserable life, I'll hit the road. By the way Poole – are you married? If so, do you have children? I am available for adoption just so you know..."

"I'll keep that in mind son – now why don't you try to do your job?" Poole dismissed Water.

Water got up and handed Poole the paper with the two names he'd written down while they'd been bantering and walked out of the squad room.

Poole turned in his chair and started attacking his computer in his unsophisticated, yet effective two-finger-assault-style. He googled Benjamin Walker without getting any hits. The National Crime Investigation Center came up empty as well. Checking the DMV website revealed nothing new on Walker. Poole started on the first professor before he was interrupted by his phone.

"Poole."

"Hey Poole, you have a visitor coming your way. If I caught the name correctly it was 'Angel of Injustice'".

"The defender is here already?"

"Yup, coming your way as we're speaking." The desk sergeant replied with a chuckle before hanging up.

Poole gathered himself out of his chair and went to the hallway leading to the interview room.

"Counselor, I am Det. Poole. I assume you're here for Benjamin Walker?"

"You should never assume, but yes, I am here for my client Mr. Benjamin Walker." The public defender replied in a clipped, almost British like accent.

"And your name is?" Poole questioned.

"Mr. Samuel Cloud."

"Yeah, I figured you're a man."

"Excuse me?"

"Never mind, this way please." Poole was leading the way to the interview room.

Standing in front of the door to the interview room Poole told Mr. Samuel Cloud why they wanted to question Benjamin Walker in the murder and disappearance of three girls. Poole had to interrupt his monologue a couple of times to move away from the attorney who seemed to know nothing about personal space, inching closer towards Poole while alternatively fixing his yellow tie or staring straight at Poole's left ear. Poole had encountered his share of attorneys and irritating people – this one was certainly making the top 10!

When Poole was done; Mr. Samuel Cloud requested, while looking straight at Poole's belt buckle: "Det. Poole, would you be so kind to ensure that all listening devices are turned off before I confer with my client?"

"Wouldn't have it any other way - Counselor." Poole responded before opening the door to the room.

'What an idiot' was what immediately crossed Poole's mind before he headed for the observation room. Was that punk for real British or just pretending to be Royal?

Knowing that he would never be able to use any of the information he was about to hear, Poole left the intercom on in violation of established policy. While he knew full well that it might cost him his job, his pension should be safe. His Royal Highness had seriously rubbed him the wrong way.

"Hello Mr. Walker, my name is Mr. Samuel Cloud. I am with the Public Defender's Office. Have you been read your Miranda Rights by the arresting officers?" the attorney opened, while swinging his brown leather briefcase onto the table, before taking a seat.

Walker stared at his attorney who was about 5'6" wearing blue shoes, gray trousers, a white shirt, yellow tie, and a blue blazer.

"You're my attorney?" Walker had to stifle a laugh; this guy looked like the ringmaster at the Ringling Brothers Circus.

"Yes sir, I was randomly assigned to your case and happened to be only a short distance away, at another important meeting, when I got the call. It would give me great pleasure to listen to what exactly transpired today, as well as any events that led up to your unjustified arrest." The ringmaster announced to his audience.

Benjamin took a minute to collect himself, making sure he had his natural instinct well contained, the one that asked him to laugh into the little man's face, before he explained to his attorney that he was innocent and not even sure why exactly he had been arrested. Mr. Samuel Cloud looked down at his legal sized notepad: "Did you know any of the dead girls?" Ringmaster inquired shifting his gaze expectantly at Walker.

"Since the detectives didn't tell me their names – I wouldn't know." Benjamin looked him straight in the eyes.

"Their names are Sandra Restrepo, Sabine Sander and Graciela Manciani. Tell me what you know about them. Remember, I am on your side, but can only protect you when I know everything there is to know!" Cloud came back.

"Some of them may have been in my classes. I don't know. I know Sabine was in one of my classes. I've noticed her, but don't know her." Walker allowed.

"Okay, so let's allow the detective in to ask you a few questions. Make sure not to answer any of his questions before I tell you to!" Winter instructed.

"I have nothing to hide." Benjamin objected.

"That's not the point. There are certain answers that may be construed against you once they are out. I am a highly trained professional – and am doing this for a living. So please, do as I say!" Cloud responded while straightening his yellow tie.

Poole had heard enough and turned off the intercom before hustling back to the squad room. He had barely planted his rear end into his chair when Mr. Samuel Cloud appeared to inform him that his client was now ready to be 'questioned by the authorities'.

Poole had actually heard enough to agree with Water's assessment that Walker was not the guy, but decided to go through the motions just to have some fun with His Highness.

"Mr. Walker, where were you when Sabine was abducted on Monday March 2nd at around 11:00 p.m.?" Poole asked the one real question he had.

"Don't answer that!" Cloud jumped in. "We don't even know for sure that the girl was abducted!" he added for Poole's benefit.

"Yeah, but she is missing – isn't she?" Poole shot back.

"No, we know that you have not been in touch with her. That is all we know at this point, while you presume that a crime has been perpetrated, there is no evidence of any such occurrence." Cloud responded in an almost angry voice.

"Semantics counselor; let me rephrase: Where were you when Sabine may have disappeared?" Poole came back; simultaneously shaking his head looking at Mr. Samuel Cloud.

"Don't answer that!" Cloud almost shouted in order to stop Walker from responding. Benjamin was semi surprised by his attorney's outburst and just sat back in his chair. Poole was as puzzled as Walker over the attorney's unexpected explosion.

"Wow counselor – just a simple question." Poole's facial expression showed his utter disdain for Mr. Samuel Cloud.

"Regardless, my client will not answer this question on his attorney's advice." Cloud insisted. "Is there anything else you want to ask my client?" Cloud continued.

"Why was your client staking out Prof. Martin's house?"

"He's my professor; I had a question regarding the upcoming final." Walker responded before his attorney had a chance to object.

"Couldn't do that in class? Your Professor told you students to drop by his house?" Poole looked puzzled.

"No, not really, but I need to improve my grade, so I figured I'd give it a shot." Walker replied.

"That should be enough of this nonsense Detective. My client has answered enough questions. Do you have anything else?"

"Technically he has only answered one question, but I've had enough answers from you to say: 'No thanks, I am done.'" Poole concluded the interview.

"I assume my client is not under arrest." Not a question, but more a statement by Cloud while he was getting up from his chair straightening his tie again.

"Just one more - if it may be answered by your client. Why did you run from the police?" Poole had changed his mind and looked straight at Walker with a smirk on his face. Cloud held up his hand and conferred with his client by whispering into his ear and receiving an equally obscured answer.

"He did not run from the police Det. Poole; he was merely running from people that were chasing him in an unmarked car!" Cloud responded with a smile on his face.

"Well then, no more questions. Please make sure though that your client doesn't leave town; just in case we have additional questions" Poole responded while planting a smile on his face that belied his true feelings towards the attorney.

"No problem Detective. Mr. Walker will be available, provided that I will be notified in a timely manner prior to any questioning." Cloud responded while dropping his note pad and pen in his briefcase.

"Sure thing, counselor." Poole replied by putting an emphasis on counselor before he got up and opened the door to the interrogation room; waiting for his guest to leave before heading back to his desk.

Chapter Sixty Seven

Benjamin Walker,
Miami (Sunday, March 8th, 2015, 4:15 pm)

"Don't go near your Professor's house, don't try to contact Sabine in case you know where she is, and don't leave town. Anything unexpected arises – give me a call immediately!" Cloud instructed Benjamin while handing him his business card outside of the police station.

"Yes sir." was all Benjamin could come up with.

Benjamin went back into the police station and asked the desk officer to call him a cab. Walking back outside he considered his next move. He was, by now, almost convinced that Prof, Martin had something to do with Sabine's disappearance. Going back to Martin's house was a risky preposition at best. On the other hand – how else would he be able to confirm, or rule out, Prof. Martin as the guy who abducted Sabine?

The yellow cab pulled up in front of the station and Benjamin got in and instructed the driver to take him to his car. Realistically he should have asked the cops to drive him back to his car, but he figured that he already had his fill of cops for a day. Sitting in the backseat of the cab he was reviewing his options. None of them were too appealing. He could go home and wait for the cops to find Sabine – if they ever did. There certainly was no guarantee that they'd find her alive. He could forget about Sabine and just move on. He could go back to Germany and start anew. Or he could just roll the dice, go back to Prof. Martin and make the guy confess. Well, he had to admit to himself, there was of course the chance that he was wrong about Prof. Martin - but he didn't think so!

Before the cab reached his car he'd made up his mind. He was going to confront Prof. Martin. Paying the cabdriver he exited and walked over to his car. Having checked his gut feelings, he knew there was only one way to go – back to Prof. Martin. Looking at his watch he figured that it was still early enough to pay Prof. Martin a visit.

Before too long Benjamin found himself in front of Martin's house. He turned the headlights off and stared at the house. The lights on the porch were on. Not thinking twice he pulled into the driveway and parked his car. Upon exiting he decided to look into the backyard before ringing the doorbell. Unfortunately most of the yard was invisible due to a bunch of areca palms, so he returned to the front door and rang the bell. It took about two minutes for Martin to answer the call.

"May I help you?" Prof. Martin asked when he opened the door.

"Prof. Martin, I am in your class, but that's not why I am here. I am curious to know if you've abducted Sabine?"

"What? I don't know what you're talking about, but I've seen you in my class. What's your name again? Well, come on in." Martin responded confused but seemingly collected and pleasant.

"Thank you. Benjamin Walker."

Martin directed Benjamin towards one of the sofas in the nicely decorated living room. Sitting diagonally across from Benjamin he asked:

"Why are you're here again? Don't answer that, I've heard you the first time, but just can't believe it!"

"I saw you in the parking lot in front of her apartment!" Benjamin informed him while sitting on the edge of the sofa ready to jump Martin.

"Mr. Walker, I honestly believe you have read too many bad novels! I went over to Ms. Sander's apartment to drop off a paper for extra credit that she had given me."

"Late in the evening - without exiting your car?"

"Well, I realized that while I was going through my papers that I had forgotten to bring it. And unlike you I have to work for a living during the day and when I am not in class." Martin responded with a smirk on his face.

"Not that it matters – but so do I." Benjamin came back immediately.

"Now that we have established that we both work, what else can we discuss?" Martin inquired after a brief pause looking expectantly at Benjamin.

"Where is she? I know that you have something to do with her disappearance!" Benjamin confronted him.

"Mr. Walker, let me ask you: Why would I abduct Sabine – or any student for that matter?"

"Don't know, maybe you're a serial killer, and you get a kick out of abducting people!" Benjamin knew right then and there that he wasn't going to pass Prof. Martin's class but couldn't have cared less.

"Mr. Walker, may I call you Benjamin? Well, if I was the monster that you make me out to be, I would be way too smart to be caught. Hypothetically speaking, of course, if I had abducted Sabine, or any other student for that matter, I would have the means and the brains to keep her concealed. But why would I do that? To make them love me? To keep them as slaves in my sex chambers? And why are you so interested in Sabine anyway? Are you guys an item?" Martin wanted to know while comfortably leaning back on his black sofa.

"No, she's just a friend." Benjamin lied. "However, I do care about her!"

"Are you playing the noble knight confronting the dragon, in the process risking his life, all to defend the honor of the princess?" Martin retorted with sarcasm dripping from his voice.

"Am I risking my life by talking to you, the proverbial dragon?" Benjamin shot back.

"Easy now Benjamin. So far we've been having a semi-civilized conversation. Don't turn this ugly, or I will have to call the police." was Martin's smooth response.

"Go right ahead, they've already cleared me as a suspect!" Benjamin lied. "Not sure you've been cleared!"

"All right then – out of my house Mr. Walker." Martin directed him while getting off the sofa. "You are now officially overstaying your welcome. Give my regards to your friend Sabine – if you ever find her." Martin responded in an angry voice, and regretting his outburst immediately. "Sorry about that remark. I truly hope she will be found soon and unharmed. She's a very lovely girl."

Benjamin trotted over to the front door followed by Martin who kept back a couple of steps. Turning around he said: "This isn't over. I still believe you are involved in her disappearance, actually now more than ever. And I will prove it!"

"Good luck – and good bye Mr. Walker." Martin responded while opening the front door to his house.

Benjamin walked out of the house and down the driveway without turning around. When he reached his car, and just as he was about to turn around, he heard the click of the front door. He quickly got into his car, and for good measure, left some rubber on the guy's driveway when he pulled out.

Benjamin's visit left Martin somewhat concerned. Was the kid just running his mouth – or had he indeed been cleared by the police? Was he a suspect, and if so, when would they question him again? Not that he was concerned, but he could certainly do without the distraction. Maybe he should give the cops a clue. Now there was a great idea. He could plant the parking stub he received when entering the Dolphin Garage at Miami International Airport, where he'd left Sabine's car, at Mr. Walker's residence. Walking over to his laptop he marveled at his own cunningness and intelligence. It shouldn't take him too long to find out where Benjamin lived, after all, he did have access to the University's computer system. Bingo, he wrote the address on a small pad of paper next to his laptop and ripped it off.

He was excited. He would plant the evidence in Benjamin's apartment and then – should the cops ever show up again – point them indirectly at Mr. Walker's apartment. He noticed that his excitement had spread to his loins. Time to go for a little walk!

Chapter Sixty Eight

Benjamin Walker and Jerome Water,
Miami (Sunday, March 8th, 2015, 5:03 pm)

Angry wasn't the word to describe Ben's state of mind after leaving Martin's house. The guy had to be guilty. His demeanor, his body language and the smug look on his face. While he had no proof, he knew the guy was responsible for Sabine's disappearance. Driving down Killian Drive towards 117th Avenue he realized that he wasn't going to be able to solve Sabine's disappearance by himself.

The first Detective, the younger one had been pretty cool. Remembering their encounter he started digging in his jean pockets for the business card the guy had given him. Detective Jerome F. Water it read. Pulling over to the side of the road he decided to give the guy a call.

"Detective Water" came the answer after a few rings.

"Yeah, this is Benjamin Walker – your main suspect in the disappearance of Sabine Sander." He responded with sarcasm.

"How can I help you?" Water responded without missing a beat.

"Do you want to find out who abducted Sabine?"

"Naturally – it's my job and furthermore what I would really like to accomplish!"

"Alright then – I know who is holding her!"

"Who?"

"Prof. Martin is keeping her!"

"Where?"

"Don't know yet, but he's definitely the guy who abducted her!"

"And you know this how?"

"I just do. I was over at his house and he was really smug about her disappearance. He was almost hinting towards the fact that he's holding her captive somewhere!"

"Benjamin, let me get this straight – you went back to Prof. Martin's house – knowing that that's an arrestable offense?"

"Yeah well, you guys weren't doing anything!"

"Never mind - we need a little more than your suspicion to obtain a warrant. Not that I don't believe you – it just isn't enough for you – the main suspect - to say so!" Jerome responded.

"How about you search his house?"

"Again, we need probable cause for a warrant."

"So you just gonna do nothing?" Ben was incredulous.

"I didn't say that Ben." Water came back.

"Sure." Ben hung up.

Hitting his steering wheel with both fists he yelled a few obscenities before hitting the gas hard, peeling out of the grassy area he'd been parked in, leaving a fishtail mark of dead grass behind.

As soon as he hung a right on 117th Avenue his cell phone rang. Snatching it from the passenger seat he looked at the display: Water.

"Yeah." he answered.

"Benjamin, don't do anything stupid. You go near Martin's house again and you're out of the race. Let us handle this."

"What are you going to do?"

"I don't have a fucking clue, but we'll come up with something. You stay put. Go home, I'll call you." Water responded.

"You're joking!"

"Hardly, stay out of this. I promise I'll call you." Water begged.

"Alright, but don't take too long."

Chapter Sixty Nine

Jerome Water and Prof. Martin,
Miami (Sunday, March 8th, 2015, 7:19 pm)

As soon as Water hung up he hit the speed dial for Poole.

"Poole, Walker just called me. He was over at Martin's house and believes that Martin has Sabine hidden somewhere." he opened.

"Did you arrest him?"

"Can't arrest him over the phone can I?"

"Jerome, it's too early in our relationship to get mouthy with me!" Poole shot back.

"Sorry Poole, I just happen to think that Walker may be right. Franco and I liked Martin as well. Why don't we stop by and ask him a couple of questions?"

"Okay, where are you anyway?"

"Having a romantic dinner at a lovely restaurant. I'll meet you in front of Martin's house."

"What's the girl's name? Wendy?"

"Burger King."

"Very intimate – hot date. I am finishing some paperwork so you're on your own, but I'll send a couple of uniforms to back you up." Poole ended the conversation.

Disposing of his leftover's into the somewhat dirty garbage receptacle by the door he headed for his cruiser.

Pointing his vehicle towards Martin's house Jerome thought about Benjamin's call. There was no way that Benjamin was involved in Sabine's abduction – or was there? As he had learned, criminals sometimes inserted themselves into the police investigation. However, he didn't think that Benjamin was one of them.

When he arrived at Prof. Martin's house the squad car was already parked in the driveway. Parking on the right-of-way in front of Martin's house he approached the officers.

"Det. Water." Jerome opened while flashing his badge.

"How long have you been here?" he continued.

"Just got here." one of the officers responded.

"Let's do this. He's not a suspect, just a person of interest. So why don't you just hang here?"

"Sure thing Detective." the second officer, Gomez according to his name tag, volunteered.

Jerome walked up to the single family home and rang the doorbell. After a couple of minutes Martin opened the door looking surprised.

"Detective – what can I do for you?" Martin asked.

"Sir, if you don't mind, I have a few questions."

"Sure."

"May I come in Professor?"

"What exactly is this about if I may ask?

"I just have a few questions."

"Please step in."

Once inside the spacious living room Martin pointed towards the sofa for Jerome to have a seat. Deciding to keep the initiative Jerome remained standing.

"Professor Martin, we have received confidential information that you may know something about Ms. Sander's disappearance."

"Ah, let me guess! You're referring to the crackpot Walker who just an hour ago forced his way into my home to accuse me of having abducted Ms. Sander?" Martin replied while looking at Jerome.

"I am sorry sir, we cannot disclose our sources. Would you like to file a complaint against Mr. Walker for having forced his way into your house though?" Jerome inquired.

"How am I supposed to answer such a ridiculous and utterly incorrect accusation without knowing my accuser?" Martin replied with a puzzled look on his face.

"Prof. Martin, did you have a chance to think about the night of Ms. Sander's appearance? More to the point, if there was anything you did that night that would verify your alibi?"

"Detective, as I've told you - I live alone – so no. Maybe one of my neighbors saw me come home, but I wouldn't know. Ask around. But seriously, why would I abduct Ms. Sander? I am a successful entrepreneur and teach at FIU. Don't you think that there would be easier ways for me to make the acquaintance of a young girl?"

"Would you object to me taking a look around your house?" Water answered.

"I will allow you to look around without a warrant in the spirit of cooperation and because I hope that Ms. Sander is fine. However, please be advised, that I will not stand for you or your Department tarnishing my reputation with unwarranted allegations. So go ahead, but make sure you guys tread lightly from here on out." Martin informed Water with a stern look on his face.

"Thank you Professor, I appreciate your voluntary cooperation." Water replied with a serious face while thinking that if Martin was involved at all, it would be difficult to trip up someone as smart and smug as him.

Doing a search from room to room took Water about ten minutes. Having checked every room, closet and other potential hiding space he returned to the living room where Martin had remained.

"Satisfied Detective?"

"Yes, thank you for your cooperation."

"The next time you stop by unannounced; please make sure to bring a warrant." Martin said with a thin smile on his lips while pulling the front door open for Water.

"I'll make a note of it." Water responded with a courteous nod.

Once outside of Martin's house Water thanked and dismissed the patrol officers and called Poole.

"Hey Poole. Wild goose chase. I found nothing in Martin's home. His alibi is iffy, but plausible."

"Yeah, so we're back to square one?"

"Looks like it. While I stand by my assessment on Walker, maybe we should get a warrant for his apartment. Just to cover all our bases."

"Good thinking. I'll write it up."

Chapter Seventy

Prof. Martin, Miami (Sunday, March 8th, 2015, 11:15 pm)

Unbeknown to himself, he was getting lucky. The patrol officers watching Benjamin's place had gotten a call to respond to a robbery only a few minutes before he pulled slowly into the almost filled parking lot in the front of the apartment complex.

Rolling into the parking lot he scanned the cars in the lot. None seemed to be occupied. Benjamin's Mustang was nowhere to be seen. He knew that he was no locksmith, but he had watched a couple of internet posts on how to unlock a front door – the ones that didn't have a deadbolt engaged – and was hopeful and comfortable about the task ahead. He had to get into the apartment and plant the seed that would lead the cops to be convinced that Benjamin was their man.

Getting out of his car, after turning off the dome light, he scanned his surroundings. He couldn't detect anyone, but didn't want to take any unnecessary risks so he remained standing still next to his car for a few seconds. No movement that he could detect. Not surprising at this time of night.

He slowly and carefully made his way through the parking lot towards the first building. Looking at the buildings' number he deduced where Benjamin's building would be located and started walking in that direction until he heard some loud laughter. Stopping in his tracks he ducked down, pretending to tie his shoe laces. The laughter had stopped and no one had appeared into his field of vision. Advancing carefully towards the building he wondered about life.

How exactly did he end up burglarizing someone's apartment? Necessity! Now quit thinking about the implications and move on he told himself.

Reaching Benjamin's front door he quickly put on some latex gloves, took out his credit card – the one he hardly ever used – and jimmied it in between the door frame and the door. To his surprise the door unlocked! Go figure! He was a regular burglar!

He eased into the apartment and closed the door. Not daring to turn on the lights he took out his cell phone and brought up the flashlight app. The apartment was small but reasonably clean and organized. A small sofa, coffee table, two side tables, midsized TV on a small dresser, small stereo system with speakers and a table with two chairs in the dining area. He moved into the bedroom where he found a queen-sized bed a nightstand and dresser. He focused on the nightstand where he detected a book. He hadn't expected to find a novel by John Irving, but didn't really care about what Benjamin's reading pleasures were anyway. He quickly took out the parking garage stub he'd received at the airport, wiped it with the bottom of his shirt and inserted it into the middle of the book.

Pleased with his accomplishment he went back to the living room and quietly exited the apartment, slowly pulling the door shut. He didn't encounter anyone on his way to the parking lot and let out a sigh of relief when he sat back in his car.

Pulling out of the lot and accelerating on Bird Road he noticed a dark Mustang in the left lane. Angling for a better view he twisted to look over his shoulder but couldn't see the car. Switching back to his rearview mirror he still failed to see the Mustang. A quick glance into his outside mirrors also yielded no result. Almost panicking he sped up to get a better view of his rear. Still nothing. Hitting his brakes he realized that the Mustang must have made a left turn a while ago. Cursing himself for being such an idiotic paranoid he continued towards his home. He was in a good place. He'd planted the evidence that would be hard for Benjamin to explain. Yup – he was in good shape indeed.

Tamargo couldn't believe his eyes. The dark clad figure emerging from Benjamin's apartment was definitely not Benjamin. Wearing a hoodie and nervously looking around didn't do anything to dispel Tamargo's suspicion, but confirmed his belief that he was watching a burglar making his way back from Benjamin's apartment and now approaching the parking lot. Sliding down in his car seat he waited for the guy to get into his car which was parked not too far from him. A BMW no less – what had the world come to? Burglars driving fancy imports? Starting his car as soon as the other car exited he sped out of the parking lot following the car westbound onto Bird Road. Glancing at his dashboard clock he figured he'd give Water a break and not call him about this unexpected development just yet. The driver must have been drunk or on some other illegal substance judging by his erratic driving. Staying well behind the BMW he followed him for about fifteen minutes.

When Tamargo's prey pulled into the driveway of a familiar house he again considered calling Water but figured that he was going to handle it without calling in the cavalry. He turned off his headlights and pulled in behind the other car. Quickly getting out he loudly said: "Hey, wait up." before his person of interest disappeared into the house. Shaking his head in disbelief he walked up to the front door and rang the bell.

The door was almost immediately opened and he was greeted with: "I know you! What are you doing here? Are you stalking me?"

"And a good night to you sir. To answer your question: hardly, I was following you after you exited Mr. Walker's apartment." Tamargo responded without much emotion but with a generous dose of sarcasm.

"I have no idea what you are referring to, but I don't want to be inhospitable – even at this time of night. So please, come on in."

Tamargo was slightly surprised by this calm and collected response, but stepped into the foyer of the house. His host motioned him towards the seating area in the living room before closing the door behind Tamargo.

While walking towards the living room Tamargo suddenly noticed a shadow approaching him quickly. Right then he received a blow to the back of his head. Dropping hard onto the tile floor without being able to break his fall knocked the wind out of him. Flopping onto his back he discovered his host standing over him raising a baseball bat like a pro golfer on the tee. Trying to reach his gun in the hip holster before being knocked into oblivion he rolled onto his left side. The second blow hit him on the right shoulder with such force that he continued his roll – now involuntarily – over onto his stomach. Realizing that he was in deep trouble, he struggled to continue rolling to gain distance from his attacker.

The searing pain from his shoulder, when he rolled over it made him cry out in pain. Trying again to reach his gun he realized that he wouldn't make it in time before his assailant would hit him again. Raising his left arm to block the blow he was taken by surprise when he received a kick to the head delivered with expert force. Fighting to keep his focus, he blinked his eyes rapidly and reached for his holster again.

The last thing he saw, before his lights went out, was the blurred image of a baseball bat approaching him at warp-speed.

Chapter Seventy One

Prof. Martin and Franco Tamargo,
Miami (Monday, March 9th, 2015, 2:11 am)

There was blood and, what he figured to be brain matter, on his floor. Luckily he had an extra sheet of thick blue vinyl tarp that he kept as part of his sad-departure-supply. Last time he went to Home Depot he was so angry about the sad departure of his last guest that he had made certain to have a good supply on hand for potential future mishaps. Rolling out the tarp next to Tamargo's lifeless body he reflected on the recent events and his future steps. It took him a while to get the guy onto the plastic …. He took the car keys and gun from the body before he wrapped the man into a tight bundle. Using a couple of rolls of duct tape he secured his package. He made sure the front porch light was turned off before he investigated the rather large trunk of his departing visitor's car. Yup – that would do, heck he could pack another couple of people in there. Making sure none of the houses across the street had any lights on; he manhandled his visitor out of his house and into the trunk. Exhausted and sweaty he decided to take a shower. Maybe he should also relieve his anxiety!? Yeah, that was an excellent idea. There was still plenty of time to dispose of the body before the new day dawned.

Chapter Seventy Two

Sabine Sander,
Miami (Tuesday, March 9th, 2015, 2:45 am)

There had been more blood after his last assault. The pain had been bearable, but the shame was about to kill her. She needed to get out of this place. There was no way she was going to be able to continue to take his abuse. Correction, even if she was able to take it, the ultimate outcome was going to most likely end in her demise anyway. So why prolong matters? She was going to fight him tooth and nail next time he came near her!

Unfortunately next time came way too soon. She hadn't been able to come up with a plan, didn't know how to overwhelm him. Too late – here he was. Dressed in his usual hideous attire he stood in front of her before she was able to adjust or even comprehend his sudden appearance. He again put some clothing down on the mattress that by now had a number of blood stains on it.

He pointed at the robe that looked like a nuns outfit and gestured for her to put it on. This time she put on the robe quickly, trying to avoid the humiliation of another rape. She shivered, not knowing if her simple gesture of obedience would be enough to appease him.

He looked at her, stepped back a couple of feet and said but a single word: "Slut!"

Before she realized it, he'd closed in on her, threw her onto the mattress, and turned her onto her stomach. He swiftly pulled up her robe and penetrated her.

No one should ever have to be subjected to this kind of pain and humiliation! He had raped her in an unusual way. When he was done, he had actually laughed before walking over to a bag that he must have carried in earlier to retrieve a couple of baby-wipes. He held them out to her, but she refused to take them from him. He dropped them on the mattress.

"Take off the robe." He demanded.

When Sabine didn't move immediately he bent down and pulled it over her head, turned around and left.

There had been much more blood after this assault. The pain was bad, but the feeling of utter humiliation and helplessness was more than she thought she'd be able to take.

She didn't even try to clean herself, just rolled over on the mattress and cried, eventually, mercifully falling asleep.

Chapter Seventy Three

Prof. Martin, (Monday, March 9th, 2015, 4:25 am)

Taking the Turnpike Extension to 826 and then switching over to the Dolphin Expressway, it took him about twenty minutes to the airport in the dead of night. He was wearing a dark blue baseball cap and kept his head low while passing by any of the security cameras that he'd discovered on his previous excursion to the airport.

Driving up to the top floor of the Flamingo garage made him snicker. If Walker didn't have an alibi for tonight, he figured the cops would connect him to this second body as well. Game over for that little fuck. It was way too late to catch the Metro, so he decided to walk over to domestic arrivals and to grab a taxi. Keeping his head low he made his way through the garage towards the taxi stand. His driver was an old Cuban who tried to start a conversation about the days before Fidel Castro, but fell silent when there was no response.

He had the taxi driver drop him off in Coconut Grove, from there he was able to get another taxi to take him home. He was looking forward to a couple of hours of sleep before continuing to work on his project.

Chapter Seventy Four

Jerome Water, Miami (Monday, March 9th, 2015, 9:00 am)

"Hi Melody, sorry to be back so soon to bother you again." Water apologized while walking up to her desk.

"No bother at all, I am happy to see you again. I mean… sorry, happy to help you with the case. It is about the case – right?" Melody sounded like a 5th grader talking to a boy that she'd just met in the schoolyard.

"Good seeing you too! Ah, yes, it is about the case. I have a few more questions that I'm hoping you will be able to help me with." Water's face had turned a beautiful crimson red.

"Anything you need Detective."

Remembering Tamargo's remarks Jerome quickly scanned her desk. Yup, there it was; the picture of her dog. Sure enough, no ring on her fingers. Feeling like a fool he gathered his thoughts and said: "Hmmh, Melody, before I continue abusing you with questions – when this is over – could I interest you in having dinner with me?" directing his eyes to the floor his heart was sinking to the bottom of his stomach and he was afraid that he might have an acid reflux moment.

"That would be great! I was hoping that you'd ask me before I would have to..." Melody replied quickly with a smile as sweet as honey.

Yes! Was Jerome's first thought while breathing a sigh of relief. He'd gone out on a limb here. While he knew that he was a decent looking guy – some people, other than his parents, had even told him he was good looking – he was still not as confident about himself as he'd liked to be. But hey – she had said yes!

"Well, could I ask you for your phone number then?" he asked while blushing again. Melody thought that he was the cutest guy she'd ever met. Gentle, shy, and handsome as hell!

"Sure, here's my card. Let me put my cell phone number on the back." she answered while scribbling it on the card. Handing it to him she asked: "So what else did you need from me?" Melody inquired before regretting her words when she noticed Jerome blushing again.

"Aahhem, would you be aware of any complaints by students logged against Prof. Martin or Prof. Rupert?" Jerome mumbled while trying to keep his facial coloring under control. Not that he'd ever figured out how to do that.

"Sorry, but that information would be in their personal files with HR. However, if this is a police emergency, I would probably be able to hack into the files!" Melody responded looking at Jerome expectantly.

"I can't ask you to do that. There is no warrant and it would be illegal."

"Okay, so maybe I could just hit a few wrong keys!"

"What?"

"Sometimes I am really clumsy – I hit the wrong keys – stuff comes up on the screen. Sometimes people happen to be in my office. Sometimes they happen to stand behind me looking at my computer screen…!" she said with that sweet smile on her face while winking at him at the same time.

Knowing that he was knee deep in legal quicksand he nodded his head in agreement.

Melody wiped the hair out of her face and went to town on the keyboard with her pretty hands flying; and in no time Prof. Martin's personal file was displayed. Scanning it quickly Water couldn't detect any blemishes. On the contrary, he had received high scores on his reviews by students as well as his Dean. Melody quickly brought the other professor's personal information up on the screen. Again scanning it as fast as he could, Jerome learned that the guy – no surprise here – had been warned to stay away from the female students.

"Oops, sorry to have stood behind you while you were working…" Jerome said while stepping away and nervously pulling on his left ear.

"You can stand behind me anytime you want Detective." Melody had turned in her chair and gave Jerome a smile that could have melted a glacier. Feeling his face blushing, he turned and walked back to the front of her workstation. Maybe he should see a doctor about this damn blushing problem.

"Okay, gotta run. I'll call you as soon as I can."

"Can't wait." she responded.

Realizing that this new information wasn't going to help them at all, he started heading back to the station. Halfway to his car he remembered something Prof. Martin had said and turned around to see if Melody would be able to retrieve this kind of information.

Chapter Seventy Five
Jerome Water and Eric Poole,
Miami (Monday, March 9th, 2015, 10:01 am)

"Where's Tamargo?" Poole opened when he walked into the squad room seeing Water at his desk.

"Don't know, he hasn't called me and we're not bunking together!"

"Wow – early in the morning – yet you're ready for stand-up comedy." Poole snorted.

"Sorry Poole. I haven't heard from him, which is a little strange. Let me call him." Water soft balled while hitting the speed dial for Tamargo on his cell phone. After having endured twelve rings the call went to voice mail.

"No answer." he informed Poole.

"Fucking civilians, no work ethics what-so-ever. Magnum P.I. is probably sleeping in.

Okay, so we'll have to wait on his report on Walker's apartment. Anyway, I had the foresight to put out an APB on Sabine's car. Guess what – they found it in the long term parking garage at the Airport. So why don't you take a drive over there and observe the guys?" Poole subtly ordered Water.

"On my way." Water responded.

"Flamingo garage, top floor." Poole called after him.

Water went straight for the top floor of the Flamingo long term parking garage at the Miami International Airport. Pulling up outside of the yellow police tape he parked and walked over to the Sergeant in charge of the scene.

"Good Morning Sergeant. Detective Water, I am investigating the disappearance of the owner of this car."

"Welcome to the exciting scene of her car Detective." Sergeant Garcia responded without much enthusiasm.

"Anything besides the presence of the car itself? Blood, fingerprints, or the big gun that'll break the case loose?" Water asked hopeful.

"Wouldn't that be nice? Sorry, wish I could give you a hand here, but there was no visual blood, no weird items in the car, nothing in the trunk. However, CSI isn't done, so keep your fingers crossed. However, I wouldn't hold my breath. It looks pretty clean." Sergeant Garcia responded before walking over to the CSI unit personnel.

Water walked around the car trying not to interfere with the lab rats and came away with the impression that there wasn't anything he was going to find that they hadn't already discovered. Disappointed he headed back to his car while dialing Tamargo's number again. Still no response which somewhat started to concern him. Tamargo was an experienced ex-officer who wouldn't drop out of sight like this. He decided to drive by Tamargo's house later on to find out if he was wrong about the guy.

"Hey Poole, I'll check with airport security. Maybe they have the driver of Sabine's car on camera."

"Great idea. I already called them. They are expecting you." Poole replied.

"Thanks Daddy." Water replied before disconnecting the call.

Water made his way up to the third floor of the airport administrative office to talk to security. As promised, they were expecting him and had already started to scan the recordings from Monday 3/2/15, 11:00 p.m. to Tuesday 9:12 a.m. when Water walked in. He spent the next hour straining his eyes to focus on the screen showing all cars entering the garage at an accelerated speed to reduce viewing time. He was about to get a major headache when Sabine's car appeared on the screen on Tuesday at 11:47 a.m.

To Water's dismay the picture was grainy and didn't show more than a white male with a baseball cap drawn deep over his eyes driving into the garage.

"How about the outside entrance to the garages? Are there any cameras?" Water asked hopeful.

"Sure, let's switch over to them and deduct about three minutes." the technician responded.

Watching the feed in slow motion they again saw Sabine's car, but the picture was even worse than the previous one.

"So much for our high-tech security systems protecting our most vulnerable infrastructure!" Water allowed his frustration to show.

"I'll make sure to bring it up in our next budget meeting with the Director." was the sarcastic answer of the technician he was sitting next to.

"I'm sorry man, just having a bad day. Thanks for your help." Water apologized before leaving the room with a couple of printed still shots of the unidentifiable driver.

"Go get 'em Tiger!" came the smartass reply.

Water ignored it and exited the crammed room.

"Poole – I struck out again. Video is useless - it could be Walker, Martin, or any other white Anglo left in Miami."

"Shit, I'd hoped for more than that."

"Same here."

"Alright, I am doing another search of the internet and other available sources for information on the professors and Walker. Why don't you roll back in and give me a hand?"

Water decided to take a little detour and drove over to Tamargo's house. Parking in front of the house close to Tropical Park he immediately noticed the absence of Tamargo's Marauder. Where the hell was the guy? When repeated rings and knocks on the front door yielded no immediate response, he started to get a little concerned about his new friend, and walked around the house to the back. Pulling on the back sliding glass door handle he realized that the house was locked down solid. He walked back to the front, knocking on every window he passed. Strange indeed.

Water decided to call Poole for advice when his phone rang. "Hi Melody." he answered when he saw the caller ID.

"It wasn't easy, and you now officially owe me dinner – but I got the information. Prof. Martin sent in the grades on Sunday – the night before Sabine disappeared!" Melody informed him.

"Thank you so much Melody. Dinner and a Movie it is. That's the least I can do – scratch that – what I want to do!" Jerome started to smile to himself while delivering those lines.

"Let me know when." Melody responded before hanging up.

Water dialed Poole's number. "Hey Poole, I'm at Tamargo's house. No car, no response at the door. You know him better than I do. What's wrong with him?" Water inquired after Poole answered his call.

"How would I know?" Poole answered and then fell silent for a while.

"It's not like him man. Snoop around and look through the windows. I'll stay on the line."

Water walked around the house again peeking into every window without seeing any movement. Living room with a sofa, love seat and large flat screen TV. A kitchen absent of any dirty dishes or any clutter on the countertops or in the sink. Bedroom verticals were closed. There were no signs of forced entry, nor any other signs of foul play.

"Poole, there's nothing here." Water reported back.

"Okay, maybe he's with his girlfriend." Poole said without much conviction.

"Right." Water answered.

"He was sitting on Walker's apartment. You've got his number, right? Call him. See if he saw him last night." Poole responded.

"Alright."

"Mr. Walker." he said after five rings. "This is Det. Water. This may sound a little strange, but have you by any chance seen Mr. Tamargo hanging out in front of your apartment complex?" Water asked awkwardly.

"So you guys are still on me instead of checking into Martin? I don't believe it!" Walker replied angrily.

"No, I did search Martin's house. Nothing there. This is standard procedure. So have you seen Tamargo?"

"No." was the short, hostile response, before the call was disconnected.

Water was now officially worried about Tamargo. Where the hell was the guy?

Chapter Seventy Six

Jerome Water and Eric Poole,
Miami (Monday, March 9th, 2015, 2:15 pm)

"Hey." Water opened.

"Anything on Tamargo?" Poole wanted to know.

"Nothing. It's like he pulled a Houdini. I am actually worried about him."

"Same here. I know you guys think that Walker has nothing to do with Sabine, but I wonder if he may have held a grudge towards the two of you. Tamargo was last in front of his apartment. Now he's missing!" Poole stated.

"Yeah, but we don't know that he ever got there."

"Fair enough, but I am done guessing. Have Walker brought in for questioning. I'll find out for sure." Poole said ominously.

Water requested a patrol unit to visit Walker's apartment and have him brought in for questioning.

For once Fortune smiled upon them. Walker had been home and come with the officers without offering any resistance. Poole decided that he was going to have a talk with Walker, while Water was observing everything through the one-way-mirror.

"Mr. Walker, would you like to have your attorney present while I ask you a few questions?" Poole opened.

"The idiot? No thanks. However, I am curious as to why you're questioning me while there is a fucking pervert out there who's keeping Sabine prisoner. Oh, by the way – his name is Professor-fucking-Martin!" was Walker's vehement response.

"Thank you for your input. However, if you don't mind, the way it works here is that I ask the questions, and you answer!" Poole informed him.

"Sure, since all of your stellar police work has gotten you so much closer to discovering where Sabine is being held!"

"Mr. Walker, did you see Mr. Tamargo parked in front of your building last night?"

"Your partner asked me already. Maybe Martin got him too?"

"Please just answer my question."

"No."

"No - you won't answer my question? Or no - you haven't seen Tamargo?"

"You're wasting your time talking to me. Martin has Sabine. He may also have Tamargo. Why he would have him I don't know, but he's your guy!" Walker came back with conviction in his voice. "No, I haven't seen Tamargo since he and Det. Water brought me to your station. Does that answer your question, Sir?"

"Now there's a start. I know you harassed Martin in his own house. Det. Water is holding a protective hand over you – otherwise I would have already arrested you for that stunt."

"Guess I should thank my lucky stars…"

"Don't get smart with me son – I've been around the block a couple of times, and whether you like it or not – I can hold you on a number of charges."

Walker sat still for a minute before responding: "Sure, pin it on the guy who actually cares! You know what? I am now done talking to you. Maybe you'll enjoy another round with my friend Mr. Cloud!"

"That's entirely your choice Mr. Walker. Please wait here until we can get in touch with him to continue the interview." Poole informed him while getting up from his chair.

"Wait a minute!" Walker cried out.

"What now?" Poole asked sweetly.

"Forget the lawyer. I want you to eliminate me as a suspect so that you can concentrate on the real cancer. Yes, I have an interest in Sabine. For a while I followed her around campus and also around town."

Poole was about to inform him that this was also referred to as stalking, but bit his tongue and just nodded.

"Please continue."

"Well, the reason why I went to Martin's house was because I saw him at Sabine's place!"

"When was that?" Poole interjected.

"A few days back. He was just parked there for an hour or so."

"And you know this how?" Poole wanted to know.

"Dah, I was parked a couple of cars over. It was just creepy. I mean he's supposed to be the professor."

"As opposed to you, the other stalker, who is a fellow student?"

"Man, I knew you wouldn't believe me. Where is the other cop? The young one?" Walker was getting frustrated with Poole.

"Det. Water?"

"Yeah."

Without waiting for a sign from Poole, Water decided to join the interview.

"Hey Benjamin." He opened upon entering the room.

"No shit, you've been watching us through the mirror? So now who's the pervert?" Walker responded with relief audible in his voice.

"You didn't think the mirror was there to assist suspects in fixing their hair – did you?" Water responded keeping it friendly.

"Whatever. Okay, so yes I was "stalking' her, but I want her found!" Walker had turned serious.

"If you're really want us to eliminate you as a suspect you'll have to come clean on everything." Water took over after having received a nod from Poole.

"What do you think I am doing here?"

"Alright then – where were you on Monday the 2nd of March after 11:00 p.m.?" Water inquired.

"Man, I know how this may sound, but I can't tell you. But you've got to believe me that I had nothing to do with her disappearance. For all I care, lock me up until you find her. Just make sure you start with Prof. Martin. I am sure he's behind it." Walker leaned back looking almost exhausted.

"Come on; just tell us where you were!" Water insisted.

"Nope." Walker was adamant, knowing that his alibi had the potential to connect him to certain things that happened in Key West.

"You say you want to help us, but you're not really making a good case for yourself." Poole stated.

"Do one of those lie-detector things with me. Search my car; search my apartment for all I care!" Walker offered.

"Mr. Walker, are you waiving your right to counsel, and are you consenting to a search of your vehicle and your apartment?" Poole asked in his official voice, thankful for this turn of events since the judge hadn't signed off on the search warrant for Walker's apartment yet.

"Yes, yes, and yes. Happy?"

"That will all depend on what we find Mr. Walker." Poole replied dryly.

"Whatever, you won't find anything, because there is nothing to be found."

"We will have to hold you until we've completed our search. Is that a problem?" Poole continued.

"No, how long will it take, and when will you go after Martin?"

"One step at a time." Poole replied while getting up.

"If you're straight with us, you're dropping down on the list." Poole assured him before leaving the room behind Water, who had turned around to give Benjamin a re-assuring nod.

Chapter Seventy Seven

Sabine Sander,
Miami (Monday, March 9th, 12:14 pm)

Her captor, or monster, as she had taken to referring to him, was entering her prison again. Wearing his now usual Zorro-mask and the silk robe he came towards her. He seemed more agitated and excited than she had ever seen him before.

He unrobed and lay down on the mattress, while she was still standing next to it.

"Please join me." he requested in a husky voice.

Having experienced some previous outbursts after disobeying his 'requests', she complied and lay down on the mattress. Pulling her close into a lovers embrace he started kissing her neck. Trying to control her almost unbearable urge to vomit she turned her face away from him.

"Everyone has options in life. Everyone has to make decisions in life. The decisions will influence the future path our life takes. You have to make a decision right now. You can show me some affection or you can start reviewing your life. It's all up to you." he whispered into her ear.

It surprised her how fast the thoughts were shooting through her brain. Did she want to suffer continued humiliation or did she want to end it once and for all? Would giving in present a chance to escape later on? Dying now would certainly rob her of any potential future opportunities. She turned her face towards him and looked him straight into his eyes. He must have been surprised by her move because he pulled his own head back a few inches.

"Good decision." he whispered before starting to caress her body like a lover. His foreplay however didn't last long before she could feel his erection on her leg. Rolling her on her back he mounted her and pleased himself quickly.

Chapter Seventy Eight

Benjamin Walker's apartment and car,
Miami (Monday, March 9th, 2015, 5:31 pm)

Poole had obtained Walker's apartment and car keys and called the CSI unit to do a thorough search of both. They took Walker's Mustang on a flatbed truck to the CSI base while another team was dispatched to his apartment.

Water had gone back to the holding cell, occupied by Walker to inform him that the process would most likely take a few hours.

Poole had not only sent the CSI unit, but an additional two officers to expedite the search of the apartment. Two hours later Poole received a call that put a frown on his face. Hanging up he turned in his chair to face Water.

"Maybe we were wrong all along! They found a ticket from the airport parking garage. The timestamp matches Sabine's car entering the garage. And there goes 'eliminate-me-from-your-list-of-suspects-I-have-nothing-to-do-with-it'".

"It doesn't make sense though. Why would he suggest for us to search his apartment?" Water wanted to know.

"He's a dumb-ass criminal. That's how we catch them sooner or later!" Poole came back.

"I'm not sold on this."

"Oh for God's sake – neither am I." Poole admitted.

"Now what?" Waters inquired.

"We're back to square one."

"I don't know. How many professors do you know that visit their students at home?"

"In case you've forgotten, I am nearing retirement age, and it has been a while that I've been to school." Poole replied with an incredulous look on his face.

"Why, you look so young." Water replied before breaking out laughing.

"Funny, now go change your diaper youngster!" Poole shot back.

Waters thought about asking if it was time for Poole to change his 'depends' but resisted the urge and just grinned.

"Thinking about adult diapers aren't you?" Poole must have read his mind. "Wise choice to keep that thought to yourself!"

"I've always been a great proponent of 'shut up while you're ahead'"

"Let's review this case. We have two dead girls, a dead boy, a missing female student, a horny professor who may be soliciting sexual favors for good grades, a smart-ass professor who engages in home visits, and a love-struck student who has the receipt to the garage where Sabine Sander's car was found. Am I missing something?" Poole looked at Water.

"Okay, Prof. Rupert is a pervert who should be investigated, but he's not our guy. Walker is somewhat suspect for not giving us his alibi for the night of Sabine's disappearance, and having found that parking stub in his apartment doesn't help his case. However, he is too forthcoming to be my prime suspect." Walker replied.

"Which leaves Prof. Martin as the main suspect? However, he also volunteered to have his place searched by you – without any results I may want to add."

"Sure, but I am not CSI. I just did a cursory search. I didn't open any drawers, slipped under the bed or dusted for prints."

"So you think we should ask him for his consent to do another search?"

"Somehow I don't think he'd go for that. A search warrant may be in order." Water suggested.

"Yeah, based on what? Walker's half baked allegations?" Poole was doubtful.

"If he's the guy, there's got to be something in his past. Melody pulled up his records but there was nothing. Shit, I forgot to tell you. Martin claimed to have been grading tests and submitting them the night Sabine disappeared. Well, he submitted them the night before!"

"Melody? You checked his records without a warrant? Boy, first off: Bad move because anything you would find is inadmissible. Second: Balls – didn't think you had that kind of advanced Cowboy attitude in you. Third: Who's Melody?" Poole looked quizzically at Water.

Water laughed before answering: "Thanks for the compliments – I guess."

"And the answer to my question is?" Poole insisted.

"She works in the office. She was very helpful. That's all." Water felt his cheeks getting hot.

"Since it is unlikely that we'll get a warrant for Martin's house or his records, why don't you talk to your girlfriend tomorrow morning and see if she knows anything else about him that didn't make its way into his official records." Poole had a big grin on his face before he pursed his lips and blew a kiss at Water.

"Ah, just doing my job to the best of my ability, Sir."

"Yeah, you keep telling yourself that." Poole snorted.

Chapter Seventy Nine

Melody Rodriguez and Jerome Water,
Miami (Tuesday, March 10th, 2015, 9:00 am)

Water was heading back over to Melody's office to try to extract more information on Prof. Martin. He wasn't kidding himself though – he would have been heading that way soon anyhow. She really was very attractive and also funny – plus they had a dinner date coming up.

He suddenly realized that it had been Tamargo who first noticed their connection. Where was Tamargo? Water picked up his phone and dialed Det. Poole's number.

"Hey Poole, anything on Tamargo?"

"Nothing, but I put out an alert to all patrol units."

"I really hope he's just pulling our chain, but I don't believe my own hopes…!" Water trailed off.

"I hear you. Let me know what your girlfriend finds."

Water didn't reply but just disconnected the call. While he knew that Poole was trying to lift their spirits about Tamargo's absence – he just didn't feel like bantering.

Pulling into the short term parking area close to the Graham Center and displaying his MDPD parking decal on the dashboard, he walked over to Melody's office. She immediately picked up on his solemn expression and asked:

"Jerome, what happened? Are you okay?"

"Yeah, actually no. We don't know where Tamargo is. He somehow just disappeared."

"That was your friend who came with you before – right?"

"Yes." was Water short response.

"I am so sorry. So he just disappeared? How can that happen?"

"Wish I had the answer to that. Unfortunately, we still have a murderer out there. So I have to ask you another favor that may get you into trouble." Water looked at her questioningly. "Please know that you don't have to help me – and probably shouldn't. It may cost you your job."

"Well, now that you put it that way – no!" she said before breaking into a wide smile. "I'm sorry, just trying to lighten the mood ‑ you already took my heart! What's a job?" she smiled at him for a brief second before touching his hand that he had placed on her elevated desk countertop. "Jerome, I really hope that your friend is okay!"

"Thanks Melody." Water swallowed hard before continuing. "Is there any way that you could get 'unofficial' information about Prof. Martin?"

"Like what's not in his official file?"

"Exactly."

"Well, I know the secretary in the office of the Dean of the Business School pretty well. We have lunch together quite often. I'll give her a call and see if she knows anything." she was already picking up the phone.

"Hi Carmen, its Melody. I was wondering if you would be willing to give me an unofficial answer to an unofficial question." Melody opened the conversation.

"No, I have not been drinking since our last girls' night out...and this is probably something that could get you into trouble." Melody listened for a few seconds.

"Yeah, since our last night out I have no doubt that 'trouble' is your middle name. Is there anything that you know about Prof. Martin that it not officially known about him?"

"Sure, we could meet you by the lake."

"Oh, a friend of mine who's with the cops."

"No, no one is in trouble. He just wants to make sure he's not missing anything. Five minutes. Okay." Melody hung up the phone.

"She'll meet us out by the lake in five minutes. Don't know how much she knows though."

"Thanks Melody." Water replied before gallantly bowing and letting her walk by him.

They met Carmen on the bridge by the small body of water that separated the Green Library and the Business School building.

"Melody – you didn't tell me you were going to show up with Mr. March from the Police Academy Calendar!" Carmen opened. This time Water was in good company since Melody's facial color changed as well.

"Carmen, this is serious." she tried to recover.

"Yeah, he looks serious enough that if I had known, I'd have been smart enough to put on some make-up!"

"Hi Carmen, my name is Jerome Water. I am a Detective with the MDPD and we are investigating certain… ahem… irregularities. Would you happen to know of any complaints against Prof. Martin that may not have made it into his personal file?"

"Not to be a party pooper – am I allowed to reveal this kind of information?" Carmen inquired semi-seriously.

"Well, it's just that…" Melody started before Waters cut her off.

"No, you are technically not at liberty to disclose this kind of information without Prof. Martin's consent or a warrant that compels you to do so."

"Wow – now it sounds really interesting. What did he do?"

"Nothing. I am just conducting a background check on a number of faculty members, and Melody mentioned that you may have information that might not be in his official file." Water lied.

"But I am helping the police – right?" Carmen wanted to know while smiling and looking Water up and down.

"This is not official – otherwise I'd have handed you a warrant. So to be honest, while you're helping the police – you're also doing something illegal." Water opted for full disclosure.

"So I'd be like a Bad Girl helping the good guys – I am in!" Carmen responded with a dead serious look on her face before breaking out into a Cuban style roar of laughter.

Water exchanged a look with Melody before refocusing on Carmen. "Are you sure? You could get into trouble."

"Melody – didn't I already tell you earlier? 'Trouble' is my Middle Name!"

"You're taking a risk – but don't let me stop you – 'Trouble'." Water said with a grin on his face.

"Really, there is no second 'hidden' file on any of the staff, but there are some things I've overheard. If I recall correctly, there were allegations that Prof. Martin was dating a student. However, that was never really confirmed. Oh, wait there were actually two students that claimed that he had asked them out."

"What did his boss do?" Water asked.

"The Dean was furious. He called Martin in and questioned him for a while. I didn't really hear the whole conversation, but at one time Martin shouted that he was the only real Professor on the faculty staff and that the Dean should not listen to unsubstantiated rumors. Shortly after that the conversation was over."

"Anything else?

"Nope, that was it. There never was, as far as I am aware of, another incident. Well, at least I am not aware of any other conversation between the Dean and Prof. Martin."

"Carmen, I truly appreciate your information."

"Melody – if you ever get tired of this guy – give me a call." Carmen gave Melody a smile that exposed all of her thirty-two teeth.

"Right." Melody answered before snaking her arm under Water's and starting to walk back towards her office.

"Nice meeting you Det. Water!" Carmen shouted.

"Same here." Water responded with a smile on his face.

"So what do you think of Carmen?"

"Quite a character your friend. Must be fun to go out with her."

"You're interested in going out with her?" Melody gave him an annoyed look from the side.

"No, what I meant is that you guys must be having fun when you're going out."

Jerome thanked Melody for her help and dropped her off in her office before heading back to his car. He had hoped for something a bit more interesting and substantive than what he learned, but had to admit to himself that there could be a pattern. Professor dates college students, and then students disappear. He hit the speed dial for Poole and filled him in on the latest development.

Chapter Eighty

Jerome Water,
Miami (Tuesday, March 10th, 2015, 10:55 am)

Water found Poole hunched over sitting at his computer. Pulling up a chair from another desk, he settled next to him.

"What are you up to?"

"Detective work." was the short reply.

Inching forward Water took a look at the screen. Looked like a Newspaper article from a paper in New Mexico.

"What is this article all about?" Water wanted to know.

"Apparently Martin's wife had a tragic accident shortly after they got married. It doesn't really say in this article but I'm sure he was a person of interest to the cops down in New Mexico."

"So you think he was involved in her death?" Water asked while motioning with his head towards the screen.

"Don't know. But I will contact colleagues in New Mexico and ask for the file."

Water relaxed in his chair and thought about the situation for a minute before asking Poole: "Hey Poole, are you still holding Walker?"

"Nah, I released him a couple of hours ago. Wish I hadn't. Thomas Sander was waiting outside in the reception area. Believe it or not, he started talking to Walker and they somehow got along. Guess Walker convinced him that he wasn't the bad guy – that they are sharing a mutual interest!"

"Are you kidding me?"

"Wish I was, but it's the gospel truth."

"So what happened next?"

"They left like two long lost brothers that finally reunited."

"Damn, just when you think you've seen it all, heard it all, something like this happens." was Water's short comment.

"My sentiments exactly."

"I just hope this doesn't end in disaster." Water was shaking his head.

Chapter Eighty One

Benjamin Walker and Thomas Sander,
Miami (Tuesday, March 10th, 2015, 10:20 am)

When Thomas Sander saw Detective Poole entering the reception area with a person that clearly seemed to be a suspect, he looked at him questioningly.

"Detective Poole is this person a suspect in my sister's disappearance?"

"I'm very sorry Mr. Sander, but we cannot comment on an open investigation even to family members. However, having said that, no, at this time he is not a suspect."

Sander looked at Walker before getting up and walking over to him.

"Do you know anything about the disappearance of my sister?" he continued while appraising Walker.

"I believe I know something, but the cops are not really listening to me." Walker responded while looking at Sander curiously.

"Maybe we should have a little talk then?" Sander suggested.

"Anything. As long as it helps us find Sabine!" was Walker's response.

"How about we go over to Sabine's apartment?" Sander suggested.

"Detective Poole has my car been released, and if so where is it at?" Walker had turned towards Poole hoping for a positive answer.

"Sorry, but your car is still at the CSI unit. It will probably take them another day to put everything back together."

"Would you mind calling us a taxi then?" Sander wanted to know.

"No problem. Sergeant, would you please call a taxi for these two gentlemen." Poole answered while looking at the Desk Sergeant located behind the counter.

Nodding towards Poole he picked up the phone and called for a taxi.

"Why don't we wait outside for the taxi to get here?" Sander suggested.

"Sure." Walker answered while walking towards the exit.

Once outside the police station Sander looked at Walker.

"If you have anything to do with the disappearance of my sister, I promise you right now, that I will kill you!" Sander informed Walker looking straight at him.

"I wouldn't want it any other way."

"Now that we got that out of the way, what information do you have that could help me find Sabine?"

"Us!"

"What?"

"Help us find Sabine! So far, I have no proof, but I strongly believe that Professor Martin is involved in her disappearance. I have seen him late at night over at Sabine's apartment. When I questioned him about her disappearance he was just way too smug. And while he did not admit to having abducted her, I really think he is the guy."

"How come you observed Martin in front of my sister's apartment?"

"Okay, let's get this out of the way. I have a huge crush on your sister. And yes, I may have been, what the cops call -stalking - her. However, I have never, nor would I ever, hurt your sister!"

Sander took a long hard look at Walker, swallowed hard and turned towards the taxi that had just pulled up. Sander got into the passenger seat while Walker entered the rear. They both were silent on the fifteen minute drive to Sabine's apartment.

When the taxi pulled into the parking lot Sander quickly got his wallet out and paid the driver. Walker followed Sander to Sabine's apartment while entertaining thoughts of having made a big mistake by going into the lion's den with a guy that was not only agitated but also a lot stronger than him.

Once inside the apartment Sander was the perfect host. He directed Walker over to the sofa before walking to the kitchen, opening the fridge and offering him a Heineken from the twelve pack that was located on the lower shelf. Walker accepted and they settled down on the sofa. After a few minutes of small talk they both started to open up and talked about their background. When Sander found out that Walker had grown up in Germany they decided to switch to Sander's native language – German. It only took a few more minutes of going over each other's backgrounds to find out that they shared the same hometown.

"Let's assume that you are right and Martin is holding Sabine. The real question then is – where!" Sander brought their conversation back to the present.

"I checked the property records for Miami Dade, and his house is the only one under his name." Walker informed Thomas.

"But he could have a house somewhere other than in Miami." Sander answered while getting up to retrieve the laptop he had purchased only a couple of days earlier.

Armed with his laptop and two more Heinekens Sander sat down again. "What do you call the office that is in charge of all the Real Estate here in Miami?"

"Miami Dade County Property Appraiser's Office."

"What cities are close by?" Sander asked.

"Well, I believe the appraiser's offices are organized by counties. So the closest one would be Broward County."

"Why don't we try that one?"

A few minutes later they finished their unsuccessful search of Broward, Palm Beach and Monroe counties. They sat in silence before Sander bolted forward in his seat. "What if he has it under a corporate name?"

"Yeah, he has some investment company!" Walker replied excitedly.

"You know the name?"

"No, but I think Florida has a website with all corporations. Why don't you search for it?"

After a couple more minutes they had found the website and entered Martin's name under 'officers and registered agents'. The website immediately jumped to a page displaying all 'Martin's' that were officers or registered agents of corporations in Florida.

"What's his first name again?" Sander asked.

"Robert."

"Here it is. He has one corporation – Martin Investments, and a partnership called El Dorado. The partnership was established only a few months ago."

"Try those names on the property appraiser's site." Walker urged.

Opening up the appraiser's site for Miami Dade, Sander entered Martin Investments, but got no results. He quickly entered El Dorado into the field for the search.

They both sat back looking at each other when the result was displayed.

"No shit!" was all Sander said.

"Isn't that right behind Martin's house?" Walker added in bewilderment.

"Looks like it. This one here – right?"

"Yeah, klick on it."

"S.O.B." Sander shouted when the name of the owner appeared on the screen.

"Are you fucking kidding me?" Walker shook his head.

"Why don't we find out?" was Sander's stone-faced, yet excited, response.

"There's just one problem. If they catch me again at Martin's house I am going back on their radar."

"Yeah, but we're not really going to Martin's house - are we? We will be checking into El Dorado's property!"

"Hey, when you're right - you're right. That does leave the question of transportation though."

"There is a car rental place not too far from here. Why don't we hoof it over there?" Walker suggested.

"Why don't we take some tools with us?" Sander asked rhetorically.

Chapter Eighty Two

Jerome Water and Eric Poole,
Miami (Tuesday, March 10th, 2015, 11:55 am)

"You don't think the boys would do anything stupid – do you?" Water asked while looking at Poole questioningly.

"You know, at this point in our investigation, I'm almost banking on it. It would be nice, for the civilians to do our dirty work for once." Poole responded with a funny look on his face.

"Are you for real? Is that why you introduced the two?"

"Rookie, don't forget I always go by the book." Poole gave Water a stern look.

"How long do you think it will take Walker to convince Sander to go over to Martin's house? And if they do, what do you think will happen next?"

"Do I look like Jesus? How would I know what they will do? However, why don't we hedge our bet and camp out in front of Martin's house?"

"Okay, why don't I get a couple of sandwiches and some water from the lunch room and then we go out on our date?"

"I just wish that Tamargo was with us. I have a feeling in my stomach that something bad happened to him. Somehow I think it may be connected to Martin. If that asshole is in any way connected to Tamargo's disappearance, I will skin him myself." Poole added while pulling a cigarette out of his shirt's breast pocket.

"You won't light up that shit in the station – will you?"

"I am way to close to retirement to fuck up like that." Poole responded while showing his yellow teeth through a crooked smile.

"Should we request some backup?"

"Based on what? I think we have to do this by ourselves." Poole responded while walking towards the lobby.

They got into Water's car and drove the short distance over to Martin's house. Looking for an unsuspicious place to observe Martin's house from, they ended up parking in the same place that Walker had chosen only a few days earlier. Their position allowed an unobstructed view of the front of Martin's house. It appeared that Martin, based on the fact that his car was not in the driveway, was not home. They looked at each other and realized they might be spending quite a bit of time together.

"Poole, you never really told me how you ended up being a cop." Water opened.

"I have never told you, because you have never asked me. Besides, it's a rather boring story."

"Well, the way I see it we have a few minutes on our hands, why don't you entertain me with a boring story?"

"Since you are begging me, I will disclose my humble beginnings on the police force to you." Poole allowed before rearranging his rear-end in the passenger seat. "In high school I was - what some people would call - a bully. At times I also took some liberties with the law. There was this abandoned house in my neighborhood, and a couple of friends of mine and I decided to remove a toilet, and place a rather large amount of explosives in the sewer pipe to find out what would happen to the septic tank. We had a little pool going, and I had predicted that the septic tank would explode and open up on top like a crater. I don't mind telling you that I collected the money. Unfortunately, well, in retrospect luckily Officer Thomas was the one to respond to the explosion. All my friends were able to make a clean getaway. I however was so mesmerized by the explosion that I had stayed behind. I was already too old for the officer to give me a good spanking. He did the second best thing by sitting me down on the dirty bathroom floor and threatening me with juvenile detention and other serious consequences. Back then I was also a bit of a smartass, and gave him a little lip. Which ended up being a mistake, because he then cuffed me, put me in the back of his cruiser and drove me home. My dad blew a fuse when Officer Thomas told him about my little stunt and what the potential penalties could be. To top it off, he informed my dad that he would be financially responsible for all of the property damage. My dad asked Officer Thomas if he could talk to me for a minute and took me to the bedroom, where I received the beating of my life. Officer Thomas actually stepped in after a few minutes and stopped my dad. Told him that in his opinion Justice had been served and the case was closed for him. Anyhow, I was very impressed by the officer's compassion for a stupid kid. So after high school and four years in the Army I decided to join the Force." Poole finished with a little smirk on his face.

They both sat in silence for a minute before Water opinioned: "So deep down inside – you're a bad ass!"

"You better believe it." Poole answered dryly.

Chapter Eighty Three

Julio Touza, one of the security guards at Miami International Airport, was driving around in his golf cart in the Flamingo parking garage with a friend from out of town. While this was against regulation, he wanted to show his friend where they had just recently found the car of a missing student.

"Right there, where the Marauder is parked." Julio pointed when they got closer. Parking right behind the car Julio indicated were all the police tape had been blocking traffic from getting closer to the potential crime scene.

"What the fuck is this smell?" his friend Alfredo inquired. "Man, this is nasty." They both got out of the golf cart and approached the vehicle. "It's coming from the trunk."

"All right, step back from the vehicle." Julio informed his friend. Now back in his official capacity he crouched down and looked under the vehicle. No dead animal that could cause the smell. "This is no good. I will have to call it in. You should probably not be here, so why don't you wait at La Carreta."

Alfredo quickly walked towards the elevator, intermittently stopping to look over his shoulder to see what Julio was doing.

"Sergeant, this is Julio Touza, I think we may have a problem on the top floor of the Flamingo garage. Right in the very same parking space where we found the car of the missing student. It's a black Mercury Marauder that has a horrible smell coming from it. I could not see anything inside the car. So I assume there's something in the trunk." Julio listened for the response from his supervisor. "Yes, I've checked under the car. There is nothing." After listening for another brief period of time he responded: "Yes Sir, I will secure the area and make sure that nobody gets close to the vehicle."

Within minutes three Miami Dade County police officers pulled up their vehicles in the vicinity of the suspicious car. The officers quickly roped off the area ensuring that it wouldn't be contaminated.

Julio's supervisor also appeared on the scene.

"This is more than just a coincidence. I mean, we just had another vehicle towed from here that belonged to a missing student. Maybe we should give the detective that was investigating the matter a call." He suggested.

One of the MDC police officers immediately agreed and called Dispatch to find out which detective had been on the scene previously.

Chapter Eighty Four

Benjamin Walker and Thomas Sander,
Miami (Tuesday, March 10th, 2015, 1:22 p.m.)

After the recently formed duo of Walker & Sander had walked a couple of blocks over to the car rental station, and obtained a gray Ford Fusion for their little road trip, they set out for the property behind Martin's house.

"You know, just in case Martin is actually in that house, we should probably park the car far away outside his line of sight." Sander suggested.

"Why don't we do a drive-by first and see if there is any parking available close by. If not, we may have to park at Miami Dade College, or on Killian Drive and walk back from there."

They rode in silence for a few minutes before Sander asked Walker: "I am still not really clear on your obsession with my sister. From what you have told me you guys never even really met."

"It is complicated. My dad made the mistake of marrying someone who was wrong for him. I have promised myself to never make that mistake. And while your sister is extremely beautiful, to me she just seemed to be a very good, wholesome and positive person. When I finally decided that I should introduce myself to your sister, I found out that she was missing."

"So what you are saying is that Sabine does not even know about your feelings for her?" Sander looked at Martin in surprise. "Yup, that is correct."

"Okay, we're getting close. It is about two more blocks, but we should probably start looking for parking." Walker said when he pulled off Killian Drive.

As always in residential neighborhoods in Miami, there was no public parking available other than in front of people's homes.

After making another right turn Walker instructed Sander: "Keep your eyes peeled for the house number - 9695"

"Hey, Walker why don't you slow down? The uneven numbers are on the north side – correct?"

"Yeah, it should be coming up soon." Walker responded excitedly, while slowing down even further.

"Over there, the white house with the chain link fence." Walker exclaimed. They continued their slow drive by and noticed no car in the driveway, and no lights in the windows.

"Okay, there is no way we can park in the street and not be noticed in case Martin comes by this way." Sander announced.

"Let me continue down this street and see if there's any parking." Walker responded.

They continued their slow drive down the street, but couldn't find any available parking. Walker accelerated the car and headed towards Miami Dade College.

"Wasn't there a school back the other way? Why don't we park there?" Sander wanted to know.

Benjamin made a quick U-turn and they headed back east on Killian Drive.

After a couple of minutes he turned left and pulled into the parking lot of Miami Killian Senior High. The lot was vacant except for a couple of vans.

Retrieving the bag of tools they had packed earlier, they started walking back towards Martin's secondary property.

"There was no movement inside of the house that I could detect when we drove by.

However, Martin may still be inside. Any idea what we will do once we get to the house?" Walker inquired.

"How sure are you that he is the guy? I mean, if we know it's him, there is nothing to hold me back."

Walker kept walking for a while before answering Sander: "Man, while I am not willing to shoot him without further proof, I honestly believe, that he is involved in Sabine's disappearance."

"All right then. How about we check out his main house first, see if he is home and take it from there. Realistically, if his car is not in the driveway, there are no lights on in either one of the houses; we should be good to go to investigate the second house." Sander suggested.

Walker, who had essentially acquiesced to the fact that Sander was going to be the unelected leader of their little excursion, nodded in agreement.

When they turned off Killian Drive onto the side street where Martin's main house was located, Walker noticed the nose of a familiar car protruding past the hedges in the driveway across from Martin's house. "Shit, the cops are waiting in front of his house."

"Where?" Sander asked.

"Not in the street, they are hidden in the driveway across from Martin's house." Walker responded while briskly turning back to Killian Drive. Sander got the bigger picture quickly and followed him.

"I guess we will have to walk around the block, and approach Martin's other house from the other side." Walker offered. "This is certainly complicating matters." Sander hissed. "Don't worry, so far they have proven to be totally inept!"

"Yeah, but they might get lucky and catch us burglarizing a house."

"Nah, they are camped out in front of his house, and chances are they will sit there for hours eating doughnuts." Walker chuckled.

They continued walking in silence, rounding the block and approaching the property from the other side. Realizing that two guys walking a residential neighborhood with a gym bag looked extremely suspicious, Walker said: "Listen, when we get to the house, and there are no lights on, we need to just walk up and quickly gain access."

"Yes, I have watched a lot of police shows about life in America and know that two white guys aimlessly walking around in a residential neighborhood are extremely suspicious and

subject to being shot by neighbors on-sight."
Sander said with a big toothy smile on his face.

"Are you being racist?" Walker responded
with a smile, even though he was very nervous
about the task ahead.

Getting closer to the house, they noticed
that there were no lights on inside. Breathing
a sigh of relief, Walker shifted the gym bag
with the tools to his other hand. They found
the front gate locked and quickly jumped it.
Walking up to the front door, they weren't
surprised to find it locked.

Without wasting time they circled the house
and found themselves in front of the rear door
leading to the kitchen. Unsurprising, the door
was locked as well. Walker placed the gym bag
on the ground opened it quickly and retrieved
a screwdriver and a hammer. Luckily the door
was wooden and it only took a few hard swings
to drive the screwdriver into the door hard
enough to bust the deadbolt open. They
quickly stepped inside and pulled the damaged
door closed behind them.

"Can you believe this shit?" Sander wanted
to know when he turned around and saw the
inside of the house.

Chapter Eighty Five

Prof. Martin, Miami (Tuesday, March 10th, 2015, 1:23 p.m.)

Water and Poole had been sitting in silence for some time when they observed Martin's little BMW pulling into the driveway. "What's the game plan?" Water inquired. "How about we sit tight for a while, and see if he stays home or goes somewhere else. Since we don't really know if he's the guy, or if he is, where he is holding Sabine, I'd say we sit on him for a while." Poole responded.

"Okay boss." Water responded while staring across the street watching Martin exiting his car, scanning the neighborhood, and walking towards his house.

""I don't see him holding Sabine in his house. While I do believe that he is a pompous ass, he did not strike me as stupid." Water volunteered.

"People are stupid – and criminals even more so." Poole responded while shaking his head.

"What do you really think happened to Tamargo?"

"I don't have the faintest idea. He either drove into a canal, or was killed by Walker or Martin." Poole responded with a sad look on his face.

"So either way, there is no happy ending?" Water said while looking intently at Poole. "Afraid not." Poole opined.

Water's phone started ringing, startling both of them. "Detective Water" he answered.

"Detective, this is Dispatch. We just received a call from Miami International Airport. They have found a black Mercury Marauder parked in the very same spot where the missing student's car had been discovered. The officers that responded to the call from security wanted to make sure that you are in the loop. They wanted you to know, that there is a very strong smell of decomposition coming from the trunk of the vehicle. They are waiting for your instructions."

"Please have CSI go to the scene. We are on our way." Water answered while looking wild eyed at Poole, who had overheard the conversation. "Our worst nightmare has just been confirmed." Poole said quietly.

Water started the car and quickly pulled out of the driveway. A few more turns later he was on the Turnpike extension gunning the car towards the airport. It took them a mere nineteen minutes to get there and find their way to the top floor of the Flamingo garage. Parking their car a few feet outside of the marked area they quickly exited and walked over to the other officers. They hadn't even gotten close to the Marauder when they noticed the smell.

"This is no good!" Poole announced. "No it isn't!" Water responded.

"Do you have a crowbar in your trunk?" Poole was addressing one of the officers standing next to the car. "Sure, let me go get it." The officer responded and walked towards his patrol car. "I don't know that I have the stomach to see what's inside of the trunk." Water said.

"I hear you." Poole replied.

The officer Poole had spoken to returned with a crowbar. It only took a couple of minutes until he was able to pry the lid of the trunk open. The stench from the open trunk made everyone step back and cover their noses. Once they recovered, they all stepped forward as a unit. Inside of the trunk they saw the outline of a man covered in tarp. One of the officers put on latex gloves and cut the plastic with a knife that he had retrieved from his pocket.

"Shit!" Water cried out, when he saw the face of the victim.

"Fuck – I don't believe this shit! Let's get that son of a bitch. I'll take care of things here. You go back to Martin's house."

"I don't know." Water was torn. "There is nothing you can do here." Poole looked at Water. "Go!"

Water stood for a minute, immobilized, and overcome with grief. Taking another look at his friend he turned and walked towards his car. "We'll find him – and I'll kill the motherfucker!" Water mumbled under his breath.

Chapter Eighty Six

Benjamin Walker and Thomas Sander,
Miami (Tuesday, March 10th, 2015, 2:03 p.m.)

There was not a single piece of furniture in the house. They split up and investigated all the rooms – and found them to be utterly empty. "I don't get it." Sander said. "Neither do I." Walker muttered.

"Why in the hell would he have bought this house, if not to hold Sabine?"

"It just doesn't make sense." Walker responded. "So he must be holding her in his own house." Sander said while scratching his head.

"This property is directly behind his house. There's a garage behind this house. Let's go and see what's in it." They left the living room, walked through the hallway and entered the kitchen that was located in the rear of the house. Opening the exterior door to the kitchen they exited into the backyard.

They both walked over to the two car garage that was sitting behind the house.

"Looks like the garage door opening is blocked up." Walker said. "Yeah, I guess the door to the garage is on the side." Sander responded while walking to the other side of it with Walker following him. "That's a steel door with a very substantial bolt and padlock." Sander said once he discovered the door. Without further ado he turned around and walked back into the house to retrieve the tool bag they had left behind. Walker stood motionless in front of the door for a few seconds before he started banging on the door: "Sabine, are you in there?" He shouted. The door seemed to be very substantial and solid judging by the muffled noise his fist was making on it.

"Are you trying to alert Martin?" Sander wanted to know. "Who gives a shit?" Walker replied, while banging on the door again before putting his ear to it. "Nothing!"

Sander didn't respond, but dug into the tool bag and retrieved the hammer he had put back in earlier. "Step back." Sander instructed Walker before starting to attack the padlock. He went at it for a couple of minutes before Walker shouted: "Stop! I think I heard something." They both put their ear to the door but couldn't hear anything.

After a minute they both stepped back and Sander continued his quest to bust the padlock open. The lock was definitely heavy duty and after a couple more minutes Sander handed the hammer to Walker, who continued banging on it.

Another six strikes and the lock finally gave. Walker dropped the hammer and looked at Sander, who pushed him aside and opened the door.

Chapter Eighty Seven

Jerome Water,
Kendall (Tuesday, March 10th, 2015, 2:31 p.m.)

Upon his return, he chose the same parking space they've had before. The little BMW was parked in the driveway. He decided to get out of the car and check for lights inside Martin's house. Not wanting to alert the man, he walked to the corner of the property. Recalling the layout of the house, he saw lights on in the living room and master bedroom. As far as he could tell there was no movement inside of the house.

Water was unsure of what to do next. He slowly walked back to his car and slid into the driver seat. Leaning his head back onto the headrest he was contemplating Tamargo's fate. He had not known him for long, but had somehow gotten close to him. How in hell did he end up killed and stuffed into the trunk of his own car?

Tired of waiting in his car he hit the speed dial on his cell phone without thinking.

"Hey Poole, I think I am going to talk to Martin." he opened.

"Jerome, listen, we're all a little emotional at this time. Don't do something you will regret later!"

"Like beating the shit out of him?"

"Yeah, something like that."

"I'll be good, talk to you later." Water said before disconnecting the call and getting out of his car. Walking up to the front door he took a few very deep breaths to calm himself down. After having rung the doorbell he was kept waiting for a couple of minutes.

"Detective Water; what a surprise to see you again." Martin greeted him after having opened the door. "Don't tell me you are here to search my house again. If so, I assume you are now armed with a search warrant." He continued.

"Actually I am just coming back from the airport." Water said while watching Martin closely for his reaction.

"Okay." Martin answered coolly, but couldn't stop a slight twitch of his left eye.

"Would you like to guess what I was doing at the airport?"

"Are we playing twenty questions?" Martin came back, but did not look as confident as he had a few seconds ago.

"Let's cut the crap, you are our prime suspect in the murder of Sandra Resterpo, Graciela Manciani, the disappearance of Sabine Sander and now the murder of Franco Tamargo."

"Are you out of your mind? Just because I happen to teach at FIU does not mean that I had anything to do with their murders. And that Tamargo guy I don't even really know."

"You may think that you're really smart, but I will tell you one thing: if you had anything to do with the girls or Tamargo, I will get you."

"Are you threatening me Detective?"

"Hardly, that was a promise, and I have a reputation for keeping my promises." Water hissed before abruptly turning and walking back to his car.

He had barely gotten back into his car when his cell phone rang. He glanced at the display before picking up the phone saying: "What's up Mr. Walker?"

"Where are you?"

"I am in front of Martin's house."

"Why don't you drive down the street, turn left and find the house directly located behind Martin's?" Walker suggested.

"And what would I find there?"

"You are invited to a happy reunion!" Walker replied giddily.

Water quickly started the car and drove down the street as instructed.

Chapter Eighty Eight

Sander came into the garage like a German Storm Trooper before stopping in his tracks and quickly denying Walker access to the garage.

"What the hell?" Walker asked puzzled.

"Please stay outside!" Sander instructed before rushing into the garage towards his sister who was cowering on a dirty mattress.

"Tommy!" Sabine screamed with joy while at the same time trying to cover her nakedness.

Sander quickly opened the top buttons of his shirt, pulled it over his head and handed it to his sister. Sabine grabbed the shirt turned around halfway and put it on. Sander pulled her up to her feet and engulfed her in a bear hug. Putting her head to her brother's shoulder Sabine took turns laughing and crying. "Let's get you out of here!" Sander suggested before seeing the shackles on his sister's ankle.

"Hey Benjamin, you want to come in here with the hammer?" Sander called out over his shoulder.

Walker, grinning from ear to ear, but otherwise somewhat shy, walked in with the hammer and the tool bag.

"I am so happy to see that you're okay!"

"I'm sorry, who are you?" Sabine inquired.

"Sabine, this is your secret admirer Benjamin Walker, who has helped me find you." Sander informed her.

Walker didn't move for a few seconds, but then regained his composure and looked at the shackles.

"I don't think the hammer will be of much help." He continued before suggesting: "Maybe I should call Detective Water."

Glancing over towards Sabine and Thomas who had sat down on the soiled mattress, he realized that it was time to give them some space and privacy. He decided to make the call outside. After his conversation with Water he walked towards the street to meet him.

Water was pulling onto the swale in front of the property when Benjamin entered the front yard. He gave a short wave and continued to walk towards the street. Water jumped out of his car and rushed forward.

"What the hell happened?" He wanted to know.

"We found her!"

"Is she okay?"

"Yeah, Thomas and Sabine are still inside catching up."

"Inside where?"

"We found her stashed away, actually shackled to the floor, inside of Martin's garage."

"This isn't Martin's property."

"Yes it is, and it only took Thomas about five minutes to find out about it. How come that you guys couldn't figure it out?"

"Poole did all of the Internet searches, but I am sure that he would have never missed anything like this." But we can discuss this later Water ended the conversation and started walking to the garage.

"I am going to wait here." Benjamin responded.

Water carefully approached the door to the garage listening for Sabine's and Thomas' voices. When he was sure that they were not involved in a conversation, he turned the corner and walked into the garage. Despite the loss of Tamargo, he was overcome with joy to see Sabine and Thomas sitting on the mattress catching up with each other.

"I am so sorry to interrupt you guys. Is there anything that I can do at this time?"

Sabine and Thomas turned their heads to look at Water, and in unison said: "No thanks."

When Water started to turn Sander asked: "Do you have a bolt cutter in your car?"

"Sure do, let me go get it."

Rushing back towards his car he passed by Walker and stopped to say: "She seems to be alright. However, I believe she will need extensive psychological support to overcome her ordeal."

"Yeah, who knows what that fuck has done to her."

Water was opening the trunk of his car to retrieve the bolt cutter, when he heard a scream from behind the house. Not thinking twice he grabbed the bolt cutter and rushed back to the garage. Walker who had heard the scream as well was already running around the corner of the house.

When Walker stepped into the garage he saw a man dressed in a funny looking silk bathrobe and a Zorro mask frozen between the door and the siblings sitting on the mattress. Water almost knocked Walker off his feet when he turned the corner rushing into the garage. Overcoming his surprise quickly, Water dropped the bolt cutter and drew his gun, immediately leveling it at the masked man.

"Do not move - hands where I can see them!" Water shouted.

The masked man did not move, but stood frozen staring at Sabine.

"Turn around slowly. Do not move your hands." Water told the man.

As instructed, the man slowly turned towards Water, who had to catch his breath when he realized that he was facing Professor Martin.

"What an unexpected surprise – didn't figure to see you so soon again!" Water exclaimed, surprised and stunned at the same time.

Martin recovered surprisingly fast from having been caught in his silly outfit in the garage where Sabine had been held captive. "Wow, I was just walking around in my backyard, when I heard the commotion over here and thought to investigate what was going on."

"You want me to believe, that you always walk around dressed up as Zorro ready to go into a sauna? Water hissed at him.

"I do not really care what you think; I do have a right to walk around in my backyard." came the somewhat nervous answer from Martin.

"He is the monster!" Sabine shouted, while Thomas was getting up from the mattress. Once he started unfolding his rather large frame in front of Martin, the professor started to stumble backwards, surprised by how tall Thomas was. Walker, who had been standing in the open doorway, violently pushed him back into the garage. "You are not going anywhere buddy!" He announced while his victim lost his balance and fell forward, past Thomas, and ended up on the mattress next to Sabine. She started screaming and hitting him with her fists. Martin was lying on his belly; his robe had slid up his back exposing his bare rear end. He quickly rolled over onto his side and grabbed his robe, covering himself before starting to fend off Sabine's blows to his head.

Water recovered enough from his initial surprise to step forward and prevent Sabine from continuing her attack on Martin. At the same time he was blocking Thomas from getting to Martin.

"All right, this is it guys - everyone stays where they are." He instructed the group, while holstering his gun and reaching for his cell phone.

"Dispatch, this is Detective Water. I am requesting an ambulance and a patrol car to 9695 Montgomery Drive." He hung up his phone and addressed everyone present in the garage.

"Okay, Professor Martin you're under arrest for kidnapping Sabine Sander. Everyone else, cool it. Professor, before I put the handcuffs on you, please make sure to tie the rope to your costume." Water waited until his request was met before he put the handcuffs on Martin. "Stand right here and do not move." He instructed before picking up the bolt cutters that he had dropped earlier. Kneeling down next to Sabine he cut her shackles off. Once everyone was mobile, Water instructed them to walk to the street. While they were walking Martin started to complain: "This arrest is illegal. I have not committed any wrongdoing and was subjected to a physical assault in front of a police officer who did not intervene."

The entire group stopped walking and looked at him in disbelief. "Boy, you've really got a set of brass balls on you!" Walker stated, while Water quickly stepped between Martin and Thomas to prevent the later from getting closer to Martin.

"Detective, why don't you go ahead and this gentleman and I will have a brief conversation?" Thomas suggested. "I feel you, but unfortunately I can't do that." was the immediate response.

When they started walking again Walker somehow managed to bump into Martin, sending him to the ground. Having his hands cuffed behind him Martin was unable to break the fall, hitting the ground hard with his face first. To everyone's dismay his robe opened up again. Water gave Walker a dirty look and helped Martin back up to his feet.

"For God's sake, cut it out!" He said angrily. "My apologies, I tripped and lost my balance." Walker replied.

"Right!" Water moaned before he took it upon himself to cover up Martin's exposed lower body.

"My attorney is going to have a field day with what just transpired here!" Martin spit.

Luckily the ambulance and a patrol car arrived within minutes after they reached the street. Sabine and Thomas entered the rescue vehicle after a quick examination of Sabine. Water instructed one of the officers to secure the crime scene and to stay there until the crime scene unit arrived. The other one was to deliver the suspect, Professor Martin, to the police station.

Having taken care of the business at hand, he turned to Walker and asked: "How in hell did you guys find Sabine?"

Putting a big grin on his face, Walker replied: "German ingenuity! We searched for additional properties owned by Martin. Turns out, he owns the house and garage that we found Sabine in. And guess what – it is registered under a corporation. He was trying to hide the fact that he was using it for his obviously perverted games!"

"Didn't know you're German."

"Yeah, my mother was German."

"What do you mean was?"

"She passed away." was Walker's simple answer.

"Anyway, great job on finding out about Martin's hidden property. However, you guys

should have called me before you went in."
Water pointed out.

"Maybe, but you guys were soft balling
Martin."

"No we weren't. You've got to realize that we
have to operate within the parameters of the
law. Give me a second before we continue."
Water hit the speed dial for Poole on his cell
phone.

"Poole, we've got Sabine. Looks like Martin
is the perp. I've sent him over to the station.
Sabine and Thomas are on their way to a
hospital, and I will be over shortly to explain
everything."

"Where is your car?" He addressed Walker
again.

"Not too far from here, I can walk."

"All right, this may get complicated, so
please do me a favor and stay away from the
station. I promise I will keep you updated."
Water informed Walker while shooting him,
what he hoped to be a stern look, before
turning to walk to his car.

"Hey Water – we got Sabine alive – give me
a smile!" Walker called after him.

Turning around to face Walker, Water put on the biggest smile he could muster under the circumstances.

"Yeah, you did good – but I lost a friend!" He said before turning away.

"What do you mean?"

"Franco – he's dead!"

"Look man, I am sorry, I didn't know! The other guy that was there when you arrest me - right?" Walker responded while Water was getting into his car. Looking back one last time he replied in a low voice: "Yeah, that guy."

Chapter Eighty Nine

Jerome Water, Eric Poole, and Prof. Martin
Police-Station (Tuesday, March 10th, 2015, 3:55 p.m.)

The station wasn't too far from the crime scene, and it only took him fifteen minutes to get there. He quickly parked his vehicle in the lot and walked into the station. When he passed the Desk Sergeant, he was informed that Martin and Poole, who apparently had gotten back from the airport, where in interview room two. He walked halfway down the long hallway before entering the observation room next to the room Martin and Poole were occupying. With a sigh of relief he noticed that someone had shown mercy and had outfitted Martin with a somewhat less flamboyant outfit. While he wouldn't win any fashion awards in an orange jumpsuit, it still beat the silk robe.

Observing through the one-way mirror, he figured that the conversation had reached a standstill. Martin sat in his chair with his arms crossed in front of his chest, while Poole was playing with a cigarette. Water pushed the button that allowed him to listen to the nonexistent conversation between the two. After having muted the system again, he left the room to join Poole.

"Mind if I join you guys?" Water opened, before continuing: "Poole, you should have been there; it was a lot livelier than here. We had all the players in one room."

"Well, unless Tamargo was miraculously resurrected, I think there was an important player missing." Poole offered without a trace of humor in his voice.

"I didn't mean it that way, you know that." Water replied in a flat voice.

"I know; I'm just a little frustrated over the fact that no one is willing anymore to own up to what they have done." Poole said with a sharp look at Martin.

"I will entertain you just this one more time before my attorney gets here. I have nothing to do with anything concerning the person you are referencing." was Martin's short response before he started staring at the wall next to Poole.

"We'll be back when he gets here. Let's go." Poole spit while getting up from his chair.

"The guys will love you in that cute outfit of yours!" Water hissed at Martin before he joined Poole exiting the room.

They both reconvened in the observation room, where Water opened by saying: "I just hope, that the presence of – strike that - the fact that Sander and Walker illegally gained access to the garage does not throw a monkey wrench into the prosecutor's case. "

"That makes two of us. But why don't you tell me the whole story before his attorney gets here?"

"From what I've gathered, Sander and Walker somehow figured it out that Martin owns the property behind his primary residence. They then ventured onto that property, discovered that the house itself was empty and investigated the garage. After they broke into the garage, Martin appeared in his very sensitive get up, claiming that he had only come over because he had heard a commotion."

"Yeah right, we all walk around our backyards naked only covered in a silk robe. However, how did he get those scrapes and bruises on his face?" Poole asked while looking expectantly at Water.

"After I had handcuffed the suspect, namely Prof. Martin, and was walking the group back towards the street, Walker tripped on something in the back yard and accidentally knocked Martin to the ground." Water responded in his official voice with a sincere look on his face.

"Sounds good, just make sure that you don't change colors on the witness stand!" Poole said while looking at Water knowingly.

"It's the truth."

"Of course it is. Are you hungry? I'm hungry, let's go to the cafeteria." Poole said.

"They've installed a cafeteria while I was gone? Or are you referring to the break room with a vending machine?" Water had a puzzled look on his face.

"You have much to learn – it's all in the presentation."

After they had purchased some stale sandwiches and a soda from the vending machines, they sat down at one of the few tables in the break room. "How do you think this is going to play out?" Water inquired while chewing on a sandwich.

"Well, for starters, his attorney is going to advise him not to say anything to us. We will then put in a call to the prosecutor's office, where someone will inform us that we do not have enough to hold him." Poole responded after he had washed down his last bite with a gulp of soda.

"You've got to be kidding me? We don't have enough? We found Sabine in his garage while he was prancing around naked, covered by only a silk robe. Oh, did I mention the Zorro mask?" Water responded while almost choking on the food in his mouth.

"Welcome to the legal system buddy. We did not serve a search warrant on him. We had no probable cause. In fact, we did not even conduct the search. No, the search, and if I may add break in, was done by one of our former prime suspects and the brother of the victim. Now, if I was the defense attorney, I would ask the following: if these people had access to my property, were they maybe also the ones who kept Sabine prisoner there? Or who else has used my property for illegal activities?"

"Are you fucking kidding me? Thomas Sander holding his own sister as a sex slave?" Water wanted to know while his eyes had transformed into the size of saucers.

"You asked the question – I've answered it." Poole came back before taking a big bite out of his sandwich.

"What about the other girl?"

"What about her? We will see if CSI can find any evidence of her presence in the garage. But again, the defense will argue that Sander and Walker had access to it just the same as Martin did." They both continued to sit in silence working on their sandwiches and own thoughts.

"Why don't you go over to the hospital and talk to Sabine and get a full statement from her as well as Thomas? Make sure you get as many details as humanly possible. How she was abducted, what she was subjected to – and I am not even sure I want to hear that! Also get the detailed story from Thomas how he and Walker found out about the property and how they gained access to the garage. I am sure I don't have to tell you, this is important." Poole suggested.

"Will do. Who is going to tell Tamargo's family?"

"I will, as soon as Martin is squared away." Poole said with a sad expression on his face. He rubbed both of his hands over his face before picking up the leftovers of his food.

Getting up he disposed of the cellophane wrapper, napkin and empty soda can in the garbage.

"Break is over, we'll better get going."

Chapter Ninety

Prof. Martin,
Police-Station (Tuesday, March 10th, 2015, 4:18 p.m.)

As soon as the cops had left the interview room Martin leaned back in his uncomfortable chair. Admittedly at first sight his situation appeared to be a bit complicated. However, he had put in a call to one of, if not the best criminal defense attorneys in Miami. Robert White had worked miracles for some very notorious defendants. He knew he was going to be in good hands. Besides, what did they really have on him? He had been walking around in his backyard in a bathrobe, when he heard a noise from the property behind his main residence, which he owns. Any rightful owner would have to check into this. He was certain that he had not left any physical evidence in the garage. The blood left behind by his previous guests had been scrubbed off with gallons of chlorine. Granted, some of his DNA, in the form of skin, sweat, or maybe even semen may be found on the mattress. A mattress he would claim, he had recently put out in front of his house for disposal. How was he to know that the mattress would later on be used in a crime? Maybe he didn't even need the best defense attorney in town to represent him, but he immediately dismissed the thought. No sense in getting overly cocky. The legal system would work its way and he would be found not guilty.

He started to relax even further and put an arm over the back of the chair and a foot up on the table. Yup, the first thing he would ask Mr. White to do was to file suit against the Miami Dade Police Department for police brutality. After all he had the scrapes and bruises on his face to prove it.

Chapter Ninety One

Jerome Water,
Baptist Hospital (Tuesday, March 10th, 2015, 5:16 p.m.)

When he entered the room Sabine was lying in a hospital bed with Thomas sitting next to it holding her hand.

"Sorry to interrupt you guys. I hope you have had a chance to catch up. However, I really need Sabine's statement, and as a matter of fact, I will need yours as well Thomas." Water said apologetically, to which both of them nodded.

"Thomas, would you mind waiting outside while I talk to Sabine?"

"Can't he just stay in the room please?" Sabine asked in a weak voice.

"I am so sorry, but since Thomas has some involvement in this case as well, I cannot interview both of you at the same time. How about Thomas waiting right outside of the door until we're done?" Water gently suggested.

"Sabine, it's okay, I'll be right outside." Thomas said while getting up from his chair and walking to the door.

"Sabine, if it is not too hard for you, could you please lead me through everything that happened since you were kidnapped? I know this will be hard for you, but the more detailed you are the better a case we can make." Water inquired as soon as Thomas had left the room.

"What do you mean a better case? You have caught him already! Isn't he going to jail?" Sabine asked in disbelief.

"Yes, I know we have him already, but we still need to convince a jury."

"But I recognized him; he is the guy who raped me. He is the monster that has held me as a sex slave for more than a week. The bathrobe you saw him in, and the silly Zorro mask, that is his usual attire for when he comes – came - to rape me." Sabine was now clearly upset.

"Sabine, I know this is extremely difficult for you, why don't you just try to tell me everything from the beginning?" Water was trying to be as sensitive as possible. Looking at Sabine he realized that this may be a tall order for her. While he was sure that the nurses had washed and nourished her, her eyes still looked dazed and hollow. Though he was feeling very bad for her, he knew he had to press on for her statement. No sense in giving the defense attorney an opening by letting too much time elapsed between her rescue and her official statement. Of course, he couldn't really tell her what Poole had revealed to him earlier.

Sabine sat on her bed for a few minutes, just looking at her hands, before she started in a small and weak voice. Water had turned on the small digital tape recorder that he had placed on her food tray next to the bed. He listened in horror to her story, trying to only interrupt her, when details needed to be filled in. He knew that the district attorney would have many more, potentially painful, questions to ask. Nevertheless, he figured he didn't have to spring those on her this soon after her rescue. After about forty-five minutes Sabine was done, not only with her statement, but physically as well. Her voice had gotten progressively weaker and her eyelids were starting to drop. In a way he was almost thankful it was over. He had a hard time understanding what went through the mind of a pervert to subject an innocent girl to this kind of abuse!

"Thank you so much Sabine, try to get some rest. I will talk to Thomas for a few minutes, but he should be right back in here." Water said while quietly getting up from the chair that he had pulled close to Sabine's hospital bed. He softly walked out of the room into the hallway where he found Thomas dozing in a chair. He lightly touched Thomas' shoulder to see if he was semi–awake, and got an immediate reaction.

"Was ist los?" Thomas shouted in German while jumping out of the chair.

"Easy Thomas, I'm sorry for waking you up. Would it be okay to ask you a few questions now?"

"Sure." Thomas answered while rubbing the sleep out of his eyes.

"Have you eaten anything today?" Water inquired. "Do you want to go to the cafeteria?" He continued without waiting for an answer. While Thomas was clearly still disoriented, he started shaking his head. "I can't leave her." He objected.

"How about I get you some food?"

"Actually, that would be nice. Whatever they have is fine with me." Thomas answered gratefully while noticing the growl in his stomach.

Chapter Ninety Two

Eric Poole,
Tamargo residence (Tuesday, March 10th, 2015, 8:20 p.m.)

It was with a heavy heart that Poole was driving over to the Tamargo family's residence in the Westchester area of town. As soon as they had discovered Tamargo's body, he had started to blame himself. He should have never convinced the Captain to allow a civilian to partake in the investigation.

Carefully looking at the house numbers and finally identifying the correct address, he couldn't bring himself to stop in front of the house. Instead he circled the block twice before parking his car in front of his former colleague's parent's house. He was taking his time extracting himself from his car, and when he finally did, he saw Tamargo's mother looking out the front window at him. By the time he reached the front door, she was already in tears. She slowly opened the front door and motioned him in, pointing towards a wooden rocking chair, before heavily sitting down on a sofa. Poole had remained standing fidgeting with his car keys.

"Mrs. Tamargo, my name is Detective Eric Poole, I am so sorry to inform you that your son has perished. Please know that he is also a former colleague of mine, and I have always regarded him as a friend."

Mrs. Tamargo did not respond, but lowered her head, raised her hands in front of her face and started crying. After a couple of minutes Poole walked over to the sofa, pulled out a handkerchief and offered it to her. The woman continued to cry without even seeing Poole's gesture. Having been awoken by the noise in the living room, her husband walked in.

Looking at the scene, and not knowing what had happened, he asked forcefully: "What is going on?"

"Franco esta muerto!" Mrs. Tamargo managed to answer between sobs.

Her husband's knees started to buckle and Poole was barely able to reach him before he started going down hard on the living room floor. Not thinking twice Poole sat down next to him on the floor and put his arm over the man's shoulder. They all sat in silence for quite a while, with Poole being glad to still have his handkerchief.

"What happened to Franco?" The mother finally asked when she had recovered enough.

"I wish I had the answer to that question, but we haven't been able to get to the bottom of this case. However, I want you to know that not only I but everyone in the precinct is working on Franco's case." Poole answered truthfully.

"What I meant is how did he die?" Franco's mom said.

"He..." Poole paused for a second before continuing "received a blow to his head."

"We want to see our son!" Mrs. Tamargo replied with surprising strength, while her husband was nodding his head. Poole let out a slow breath and said: "I will give you a call tomorrow to let you know when and where you can see him."

The three of them sat quietly for a couple more minutes before Poole got up and helped Mr. Tamargo to his feet. He shook the man's hand before walking over to his wife whom he hugged gently. When he reached the front door, he turned around and looked at them:

"I know that there is nothing I can say to ease the pain of having lost your son - he was a very good man." he managed to say before he quickly walked out of the house where he felt his eyes tearing up again.

Chapter Ninety Three

Attorney Robert White,
Miami (Tuesday, March 10th, 2015, 7:50 p.m.)

In retrospect Martin was delighted to not have followed his earlier impulse to represent himself. While he was sure that by the time everything was said and done he would be out a substantial amount of money, so far Mr. White was earning his keep. It had taken him only a few minutes to have the judge agree to a bond of One Hundred Thousand Dollars, which Martin had been able to secure within only fifty minutes. They agreed to meet the next morning to go over the case and the necessary strategy to ensure Martin's acquittal.

By the time Martin got back to his house, looking forward to a hot shower and a good bottle of wine, the MDPD had obtained a search warrant and was going through his house with a fine comb. Martin was relegated to the sofa in the living room where he was to remain seated while the search was proceeding. Not being used to taking orders, he requested to see the search warrant, which the detective in charge produced immediately with a big grin on his face.

"Well, let me at least retrieve a bottle of wine and a glass from the kitchen."

"Fair enough - since you may be sitting on that sofa for quite a while." the grinning detective allowed.

Let that grinning idiot have his day in the sun Martin was thinking to himself, while uncorking an expensive bottle of Merlot. He poured himself a glass and relaxed on the sofa watching the police dusting for fingerprints and looking for blood splatters throughout his house. He allowed himself a little grin on his own, knowing that he had been very thorough. Two hours later he finally found himself home alone, and took the hot shower he had been looking forward to. Dressed in his favorite black silk pajamas he got comfortable in his bed. 'He who has the last laugh!' was his final thought before he fell asleep.

Chapter Ninety Four

Jerome Water and Eric Poole at State Attorney's office
(Thursday, March 12th, 2015, 9:00 a.m.)

Detectives Poole and Water were trying to get as comfortable as possible in the very uncomfortable visitor's chairs in the Assistant State Attorney's small office. The ADA, Roberto Garcia, was, Poole thought, approximately fifteen years old. He shot Water a knowing glance, before he asked: "Say, how long have you been working in this office?"

"Long enough to recognize a very weak case when I see one." Garcia responded in a much more masculine voice than Poole had anticipated. "Detectives, I realize that you have spent a lot of time on making a case against Professor Martin, for the disappearance – correction – murder of an FIU student, and the kidnapping of another. I am also aware that a former police officer and friend of yours was killed. Having said all that, please allow me to take you through the facts I am dealing with: the main crime scene, where blood of Gabriela Mancini was found and where Sabine Sander has been kept as a sex slave was, for all intents and purposes, contaminated by Mr. Walker and Mr. Sander." Garcia raised his hand to stop the Detectives from protesting.

"Believe me when I tell you that the first motion to be filed by the defense will be for dismissal based on the fact that Walker and Sander had presumably the same access to the garage that the defendant had. No, I do not believe this to be true however; it is my job to convince a jury of the defendant's peers beyond any reasonable doubt." Garcia finished while leaning back in his chair.

"Bullshit!" Water mumbled under his breath, while Poole was leaning forward in his chair placing his hands on the attorney's desk:

"What exactly is it that you guys expect us to deliver to your front porch so that you guys can have an airtight case? I've been doing this for a long time, so please spare me your answer. Blah, blah, blah, you don't want to waste the tax payers' money! At the end of the day, you don't want to lose a case and ruin your potential for a future career defending the assholes we're trying to put away!" Poole responded angrier than he had intended to.

"Detective, I realize that it must be very frustrating to work with an Assistant State Attorney who looks like he's in Senior High. Please let me assure you that I was in the top five percent of my class and I could be defending criminals for a lot more money than what I am making here at the DA's office. Don't worry; I am not insulted by your lack of confidence. However, unlike you, who leave the courtroom after the testimony, I stay behind and see the reaction of the jury and the judge. So if we are hinging our case on the sex dungeon only – we will lose!"

"What about Tamargo's blood in Martin's house?" Water interjected. "What about it?" Garcia shot back. "It is undisputed that Tamargo has been to Martin's house. The amount of blood found was so small, that even a law school student wouldn't have a problem explaining it away. I don't have to tell you this gentleman, but I will anyway: beyond a reasonable doubt! That is what we have to accomplish. So unless you can provide me with additional evidence, I am afraid that I will not be able to find a judge to even try this case." Garcia said apologetically.

"Essentially you are asking us to deliver to you the smoking gun – correct?" Water wanted to know.

"Yeah, that would be great, I will settle for something better than what we currently have."

"Well, then I guess that's what we're gonna have to get you counselor." Water said while motioning Poole to leave.

"Good luck to all of us." Garcia responded by way of goodbye. Once outside of the attorney's office Poole stopped Water in his tracks:

"You know something I don't?"

"Without knowing if this is getting us anywhere, has it ever occurred to you that Sabine may have picked up on some distinguishing marks on Martin's body while he was forcing himself upon her? And yes, I did forget to ask her about it when I spoke to her." Water conceded.

"Good thinking Rookie." Poole shot back.

Chapter Ninety Five

Franco Tamargo's funeral,
Miami (Saturday, March 14th, 2015, 10:30 a.m.)

Poole and Water stood in front of the closed casket of Tamargo's remains lost in their own thoughts for quite a while before Poole broke the silence.

"I don't know what the outcome of the trial will bring, but I know that one way or another Martin is going to pay!"

"I hear you – and agree. I wouldn't mind visiting him on death row once in a while." Water replied.

"Hope the Governor halts his execution a few times – last minute! Just so we can visit him again." Poole deadpanned.

The ride over from the funeral home on Bird Road to the cemetery off Miller Road was impressive. While Tamargo hadn't been on the force anymore, there were at least a hundred and fifty police officers paying their last respect to a fallen officer. When they reached Tamargo's final destination there were more than just a few moist eyes.

"Franco was a good guy. Not only was he one of us, but he was a genuine person. He left the force because he thought he could help Miami better in his own way. And he was right. Not only did he lead our investigation in the right direction, he gave his life for it!" Poole announced to Water before he turned and walked away.

"Where're you going?" Water wanted to know.

"Getting shit-faced." Poole mumbled without breaking his stride.

"Wait up." was Water's choked response.

Chapter Ninety Six

Jury Selection,
Downtown Miami, (Monday, April 20th, 2015, 9:00 a.m.)

Roger Dalton, the Judge presiding over the case was known in the legal community as tough, fair, and also very compassionate. Standing at five feet eight inches with white hair befitting a sixty-two-year-old man, he had been on the bench long enough to have honed his patience without losing his contempt for fools.

The jury selection process took the better part of three days. After the wrangling between the prosecutor and defense attorney was finally over, the members of the jury had been selected. Though it was late in the day, Judge Dalton decided to start with the instruction of the jury. An English professor could've not have been clearer on outlining what the members of the jury were allowed – and not allowed – to do. He reminded them of the severity of the charges leveled against

Professor Martin and urged them to conduct themselves accordingly. The use of cell phones or any other electronic devices was strictly forbidden within the courtroom or jury room. They were not to discuss the case with anyone else, or among themselves. They were not to attempt to visit the crime scene or to try to re-create any of the scenarios that may be laid out during the hearing of the case. In order to avoid any misunderstandings, Judge Dalton proceeded to have his instructions handed to them in writing.

He finished the order of the day by thanking the jury members for their time and reminding them that it was not only a duty, but also an honor to serve on a jury.

Professor Martin, who had been observing the procedure while seated next to his attorney, looked over at the jury box, and against his attorney's advice, gave them a big smile. Except for a blonde, fiftyish looking woman no one in the jury box responded to his overtures. The exchange was not lost on Roberto Garcia who made a mental note to address the blonde woman directly when describing in graphic details how Sabine had been sexually abused by Martin.

Chapter Ninety Seven

Trial Day 1, State Court,
Downtown Miami (Friday, April 24th, 2015, 9:00 a.m.)

The members of the jury were sitting in the jury box at 9 a.m. sharp. No small feat considering a predominantly Hispanic community. In a way they were all looking forward to getting the trial started. To their dismay, the judge, prosecutor, and defense attorney were huddled at the Judge's podium with the microphones turned off. After a brief conversation with the other participants, the Judge asked the bailiff to escort the jury members back to the jury room.

The defense attorney, Mr. White, had filed a motion to dismiss the case with prejudice, claiming a lack of evidence by the prosecutor. It took Garcia the better part of fifteen minutes to convince Judge Dalton that he would be able to substantiate his case beyond a reasonable doubt. After taking a hard look at the prosecutor and the defense attorney, Judge

Dalton leaned back in his chair, folding his hands as if in prayer in front of his nose for a couple of minutes before deciding that the trial would go on.

After the jury had been allowed back into the courtroom, the state attorney proceeded with his opening statement.

"Ladies and gentlemen of the jury, you have been asked to decide the fate of a, on the surface, valuable member of our community. I would like to thank you for your willingness to sacrifice your time." Garcia, the boy – man took a moment to make eye contact with every member of the jury, before he continued:

"You will hear the prosecution – that will be me – laying out evidence that will compel you to conclude - beyond reasonable doubt – that Mr. Martin is guilty of the crimes that we not only accuse him of, but that he has committed."

The defense attorney had jumped up from his chair looking at Judge Dalton with an incredulous look on his face exclaiming: "Are you going to allow this?"

"Please sit down Mr. White these are the opening statements. You will be allowed as much latitude as Mr. Garcia opts to take." White having accomplished what he had set out to, planted a smile on his face and sat down.

"As I was saying, we will show that a valued member of our community has abused his position of trust to abduct and abuse" – Garcia shot a quick glance to see the judge's grim expression – "one of the students he was entrusted with. That student who has suffered repeated sexual abuse perpetrated by Mr. Martin is alive and willing to testify. Her testimony will shed light on a professor who was considered a top-notch educator at one of our beloved universities. A man who was entrusted with guiding our young daughters and sons to a brighter future. He has however decided to abuse this position of trust and subsequently abducted, held as sex slaves, and in at least two cases murdered children entrusted to him. Sabine Sander, his – as far as we know – third victim has survived his perverted abuse. When I say third victim, I am of course implying that there are more victims. Dear members of the jury, you are here today, to decide if Mr. Martin is guilty of abducting, holding prisoner, and sexually abusing Sabine Sander. We not only believe, but know, that we have enough supporting evidence to prove to you that this is factual." Garcia went back to his table and had a sip of water from the glass on his desk.

"My colleague Mr. White will try to convince you that anyone could have held Sabine Sander in the garage of the property that is located directly behind his primary residence. A property that he purchased, under the cover of a corporation, which he owns. I say yes, that is a possibility – but I am asking you – what are the odds? Indeed, what are the odds of Mr. Martin waltzing around naked, covered only by a silk bathrobe, hiding his face behind a Zorro mask just happening to walk into that very sex dungeon? You will hear testimony by the police officers that have suspected, followed, and finally arrested Mr. Martin. You will furthermore hear testimony by the victim of the Accused. Testimony that will prove to you that there was only one perpetrator – the Accused! The prosecution has to prove to you that the Accused is guilty of the crime as charged. I have to prove to you not only that he will have committed the crime, but I have to do so beyond a reasonable doubt. Your reasonable doubt. I intend to do just that. Not because this is a game to me, but because I want to put away a dangerous predator that may continue to fulfill his sick, perverted sexual fantasies by abducting your daughters - if left to his devices!"

Garcia started walking back towards his desk while attempting to make eye contact with every member of the jury again. When he reached his seat, White had already walked halfway over to the jury box. Ignoring the judge and the audience he squared off to the jury.

"I congratulate my colleague on a very eloquently delivered opening statement. However, you will have to realize that that's exactly what it was. An opening statement. He is not required to provide any proof for his accusations. Luckily for the legal system in this country, he will be forced to do so very soon. This is where he will fail! Dear members of the jury; Professor Martin has been a valued member of our community for a long time. He has been a mentor and educator to hundreds of students, forfeiting large monetary rewards for the benefit of his students. He is a successful entrepreneur that has sacrificed his time to help students, one of which he is accused of having abused.

Now, I will not try to explain the prosecutor's reasoning as to why he would wish to implicate such a good man in such a heinous crime: Desperation is the only way to explain the prosecutor's move to indict Professor Martin. You will hear testimony from former and current students of Professor Martin, who will attest to his passion to help raise students' prospects to achieve higher goals. You will hear from other faculty members testifying to his dedication. What you will not hear, or see, is any shred of evidence that will implicate Professor Martin in this horrific crime. Professor Martin does not only teach at FIU, he is, as I previously mentioned, also an entrepreneur who runs a very successful boutique investment company, and therefore qualified to judge how best to invest his money. He chose to invest in real estate. In that capacity he has purchased the home behind his house. As you will hear throughout the trial, he has not yet begun to rehab the property for resale. While the prosecutor may want to make you believe that this is because he wanted to keep it as a – I believe he called it a "sex dungeon" – this is incorrect. There are reasons for investors that are beyond the scope of expertise of an attorney. And yes, that does include me. However, Professor Martin has enlightened me to some of those reasons, namely that there were too many residences for sale within a one mile radius. However, regardless of his investment goals and the details on how to achieve those goals, he is within his rights to leave that investment property unoccupied as long as he wishes to. Having said that; it is illegal to trespass on someone else's property without a search warrant. Incidentally that is exactly what happened on March 10th, when Mr. Sander and

Mr. Walker decided to burglarize Professor Martin's property.

We don't know how many others there have been that have helped themselves to the use of the house. You will hear expert witnesses that will testify regarding fingerprints and DNA collected at the scene of this crime.

What you will not hear is testimony linking Professor Martin in any way, shape or form to having been part of this crime. And let us not make any mistakes – it was a crime! A crime committed by someone other than Professor Martin. Ladies and gentlemen of the jury, when we are done listening to the prosecutor, all of his witnesses and experts, there will be only one thing left for you to do. You will go into that jury room, look at each other and exonerate Professor Martin. Thank you for your time!" he said while attempting to make eye contact with everyone of the jurors. He planted a big smile on his face while walking towards the defense table and nodded confidently to Martin.

After a quick glance at his watch Judge Dalton announced that the proceedings would continue after the weekend. Addressing the jurors in earnest, he reminded them not to discuss the case with anyone, including their families.

Chapter Ninety Eight

Trial Day 2, State Court,
Downtown Miami (Monday, April 27th, 2015, 9:00 a.m.)

Judge Dalton called the room to order 10 minutes after 9 a.m. While he was a stickler for punctuality, he had to wait for a juror who was stuck in traffic.

"Mr. Garcia please proceed to call your first witness." He opened up the proceedings when the jury was complete.

"Your honor, I am calling Detective Water to the stand." Garcia opened calmly at his table. The bailiff left the room and shortly thereafter returned with Detective Jerome Water, who proceeded to the witness chair where he was sworn in by the bailiff. The prosecutor established Jerome's position in the police department and started his questioning.

"Detective Water, would you please be so kind to describe in your own words how you ended up at Mr. Martin's investment property?"

Jerome proceeded to give a detailed rundown of their investigation into the murder of Sandra Restrepo, Graciela Manciani and the disappearance of Sabine Sander leading up to his involvement in the discovery of Sabine. To Garcia's surprise the defense attorney opted not to interrupt his testimony at all. When Jerome was done with his narrative the prosecutor followed up by asking him:

"Why did you not obtain a search warrant before you entered Mr. Martin's property?"

"When I received the phone call by Mr. Walker that the victim of a serious crime had been discovered, I had probable cause."

Turning towards the judge the prosecutor announced that he had no more questions for his witness. Before Garcia reached his chair White was on his feet approaching Jerome.

"Detective Water, are Mr. Sander and Mr. Walker colleagues of yours?"

"Colleagues? No."

"So they are not sworn police officers?"

"No."

"What do you normally call it when an

unauthorized person trespasses on property? Trespassing? Burglary?"

"Are you forgetting the fact that they discovered the victim of a brutal crime?"

"No I don't, but are you forgetting the fact that you are supposed to answer my questions?" Mr. White inquired with a smile on his face.

"Well, in this case I suppose it was a citizen's arrest that was executed by Mr. Sander and Mr. Walker."

"A citizen's arrest on a property they were not invited to be on?"

"Please forgive me counselor, but even if Mr. Martin had nothing to do with Sabine's ordeal, wouldn't he be happy to have an innocent victim released from capture?" Water answered with a surprised look on his face.

"Sure, I am convinced that Professor Martin was delighted that Ms. Sander was freed, but let us not forget the fact that you are accusing him of having imprisoned her."

"Was there a question?" Water wanted to know.

"For future reference, please let me finish my sentence and address you directly before you address the court!" The defense attorney responded without a trace of humor in his voice.

"Going back to my question, do you normally arrest people that trespass and burglarize unoccupied dwellings?"

"This was not a case of a regular trespass and burglary."

"Judge, would you please instruct the witness to answer my question?" White asked the judge with a look of consternation on his face.

"Detective Water, please answer the question." Judge Dalton instructed Water.

"Yes Sir. Under normal circumstances trespassers can only be arrested after they have been issued a warning, and an officer witnessed the trespass." Water allowed.

"Thank you, that wasn't all that hard – was it? Anyhow, Detective, are you aware of the fact that evidence collected without probable cause and or a search warrant is inadmissible in court?" White asked with a devious look on his face.

"Sir, I am just a police officer. We investigate crimes, arrest the suspect and then let very intelligent attorneys decide what we little dummies have done wrong." Jerome responded while regretting his comment as soon as it had left his mouth.

There was laughter from the audience and a small smile flickered over Garcia's lips before the Judge banged his gavel.

"So Detective Water, in your professional opinion, did Mr. Sander and Mr. Walker commit a crime?"

Water sat for the better part of a minute before Judge Dalton instructed him to answer the question.

"No. they rescued the victim of a crime!"

"How about breaking into the garage? Would that be an arrestable offense?"

"I understand they were alerted by noise from inside the garage located on the grounds of an obviously abandoned home. So without consulting with a prosecutor first, I would not arrest them for that." Water replied.

"Thank you Detective Water. I have no more questions for you." White knew when not to press a witness that the jurors found to be very likable. Garcia did not want a redirect, but reserved the right to do so at a later time.

Water stepped down from the witness chair and threw an apologetic look at Garcia before trotting out of the courtroom.

"Your Honor, we are calling Sabine Sander to the witness stand." Garcia continued the proceedings.

When Sabine Sander walked towards the witness chair, the room went dead silent. While she was dressed in a rather bright yellow blouse and black pants, there was a certain sadness offsetting the bright color. On her way to the witness stand Sabine avoided eye contact with Martin.

"Ms. Sander, would you please be so kind to describe your abduction and following incarceration by the Accused?" Garcia opened.

"Objection!" White was on his feet as if struck by lightning.

"Mr. Garcia, you should know better than to take these potshots. Members of the jury you will please disregard the last question. Mr. Garcia, please rephrase your question carefully." Judge Dalton instructed Garcia with a stern look on his face.

"I apologize. Ms. Sander would you please describe the circumstances of your abduction and subsequent incarceration." Garcia said while giving Sabine a friendly nod.

Sabine Sander described the night of her abduction, the ride in the trunk of the car and having been shackled to the floor of a pitch black room. The entire courtroom was impressed by her composure until she reached the part when her abductor had first raped her. It was at that point that she broke down in tears. Judge Dalton interrupted the proceedings for five minutes to allow her to compose herself. It wasn't lost on Garcia or White how the jury reacted to this.

"Your honor, may I request that we continue Ms. Sander's testimony after the lunch break?" Garcia inquired.

White was about to object to this request, but thought better since he knew it would make him - and by extension his client - look insensitive. Judge Dalton nodded and announced to the courtroom that they would take an early lunch and reconvene in ninety minutes.

Poole and Water were having lunch at a small Cuban restaurant close to the Courthouse.

"So how did you like your first encounter with a member of the vulture-clan?" Poole asked between bites.

"Pardon my French – Fuck him. If I ever have only my self-interest foremost on my mind – I'm hoping that someone will be kind enough to administer the mercy-shot to me!" Water spit back.

"Easy now my young friend. Everyone is entitled to a fair defense." Poole said while trying to hide his smile behind his sandwich.

"Are you kidding me?" Water was becoming agitated. "I probably blew it on the stand. It was all I could do to not spit in that a-hole's face!" He exclaimed.

"I'm just jerking your chain, man! Trust me; it never gets old being on the stand. Besides, you did rather well."

"Can't wait for the next time." Walker said before washing down the remains of his sandwich with a glass of water.

Chapter Ninety Nine

Trial Day 2, State Court,
Downtown Miami (Monday, April 27th, 2015, 1:45 p.m.)

After Sabine was informed by the Judge that she was still under oath, Garcia continued his questioning.

"Ms. Sander, I know that you have given extensive testimony about your ordeal to the police already, but the jury needs to hear it from you in your own words. Would you please try to recall the time when your abductor first assaulted you sexually?" Garcia asked her in a soft voice.

Sabine looked like a frightened doe flushed from the woods by a pack of wolves, but nodded bravely before recounting the first rape by —whom she called – the monster.

The jury, as well as the audience in the courtroom, listened with rapt attention. Garcia was secretly scanning the courtroom to gauge the reaction of the jury as well as the spectators. The reaction of the jury – which fluctuated between disgust and horror – was not lost on White either. When Sabine reached the part where her captor made her dress up, she looked directly at Martin. Sabine continued her detailed testimony, only occasionally prodded by the DA, until late in the afternoon.

While the jurors were still paying attention to Sabine's testimony, Judge Dalton didn't want to overburden them and ended her testimony at five p.m.

Chapter One Hundred

Trial Day 3,
Downtown Miami (Tuesday, April 28th, 2015, 9:00 a.m.)

After Judge Dalton called the courtroom to order, he reminded Sabine again that she was still under oath. Sabine nodded bravely and tried to get comfortable in the witness chair.

Garcia got up from his chair and scanned the jury box while approaching the witness stand. Standing in front of Sabine he recalled part of her testimony from the previous day to refresh her memory before he asked her to continue her testimony.

Two hours later Sabine concluded recounting the horrors of her ordeal. Garcia informed the judge that he had no more questions for his witness. Attorney White was on his feet before Garcia had finished his sentence. He positioned himself in front of Sabine.

"Ms. Sander, I, like everyone else in this room, am deeply disturbed but what you have gone through." White opened and then paused for the better part of a minute before continuing: "However, the perpetrator that you have been describing throughout your testimony has not been caught yet. Professor Martin is not the man that has subjected you to the nightmare that you experienced."

White as well as everyone else in the courtroom had noticed that Sabine had started shifting uncomfortably in her seat. Trying to be more sympathetic he continued: "Please don't get me wrong, I am not disputing what has happened to you, I just know that it was not Prof. Martin."

"Please allow me to touch on some of your testimony. When you were abducted at FIU, the kidnapper was wearing a mask. When, presumably the same man raped you, he was again wearing a mask. My main concern and question is: have you ever seen your kidnapper and rapist without a mask?" he continued.

"I know it's him!" Sabine almost shouted while looking straight at Professor Martin.

"I apologize for having upset you. I'm just trying to get to the bottom of this horrific crime. A crime that was not committed by my client. We all realize how hard it must have been to endure what you have been put through. But you do understand, that sending the wrong man to prison for a very long time will not correct the wrong that was done to you. Indeed, it will compound the problem. The real culprit is still out there, and right now the police are not looking for him, because they believe that Professor Martin is guilty." White paused and walked back to his table to take a sip of water.

"They don't have to look for anyone else. Professor Martin is the man who kidnapped and raped me!" Sabine responded while White was trying to swallow his water.

"Ms. Sander, please only answer the questions that you were asked by the defense attorney. I understand that this is very emotional for you, but we do need to follow procedures." Judge Dalton informed Sabine. Defense attorney White looked over to the judge and nodded gratefully.

"Ms. Sander how can you be so sure that professor Martin is the person that kidnapped and raped you? You have never seen the face of your attacker!"

"I am sure! He has a birthmark on the upper side of his penis. I saw it when he forced me to perform oral sex on him!" Sabine answered causing a commotion not only in the audience, but in the jury box as well.

"Your Honor, may we have a sidebar please?" White huffed before walking over to the judge's bench. "Counselors, please approach." Dalton answered before turning off his microphone. Garcia scrambled to his feet and stood next to White when the later said: "Your Honor, I request the last statement be stricken from the record, and the jury to be instructed to disregard the testimony." White demanded.

"Easy now Mr. White, you asked a question, the witness answered. Let's find out if Ms. Sander's claim can be substantiated." The judge said.

"Are you suggesting that Professor Martin drops his trousers in the courtroom to dispel this ridiculous accusation?" White huffed.

"Mr. White I strongly advise you to watch your tone in my courtroom. A doctor will check into Ms. Sander's allegations in a separate room."

"Your Honor, since Mr. White seems to be convinced of Mr. Martin's innocence, a thorough physical examination of Mr. Martin should prove very helpful in these proceedings." Garcia chimed in while flashing White his best college boy smile.

"Your Honor, I object to this humiliating procedure." White said. "Your objection has been noted counselor." Dalton replied.

"Ladies and gentlemen of the jury, you are excused for the rest of the day. We thank you for your continued service and we will see you tomorrow morning at 9 a.m." Dalton announced to the courtroom before instructing the bailiff to take Mr. Martin to a holding cell to be examined by a doctor.

Chapter
One Hundred & One

Professor Martin and his attorney waited for about an hour before the doctor arrived.

When Luzio Ballord, MD arrived, he introduced himself before requesting: "Mr. Martin, please be so kind to drop your trousers so that I may examine your penis." Martin looked inquiringly at his attorney, who responded:

"That's Professor Martin." White announced.

"Which is still a little shy of a Doctorate. So now that we have that out of the way, Prof. Martin, please follow the doctor's order and drop your trousers so that I may examine your penis." was the calm response from Dr. Ballord.

White gave a nod to Martin who complied by standing up and dropping his pants. "It would make my job a lot easier if you could lower your boxer shorts as well – Professor." Dr. Ballord's sarcastically observed. Martin lowered his boxers and looked at the doctor without comment.

"Thank you Professor." Dr. Ballord said while taking his sweet time to put on his examination gloves.

"Okay, so what do we have here? The underside of your penis has no birthmarks or any other noticeable markings." Dr. Ballord observed.

"Doctor, the area in question is located on top of my client's penis!" White responded with a hint of fury building.

"Oh, okay, let's take a look." Ballord replied cheerily. "Ah, a scar on top of the penis where there may have been a birthmark!" Ballord was clearly enjoying himself by now.

"Nonsense!" White exclaimed.

"Dr. Ballord, I injured myself when I zipped up my pants." Martin stated.

"Wow, does your zipper close from the top?" Ballord came back.

"What?" Martin was startled.

"Well, all of the zippers I have ever encountered in my life zipped up from the bottom to the top. Unless you twisted your penis upside down before closing it – how would you have injured the top of your penis?" Dr. Ballord inquired.

Martin started to pull up his boxers and pants before looking at the doctor to respond: "I have no idea, but that's how it happened!" he barked.

"Well, that's it then." Dr. Ballord stated while removing the examination gloves and tossing them in the garbage can next to the door of the room. "I'll file my report with the judge within a couple of hours." He looked at both of them before adding: "Careful with that zipper."

White made a mental note not to have this man on the stand if it could be prevented at all.

Chapter
One Hundred & Two
Trial Day 4, State Court,
Downtown Miami (Wednesday, April 29th, 2015, 9:00 a.m.)

Sabine's brother and Benjamin were seated behind the prosecutor's table as they had been from the beginning of the proceedings when the room was called to order.

"Mr. White, you were questioning the witness when we interrupted the proceedings for a medical examination of your client based on the testimony on the stand. Would you like to continue with Ms. Sander's testimony, or would you like to interrupt for Dr. Ballord to present his findings?" Judge Dalton inquired.

"If it pleases the court we will hear the findings first." White agreed following the strategy he had agreed upon with his client.

"Very well, bailiff, please have Dr. Ballord sworn in." Dalton instructed.

"Your Honor, we agree to have Dr. Ballord's

findings read into the records without him testifying." White announced.

"Objection, Your Honor. The people would like to hear the expert witness in Court, and I believe the jury has a right to hear this witness as well." Garcia objected.

"Mr. White, I agree, the witness will be heard in Court." Judge Dalton ruled. White looked like he'd swallowed a bee, but nodded bravely.

"Dr. Ballord, did you have a chance to examine Mr. Martin?" Dalton asked the witness. "Yes your Honor, even though he prefers to be called Professor Martin." Ballord deadpanned.

"Excuse me." Dalton came back.

"Not important. Yes, I did have a chance to examine him, and I did not find a birthmark in the area that Ms. Sander indicated. While there is significant scar tissue in exactly that place, I could not verify the existence of a birthmark. Mr. Martin explained that it had been caused by a zipper. While I am not an expert on these kinds of injuries, I have a bit of a problem visualizing how it could have happened."

"Objection, the witness stated that he is not an expert on these kinds of injuries, yet he voiced his unsubstantiated opinion!" White objected.

"Agreed, members of the jury, please disregard the witness' statement." Dalton instructed. "Dr. Ballord is there anything else you can tell us about the scar?" he continued.

"No, nothing beyond my 'unsubstantiated' opinion." was Dr. Ballord's sarcastic response.

"Mr. Garcia, do you have any questions for this witness?" Dalton shot a look at Garcia. "Yes your Honor. Dr. Ballord, you have worked as an ER doctor for a number of years, correct?" Garcia inquired.

"Indeed I have. As a matter of fact, I've spent six years in emergency rooms at a number of hospitals in Miami."

"Dr. Ballord, how often have you encountered an injury such as the one you've discovered on Mr. Martin?" Garcia continued his questioning.

"Well, sadly there are a lot of injuries to the genital areas of men and women that can only be explained by, ahem, certain sexual practices."

"Objection – I don't think the Court has recognized Dr. Ballord as an expert witness on sexual practices." White had shot up from his chair.

"Sustained. Dr. Ballord, please limit your answers to the specific injury that you discovered on Mr. Martin." Dalton said. "The jury will disregard the last statement by Dr. Ballord."

"I am sorry your Honor." Dr. Ballord looked apologetically at the judge, who glanced at the witness with a look that seemed to say: save it.

"Mr. Garcia, do you have any other questions for the witness?"

"Yes, your Honor. Dr. Ballord, how much force has to be exerted on a penis to turn it 180 degrees? And…"

"Objection your Honor!" White looked incredulously at the judge who in turn pointed a finger at Garcia and said only one word: "Sidebar."

"Mr. Garcia, would you like for me to hold you in contempt of Court? The witness will be excused, and you would be wise to watch your steps for the rest of these proceedings. Do I make myself clear?" Dalton glared at Garcia in a way that left little room for a misinterpretation of his displeasure.

"Your Honor, I apologize for having exercised bad judgment in my line of questioning." Garcia replied while looking like a little boy having been caught with his hand in the cookie jar.

"The witness is excused." Dalton announced.

The rest of the day was spent listening to forensic experts that didn't add any weight to the prosecution nor did they help the defense.

When there were no more witnesses or experts to be heard the prosecutor commenced with his closing statement:

"Ladies and gentlemen of the jury, thank you for sacrificing your time to help bring justice to the streets of Miami. Thank you for working on stopping a serial rapist from…"

"Objection your Honor. The prosecutor is trying to poison the jury with theatrics!" White had risen from his chair.

"Overruled. Counselor, you know that the rules for opening statements and closing arguments are very lenient!" Dalton responded. "Mr. Garcia, you may continue."

"As I was saying, there has been a perpetrator on the loose in our city! His name is Robert Martin! He is sitting right over there." Garcia said while pointing at Martin. "This is the man that abducted Sabine Sander and held her as a sex-slave for more than a week. She was subjected to unspeakable and hideous sexual assaults while in his dungeon! While her rescue may have not been 'by the book' according to the law, she was rescued before her captor – Robert Martin – was able to continue his sexual abuse and at the end of his sexual fantasy – dispose of her when he needed a new candidate for his perverted needs! I will not bore you by going through all the testimony we've heard. I trust your just judgment to reach the only decision possible. Guilty! Thank you for your time." Garcia concluded his closing arguments before walking back to his table while looking at every jury member.

White was again up before Garcia reached his seat and stood before the jury box in silence for a long time. He took a long look at every member of the jury before he started:

"Members of the jury, as my esteemed opponent already mentioned, there is no need to bore you with a repetition or summary of the testimony we have heard. Please keep in mind though that none of the witnesses have implicated Prof. Martin. Yes, there was some circumstantial evidence. Evidence that does not prove anything. My client's fingerprints were found in his investment property, which is to be expected. Other than that – no evidence whatsoever! Ms. Sander was subjected to a horrendous ordeal, an unspeakable crime, which wasn't committed by my client! The man who perpetrated this unspeakable crime is still out there, but instead of finding the man, we are sitting here in judgment of an innocent man! Ladies and gentlemen of the jury, please do what is right: Find Prof. Martin – as he deserves - not guilty! Thank you for your service and the rendering of the right verdict." White finished.

It was late in the afternoon when Judge Dalton informed the jury to be back the next morning to begin their deliberation. With another warning to the jury not to discuss the case with anyone he ended the proceedings for the day.

Chapter
One Hundred & Three
Verdict, State Court,
Downtown Miami (Thursday, April 30th, 2015, 9:00 a.m.)

To everyone's surprise it took the jury only five hours to reach a verdict. After Judge Dalton called the courtroom to order a needle would have been heard hitting the floor.

"Has the jury reached a verdict?" he inquired.

"Yes your Honor, we have." The foreman of the jury replied.

"Please let us hear your verdict Mr. Foreman." Dalton responded while everyone in the courtroom was moving closer to the edge of their seat.

"On the count of kidnapping, we the jury find the defendant not guilty. On the count of sexual abuse, we the jury find the defendant not guilty.

"Bullshit!" was Benjamin's clearly audible reaction which was seconded by a number of people in the audience. Dalton wasn't having any of this and called the courtroom to order.

"The jury has spoken. Mr. Martin, you are free to go." Dalton announced before the courtroom again erupted into disorder.

"This isn't over!" Thomas Sander shouted towards Martin before storming out of the courtroom with Benjamin only a couple of steps behind. They ran into Water and Poole at the elevator.

"Can you believe this shit?" a very agitated Sander barked at Water. "Thomas, as you said, this isn't over. We are trying to press additional charges against Martin. Don't forget, there are two dead girls, a dead boyfriend of one of the girls and a friend of ours who most likely were all done in by Martin." Water replied while Poole was nodding and simultaneously fishing a cigarette out of his pack.

Putting the smoke in his mouth he looked hard at Sander and Walker. "You guys stay put. No stupid stunts or acts of vigilante justice. I would hate for you guys to ruin your lives over this ass. Understood?" His question was met with silence.

"Understood?" he repeated a little louder. "Yes sir." came the subdued answer from Walker. "Thomas?" Poole pressed. "Yeah, understood." he mumbled.

The elevator arrived and they were about to get on when Poole spotted Garcia exiting the courtroom. "See you guys later." He said before pulling Water towards Garcia.

"What the hell happened?" Poole hissed when they had met up with Garcia.

"Detective, I warned you that this was not a slam dunk. There was just not enough evidence. Remember – beyond reasonable doubt? There were just too many problems. Walker and Sander gaining illegal access to Martin's property being the biggest issue." He said before adding: "Look guys, I know Martin is a scumbag and I have no doubt he's the guy, but I couldn't sell it to the jury." Garcia continued graciously accepting the blame.

"This isn't the end though – right?" Water wanted to know.

"Afraid so, double jeopardy precludes us from charging him again for the same crime. I know we have those two other girls, the boy and your friend, but I need evidence. Real rock solid evidence or the media is going to scream witch-hunt!" Garcia informed them.

"We'll get you solid evidence – even if it takes us 24/7 to find it. This isn't over." Water informed Garcia while Poole just shook his head. "Maybe it's time for me to retire. When the bad guys start winning, there just isn't much sense in reeling them in. Have a good day Counselor." Poole voiced before walking over to the staircase.

"Get me something real and I'll nail this guy!" Garcia told Water.

Chapter
One Hundred & Four

Outside State Court,
Downtown Miami (Thursday, April 30th, 2015, 2:31 p.m.)

Water caught up with Poole who was standing outside of the courthouse under the canopy lighting up his smoke.

"You know that there's no smoking within 100 feet of the building – right?" Water opened.

"Call a fucking cop!" Poole shot back.

"Easy now – I am as upset as you are, but reaming me a new one isn't going to help!" Water suggested.

"Sorry, I guess I am just getting too old for this shit. Too many victims, dead girls, Tamargo dead, Sabine tormented by this prick – I really should retire." Poole said before sucking hard on his Marlboro. Looking at the dark sky heavy with rain he nodded before turning to scan the entrance of the courthouse where a bunch of reporters were waiting for Martin to make his exit.

"Look at the vultures waiting for their next story. Can't wait to see how this reads! Will it be 'the bright Professor who was wrongly accused', or will it be 'the predator that escaped justice'? It's anyone's guess, but we'll find out soon. I for one will not watch TV tonight." Poole announced.

"Poole, come on! So we took one on the chin, but this is not the end." Water paused. "Shit, I can't believe I am giving my senior detective a pep talk!" he finished just in time to see an uptick in the commotion in front of the courthouse. Prof. Martin was making his way towards the reporters when Water said:

"Shit, Poole, over there on the right side, that's Graciela's dad!" before he started moving towards the man.

Poole dropped his cigarette and followed his younger partner.

Chapter
One Hundred & Five

The moment of truth,

Downtown Miami (Thursday, April 30th, 2015, 4:59 p.m.)

Poole and Water rapidly walked towards Luigi Manciani who stood statue-like with a look of bewilderment on his face.

Water called out to Manciani while still a good distance away: "Mr. Manciani, Detective Water. You remember me?"

Manciani either didn't hear him or decided to ignore him. When the man's face started to contort into a mask of hatred Poole pushed Water and shouted:

"Run!" to which Water broke out into a mad sprint.

"No!" he screamed when he saw Luigi Manciani reach behind his back and pull out a gun. The next few seconds would be engraved in Water's mind for eternity. Manciani started moving towards Martin while raising his right hand holding the gun, pushed a reporter out of his way and fired the gun multiple times, instantly dropping Martin like a bag of potatoes.

When Manciani saw Martin going down he turned the gun on himself and shouted: "Graciela – I love you!" before inserting the barrel into his open mouth and pulling the trigger, spraying blood and brain matter over a bunch of reporters in his vicinity.

Water reached the gaggle of screaming reporters that had scrambled back and kneeled down next to Manciani. He quickly took off his jacket and placed it over the obviously dead man's face. There was no need for the slowly recovering reporters to take TV-footage or pictures of this poor man – and Water's was making sure of that.

Poole had reached the crowd and started pushing the reporters back while glancing at Water.

"You're alright?" he asked. "No, I am not. And obviously neither is Mr. Manciani!" Water replied.

Chapter
One Hundred & Six
Sabine, Thomas Sander and Benjamin Walker
(Friday, May 1st, 2015, 1:30 p.m.)

"Sis, I don't think you've ever really met Benjamin." Thomas told Sabine after allowing Benjamin into Sabine's apartment.

Benjamin stood by the front door unsure if he was allowed to proceed. Thomas waived him in further while Sabine said:

"Yeah, from the garage and you were sitting next to Thomas during the trial."

"He also – as I told you – helped me find you!" Thomas added.

Sabine rose from the sofa and walked over to Benjamin. "Thank you!" she said simply before giving him a hug that made his knees go dangerously soft. "Do I know you from somewhere else? You look familiar."

Thomas looked at Benjamin but didn't say a word. "I, ahem, you may have, ahem, maybe at

FIU. Oh shit! I used to follow you around on campus." Benjamin admitted before turning for the front door.

"Wait!" Thomas instructed Benjamin before turning to his sister.

"Benjamin is what I would call a love-struck-fool!" Thomas continued.

"You're the creep?" Sabine exclaimed without conviction.

"I am so sorry! Yes, I did follow you around on campus, but I ..." Benjamin's response petered out.

"Don't worry; Thomas told me everything before you came over. He's just played one of his cruel educational jokes on you. He did it a million times to me when I grew up!" Sabine informed Benjamin.

Before Sabine had finished her remarks Thomas had gotten closer to Benjamin and put an arm around him. "Ben, it's all good."

"I am sorry!" Benjamin declared before bidding his goodbyes.

"Tom, you scarred him." Sabine felt sorry for Benjamin.

"Don't worry – he'll be fine."

Chapter
One Hundred & Seven

Benjamin Walker and Jerome Water,
Station (Friday, May 1st, 2015, 6:30 p.m.)

Benjamin had been waiting outside of the Police Station for about an hour before he saw Water walk to his car after his shift had ended.

"Hey Jerome!" Benjamin called out.

Jerome looked around to find the body connected to the voice calling out for him. "Benjamin, how are you?" he responded once he detected Benjamin a couple of cars away from his own. "What brings you over here?"

"I need to ask you a favor." Benjamin opened while walking up to Jerome. "Sure man, what do you need?"

Benjamin filled him in on his experience with the drunken man that had assaulted him.

"What are you sweating this for? The guy has obviously not filed any charges. Trust me – if he had, we would have kept you back then!"

Jerome answered with a devious smile on his face. "Just kidding – it's all good. You've redeemed yourself. Just stay out of trouble." Jerome added while giving Benjamin a friendly punch to the shoulder.

Jerome quickly entered his car. No way was he going to be late for his first date with Melody!

Chapter
One Hundred & Eight

Conchita had been told by her supervisor to clean room 203. When Conchita entered the room with the towels and cleaning items in her hands, she expected the usual – a messy room. Boy was she wrong! A girl lying naked on the bed was something she hadn't encountered before – and she was not new to this business! She was laid out spread eagle, cuffed to the edges of the bed. Since there were no bedposts, whoever had tied her up, had used cable-ties to secure the cuffs to the bed frame.

Conchita thought that the girl was beautiful – well, her body was, since her head was covered by some leather mask, not that she was into naked girls – but she was also immediately terrified by the scream the girl let out once she had stepped into the room. She'd dropped all of her supplies and ran from the room.

She didn't stop running until she'd reached the lobby which was housed in a building quite a distance away. Breathless she'd told the manager what she'd found. The manager had immediately contacted the Key West Police Department, which in turn had dispatched a unit. Ten minutes after Conchita had discovered the naked woman the officers had freed her from her constrains.

The EMT unit had arrived only five minutes later and determined that the victim was unharmed but severely dehydrated. They took her for evaluation to the hospital on Stock Island.

The End

Acknowledgments

Numerous people have helped me complete this book. Here are a few I would like to extend my heartfelt gratitude to:

Anja and Achim Boos, Martha Castro, John Dalton, Thomas Seidenkranz, Sharyllin Shaw, Jorge and Martha Tamargo, Magaly Tamargo, Tara Tamargo, Oscar A. Vidal (LithoEagle.com), Thorsten Woelki.

READ ON

FOR AN EXCERPT

FROM THE NEXT

JEROME WATER CASE

BY FRANK H. WEISENER

THE SOLUTION

AVAILABLE SOON!

THE SOLUTION

Chapter One
The First Hit

"Daddy, look at all the pretty clouds!" Kirsten screamed on their way from the shuttle bus into the airport building at Miami International.

"Yeah, I see them." Hans Schlager answered his nine year old daughter while admiring the crystal clear blue sky laced with small puffy clouds.

"Move over! Clear a path!" were the shouted instructions by a security detail clearing the way for a dignitary approaching the terminal.

Schlager and his family were able to move out of the way before a gaggle of Miami Dade Police Officers pushed all remaining pedestrians off the sidewalk. A tall African-American male climbed out of a limousine into the pleasant breeze that was making Miami the most desirable place during the month of January.

Schlager realized that he knew the man's face from somewhere. He starred at the man while going through his memory bank - he definitely knew the guy from somewhere. Was he a movie star? No, he was too ugly for that. What was that red dot on the back of his head?

When the man's head exploded into a mass of red and white matter, Schlager turned and forced his daughter and wife to the ground. He didn't have to wait for the sound of the shot to reach his ears to realize that the man – he had just realized that it was Ben Dullton, the African-American Activist who had a tendency to appear wherever there was a Civil rights issue involving black Americans – was dead.

Most of the Police Officers had either hit the ground or taken cover inside of the terminal when Schlager looked up again. Kirsten, whom he had tucked under his rather massive body, was stirring for air. "Sorry honey, let me help you up." He offered while looking at his wife who was lying prone next to him. "Baby, are you alright?" he shouted.

She started moving while looking at him with an expression of total bewilderment on her face.

The Police Officers had started to move towards the dead dignitary. Schlager was surprised by how massive the destruction of the man's head was. Like a water melon that had been hit by a baseball bat.